Cafe Macabre:

A Collection of Stories and Art by Women

Edited by
Leah McNaughton Lederman

SOURCE POINT PRESS

This book is dedicated to those of you up too late or up too early, creating.

All of us worked together to bring this to you. Special thanks to everyone for their cooperation and patience, and specialer thanks to Dirk Manning as project manager, and to Drena Jo and Katrina Roets for their keen eyes in proofreading.

Thank you for backing this project on Kickstarter!

Andrew & Alexis Molnar

Nathan R. Plunkett

Jason Kornhausl

Mirva Lukkari

Gigi Lin

Chadwick Gillenwater

Nicole Davis

Dustin Carr

Micah Benjamin Faulkner

Laura Lemermeier

Lopez

A.K. Tosh

Jason Plowman

Lonnie Velliquette

Chandra Connor

Jessica McBee

Joanna Closter

Robert Harrison

Brian Lau—Creator-Writer—Inferno City Firehouse

Count von Kit

Coriander Friess

Paul Dulski

Everything Horror Podcast

Vlrapatz

Sean Seal

Mr. Ricky Main Squeeze Lederman

Alisha Wielfaert

Gail Koontz

Tay Ramsey-Hoover

Phillip Buck

EnigmaEndeavorsProduction

Dirk Manning

Carrie Castro

Tara Maslowski

Howie Noel

Rob Farinholt

Sally

Joyce Baker

Cathering White

Paul Gori

Gene Ha

Brad Thompson

Chris "Pepsiman" Saguisag

Table of Contents

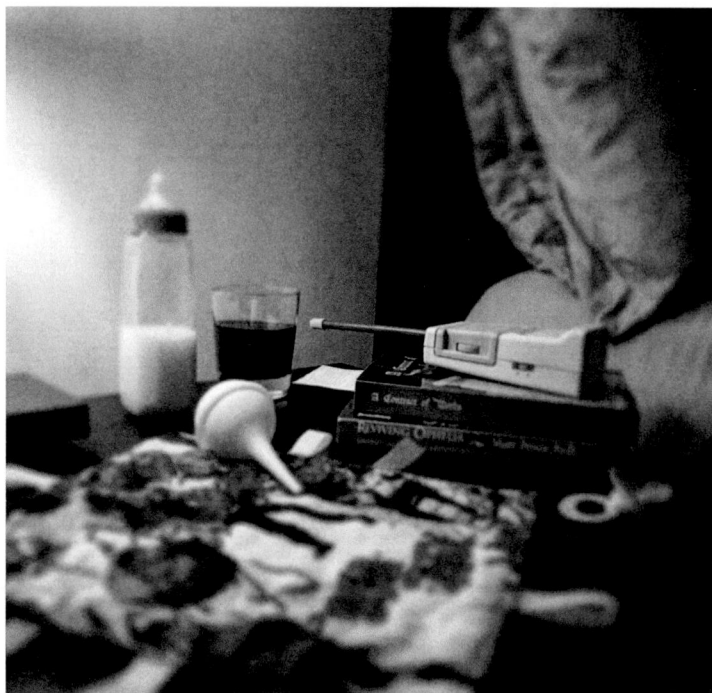

The House Awoke

Leah McNaughton Lederman

The floorboards and windowpanes creaked, though no footsteps or wind wails provoked them; no natural cause. The house was excited. For ten years, there had been no movement inside its walls aside from the minute clicking of minor pests, the staple of emptiness. Seconds ticked silently, marking iambic foreverafter.

Flies that had long been dormant, snuck in from the cold, now roused to life again from the flurry of the move-in. They buzzed from their corners, tiny shocks at first, then took flight so as to lay their eggs in something fresh, the refuse of new inhabitants. They assaulted the discarded takeout bags on the counter and circled the wonders of the newly-occupied lavatory. It was a Muscidae festival, and within days they planted a new generation in the garbage can and sink while the new residents busied themselves with the setup of the house.

The house.

Only one of three on the small street, it boasted ten acres of accompanying lawn, the disheveled grass and trees yawning away from the back door. It was an adventure waiting to happen, it had always thought, and now, perhaps, its denizens would enjoy all that it had waited so long to offer.

The last residents were no good. They offered nothing to the walls but their foul mouths, and jarred the foundations with slammed doors. The house was not sure why they had come, but it made sure they were gone before their pollution became permanent. There had already been too much sadness.

The new mother was kind. She hummed to herself and painted with soft rollers that tickled to the beam, offering bright colors and curious pictures. She stroked the floor and sanded and stained. She wiped her sweat with the same cloth she'd used to cover her hair, and laughed when her son ran into the room. He called her "Mommy" and she smoothed his blonde locks then shooed him away so she could continue to work. He bounded away and out the door, hitting sticks against the ground and jumping so that he could be as tall as the trees.

The man, her mate, also worked. He brought in box after box and slapped the young mother on her bottom. When she shrieked, the house quaked, remembering old noises, but it melted into a laugh when it saw that the man and woman stood together quietly, stroking her belly together.

The belly, it grew.

The house watched as room after room was swathed in paint and beds and couches and chairs, the child's drawings and music and hope. Sometimes the house giggled right there along with them, or breathed a purr in the moments of quiet after the boy was asleep, when the mother worked alone in the rooms. It offered a "Shhhh, shhh" as it imagined a peaceful woman would.

The young mother felt it when the house breathed. She'd stop her movement for a moment and look about. Sometimes she'd walk to the window and close it, thinking the chill came from the wind outside. The house just wanted her to know that it loved her, and was so happy she'd come to breathe life into it. No one else had loved it like she had. At least not for a long time.

It had been erected by a small family, just like the young mother's. They didn't have the money to do much else, but they filled its halls with their love for each other, until that sense was overtaken by a sense of dread. The child they'd brought with them was ill. It coughed long into the night and the parents took turns carrying it in their arms and sitting alongside its heaving frame. Doctors visited and left with long faces, until one of them removed the tiny babe in a small box made from the same wood used to build the house.

The rooms dissolved into pain shortly after, each wall of the house racked with the sound of sobs, the crashing of glass bottles. The man took to drink, and the woman just cried. He hit her, and screamed at her that the child was dead because she'd coddled it too much, hadn't let it breathe.

While he was away from the house the woman wept, and they carried on like this, mourning silently, violently, for years. One day it was done and they walked out. The woman with a few bags, the man with fewer. They left behind anything the child had touched.

When finally the new family brought into the house their new baby, the young mother and father took turns cradling it and singing to it. They had all sorts of devices, new to the house's walls, that beeped and echoed, but the child was the same as any other. It cooed and cried.

The house did not trust the man, whose touch was too rough, his voice too loud. The baby kept them up at night and the man stomped in his tired anger, snapping at the baby boy and snapping at his wife. The house did not trust the woman, who smothered the child in her breast and cried too much to be happy. She let the baby cry and walked away from it, checking in now and then from a faraway room on a tiny machine.

The house could not lose another baby in its walls. It would care for the child if its parents could not.

It was long past dark and the two children were asleep. The man walked in from his work in the yard but the house did not want him to see the baby anymore, and so it yawned and its walls opened and it swallowed him, leaving only a short yell behind before he was gone.

The young mother woke and sat up from her pillow. She leaned to the nightstand and checked the machine, listening. It told of the sounds of the baby but all she heard coming from its room was "Shhhh, shhh."

The woman smiled and settled back into her pillow, relieved that her husband had taken care of the crying baby.

4

Steps

Kari McElroy

H er reflection stares blankly back at her. Perpetually damp eyes scan a reflected chin delving near-seamlessly into her neck, up to a nose reddened by allergies regardless of season, up further to the same damp eyes now pinched in wrinkle-forming consternation. The eyes continue their trace to the shower-dampened hair framing her features—damp or not, it will remain lank. Sparrow-brown hair, hair for which her father branded her with the nickname she's never shaken: Little Bird. Small, meek. Easy prey was implied.

In movies and books, a man often tells his love interest he wishes she could see what he saw. Lily wonders if someone will ever say that to her. Or maybe they see precisely what she does, so it's not worth mentioning.

She tucks dripping strands of hair behind the ears she wished someone would have let her have pinned. As it stands, they poke out from her skull like two round little pancakes. She sighs.

Her husband, Dean, steps out of the shower and

flicks her left ear a dash harder than she imagines flirtation should be. "Your handlebars are showing," he says, taking his place beside her at the Jack-and-Jill sink. Lily shakes her hair down so the thin crop covers her ears as well as can be expected.

She slides a wicker box of cosmetics from an open shelf beneath the sink. The movement ignites her fitness tracker, a flare of digital light from her wrist. 5,952. She holds her wrist up to Dean. "It happened again."

Dean doesn't pause his shaving as he flicks a glance to the device. "So?" The razor glides over his chin, a sound like dry fingers running over paper.

"So it keeps happening."

Dean flips his razor to the sink, splattering used shaving cream and tiny weekend stubble remnants over the concave side and counter. "You get up to pee. I don't know."

"Five thousand," she glances at her wrist, "Nine hundred and fifty-two steps worth?"

Dean slaps another spent row into the sink. "Jesus, I don't know. It's a fluke. Don't waste brain space on tech fuck-ups." He laughs, tilting his head back to grate the razor along his neck. "You don't have the real estate to waste, you know?"

She tips a glob of liquid foundation into her fingertips. Maybe he's right. About the fluke. And maybe the rest.

≈≈≈≈≈

Work rattles along its daily track. Purchase orders, paperwork, boxes checked. Lily raises her wrist.

Steps

6,723. That seems right. She doesn't walk much at work. Her cubicle requires little standing, fewer steps. If she has to reach something out of her wingspan, she rolls her chair.

"Did you get that order out to St. Helen's?"

Lily glances up. Marcus leans over the top of her cube. It's unnecessary; the open entry way is broader than the space he has to lean and he doesn't look at her anyway. He swirls coffee in his thermos, gazing at the lid as though he can see the liquid churning.

"Yes. Tuesday." There's more to say. She must have more to say. She could ask about his kids or how his week has been or . . . Or anything. What do people talk about? Small talk, nothing talk. But she can't say it, big or small.

"Cool." He pushes off her cubicle, shuddering the thin framing.

※

"It's easier if you do it this way." Dean holds his knife at an angle, slicing the air before him with quick efficiency. "'Cutting on the bias.' It's a pro move."

Lily looks to the straight cut line of carrots under her own knife. "I mean . . . This way is working."

Dean shrugs with a snort barely louder than a breath, but her chest tightens with irritation. "Lots of things work, hon, but that don't make it the best." He returns to his cutting board, angle-slicing through a zucchini. "Little things add up to big things. You fix a bunch of little things, suddenly your days go a helluva lot smoother."

"I guess I didn't realize so many things needed

9

fixing." Quiet, under her breath, not so he can't hear her, but a signal to both that a response is unnecessary.

She tilts her knife to finish slicing the carrots. Dean's dices hit the board harder as he reaches the end of the zucchini. Reaching for an onion, their hands collide. In a movie, their fingers would have entwined, maybe with a nervous giggle depending on the newness of their love. Maybe dinner would be forgotten as he pulled her hand toward his chest, their bodies falling into a rhythm of togetherness.

"Jesus, ya moose," Dean grunts, tearing the onion from her grasp. "You just start on the meat, okay?"

She retrieves a package of chicken from its thaw in the refrigerator. "My steps at work seemed on track today, which makes me wonder even more about this morning."

Shearing the onion in two, Dean's knife hits the cutting board with a clack that pulls Lily's shoulders to her ears. "You're still on this."

"It's strange, you have to admit."

"Sure: it's strange as shit that you won't let it go." He works quickly through the dicing, the kitchen consumed only by sounds of metal on bamboo as the knife strikes, the wet glide of onion separating from onion, wrinkling cellophane sliding off the chicken.

"If you're that bothered by it," he says, scraping the diced vegetables into a bowl, "we'll set up a camera."

She glances up.

"Guy at work said he caught his wife cheating by rigging up an old cell phone. Made it into a camera. It snaps a picture every 15 seconds or something when it senses motion. Not a movie, but you get an idea at least. He sure did, anyway, poor bastard."

"You talked about me at work?"

Lily assumed Dean's coworkers knew he was married, but that was probably the end of it. She never met any of them, was never invited to work functions or holiday parties. They had them. Dean went. If there was a list, though, her name was never on it. Other spouses probably were. Or maybe everyone at the plant was like Dean: compartmentalized. A place for each person in his world. Her place was out of sight.

"I mentioned you'd gotten into a tizzy about a glorified pedometer, yeah." He shrugs. "Consensus was, best way to quit your bitching is to solve the damn problem."

***

"All right, here we go." Dean makes a final adjustment to the phone propped against a stack of books, checking the screen before straightening himself. "Aimed directly at your side of the bed. You're gonna see exactly what you do every night: snore and fart and that's it."

She reddens. "Thanks," she murmurs, glancing at the darkened screen. Self-voyeurism, she thinks. A shame twinges her heart; she doesn't know why.

***

"Wake up." Dean pokes her, a sharp jab to her clavicle. "You're gonna be late."

"Mmph. What time is it?" Lily's back twinges in protest as she sits up slowly, blinking away bleariness.

Dean, already showered and dressed, yanks the blankets from her body. She flinches, hands flying to cover anything revealed by shifting pajamas. "Time for you to get your lazy ass out of bed so you don't lose your shitty job."

Her eyes find the dresser the phone was propped on: "But—but it's gone."

Dean's voice, abraded with irritation, emerges from the closet where he rummages. "What's gone? Your shitty job?"

"No—the phone." The books are scattered across the dresser and floor, the phone nowhere in sight. She checks behind the dresser, under the lamp.

"You. Don't. Have. Time," he says, emerging from the closet with a pair of steel toe shoes.

She checks her activity tracker. 7:45. Shit. She has 10 minutes.

She taps the tracker once. 7,396 steps.

Another tap. 146 active minutes.

Lily types the wrong order in for the third time. With a deep sigh, she clears the spreadsheet cell and retypes, checking against the form. A minor success, but she'll take it. She checks her wrist. It's only 10:30. She sighs again and glides her chair away from the desk, spinning to stand. 8,426 steps. She straightens her back and attempts a confident stride that doesn't last past the edge of her cubicle. Her shoulders instinctively round, a useless protection against consternation. She shuffles the remaining steps to the restroom. 8,502. Chooses between the two stalls, urinates, washes hands, returns to desk. 8,634.

Steps

Back in her cube, she stares at her fitness tracker. 7,396 steps overnight. She slumps in her chair and practices flinging her arm over her eyes, as in sleep. Steady 8,634. She rolls to the side in her chair, tucking her arm under her chin. Release: 8,635. Okay. Maybe she did that 7,396 times.

"Um." A small throat noise from behind her. She straightens and whirls in her seat. Marcus is actually looking at her.

She holds up her wrist. "My, uh, my—my tracker. It—it's counting weird."

Marcus cocks his head. "Yeah, okay . . . "

Blood pulses against the surface of her skin. "I've just been thinking about it."

"Sure." Marcus shifts and he glances to his hands, probably wishing he had his thermos to look at. "How about that shipment to Nerino's?"

Through the front door, Lily finds Dean sprawled in his easy chair, remote in hand.

"I'm so tired," she moans, tossing her keys and purse on an end table. She falls on the couch, allowing the velocity to carry her feet up beside her. "Marcus was—"

Dean holds up the missing phone, twisting it side to side.

"Oh my god, where'd you find it?" She springs up, leaning forward. Closer, the phone isn't right. She leans more. "Oh no." A spidering crack glints facets off the screen. A hunk of glass is missing from the middle. "What—"

13

Dean gestures to the TV and presses play. Her figure on the screen sits up, stop motion jerkiness jarring her limbs in unnaturally quick angles. Her hair falls around her shoulders in a waterfall of string. She's still for several frames. 15 seconds between each picture. She sits, unmoving, flash after flash. Several moments later, her figure is gone.

"Wh—? Do you—?"

Dean waves her away and nods at the screen. He presses a button and the scenes skip forward, picture after picture of her empty side of the bed. Play. She reappears in the screen, standing by his sleeping figure. 4, maybe 5 flashes: just standing. In an instant, she's across the bed, crouched in her spot. The phone flashes white as her hand closes on it. The feed cuts.

Lily's fingers are numb. She searches her hands for any sign of what she'd done to the phone. No marks to be found. "I—oh my god, Dean, I—"

"Do you know how much we could've sold that phone for?" Dean glances up. It occurs to her that he hasn't looked at her since she walked in. "I was waiting to put it on eBay, but I let you use it for this horseshit and look what you did."

"I'm so sorry, I—"

"I don't need you to be sorry. I need you to work your shit out." Dean stands, tossing the remote on his chair. He picks up a box from beside the lounger and hurls it at the couch, missing her by inches. "Motion-activated camera. Set it up yourself."

Steps

Lily flings the comforter to Dean's side. The night isn't warm, but tonight the heavy down stifles her. Her feet kick the remaining blankets aside. Dean snorts sharply beside her before his breath falls back into rhythmic sleep sounds. Shallow clicks at the back of his throat crescendo quickly into deep throated snores. That he ever criticizes her sleep . . .

She rolls to face him. His hair burrs close to his scalp, a short widow's peak pointing lazily to his nose. When they met, his hair was longer, a parted mop flopping boyishly across his forehead, flinging with every movement of his head. She's almost sure he had liked her once. Or maybe he hadn't. Maybe she just stumbled into his path when the stars collided to convince him he needed to settle down.

Her hand reaches to brush hair that no longer exists from his eyes. She used to fall asleep looking at him just like this. Fewer lines splintered from his eyes, and the furrows on his brow weren't so deep, but she remembers this face. Her fingers reach his forehead. A sleep-heavy hand reaches from his side to brush her away. A mosquito.

A red light on the camera flashes 3 times and changes to a steady green. It's connected. Lily folds her legs under her on the couch and surfs television inputs to AV1. The camera's menu lights the screen. Dean's weekly golf outing leaves her hours to watch the footage. She scrolls the options. Last 3 hours? No. Last 6? Last 12. That covers it. She fast forwards past somnolent Dean slapping her hand away. She fell asleep soon after.

Within a few moments of black and white night footage, her attention starts to drift. She checks the buttons on the camera and finds an option to skip ahead 5 seconds. She taps the button once. Again. Again. Again. Stop motion footage of languid tosses and turns, mouths falling open in gaping sleep breaths. She stops skipping when she sees Dean's hand brush against her back. He recoils quick as he touched her, as repulsed by her in sleep as he is in waking. Lily skips forward again, her thumb striking the button harder than necessary.

She releases the button when her onscreen figure sits up in bed, a sharp upward jolt. Her heart quickens as she leans closer to the television, watching herself. Her screen self slides one, then both legs over the side of the bed, ghost-white hands grasping the edge of the mattress. There it sits frame after frame, a motionless screen twin.

On the couch, Lily sits back, an indecisive finger fluttering over the skip button. A movement on the television stills her hand. Her screen self has begun to turn its head, a notching jerk-motion so slow, she checks to see if she somehow set the footage in slow motion.

No. The head continues to ratchet, body shifting only as much as absolutely necessary. Its eyes are open, open and unblinking as they land on Dean's body curled on his side. She begins counting the seconds her screen self goes without blinking.

30.

46.

58.

Dean's body flops like a fish to his back, the

bedframe shuddering. From her side of the bed, Lily's screen double flies off the mattress fast as it had been slow before, a single leap so graceful she doesn't need volume to know it has landed silently. She never knew her body could move so lightly, so decisively. Her black and white doppelganger, a lithe stranger using her body in unfamiliar ways, keeps its eyes on Dean. Its shoulder blades pull together, forcing the head forward, pivoting to track its target as it prowls off screen.

The pajamaed figure appears a moment later on Dean's side of the bed. Silent feet glide close to him. He doesn't move. Lily watches as her body freezes over him on the screen, neck bent a sharp 90 degrees down to watch him. Her hair rippled with the initial movement, but now it stays as rigid as the rest of her, not the slightest tremor to break its hold until finally, one foot shatters the pose. It slides left. The screen twin begins pacing. Back and forth, back and forth, head bobbing like a cobra, shoulders braced with ready tension. Lily can't always see its eyes, but she is sure they don't blink.

It paces so long, Lily begins to skip forward, her sleep-self jumping point to point within the same line, steady steps along an invisible track. It stops again. She resumes normal speed.

Again, a foot breaks rank. It lifts to the bed's sideboard. The other creeps silently behind, body folding to an accommodating perch, a soundless bird hunched over Dean as he sleeps. Its head cocks; she wonders what it's thinking. It pulls itself up onto the bed, one leg stretching sidelong across Dean, the other pulling up beside him.

17

It crouches low over him, and the ghost fingers float to his chest where his hands rest. They pick them up from his body, soft and slow. Its gaze never strays from his face even as the quiet hands pull his wrists together. He doesn't stir. The sleep twin nods and hops off the bed, sauntering off screen.

Lily waits for it to return to her side of the bed, but the night room is still. She counts her breaths as she watches the empty screen. The inhalations grow louder and faster in her ears, huffing. She loses count, starts again. She skips ahead; 5, 10, 15 seconds. Bursts of emptiness; she presses the button again and again until the stranger, her other self, returns.

It glides open her bedside drawer and reaches in, depositing something in the deep recesses. It closes the drawer with care and climbs into bed, pulling the blankets around itself and tucking back into a corpselike sleep, unmoving the rest of the night.

Lily fast forwards to the morning. The video cuts back to the main menu. She drops the camera to her side and stares at the screen. She doesn't know how long she sits frozen before leaping from the couch— far less gracefully than her screen self. She runs to the bedroom and flings open her nightstand, pawing past ear plugs and antacids, magazines she'll never finish, a box of tissues. She shoves it all aside until her hands land on the unfamiliar. She pulls it out, already knowing: a roll of duct tape.

✂︎✂︎

Her knife slices slanted through chicken breasts cooked tenderly in cumin, paprika, cayenne and more. Lily never cared much for the spice of Mexican food, but Dean loves it. At least once every other week he stops for carryout at the Mexican place on his way home from work, crashing through the door with stacks of Styrofoam boxes venting spiced steam that hurts her nose. He orders refried beans for her. He says there's no spice, but she's sure it seeps in by osmosis. She takes a few obligatory bites, dimming her hunger just enough to pretend to be appreciative for his providence. Invariably her empty stomach squalls by bedtime; Dean blames the beans.

But today there will be no pretending. Lily wants to make this for him. She wants to see pleasant surprise lift the lines on his forehead when he returns from golf. If she ever made him happy, maybe she can do it again. Maybe a train can jump the track for a better one.

She stirs a bubbling pot of Spanish rice and her fingers flip the dial to a simmer. The waves of her consciousness dredge up the duct tape again. She shakes her head, hoping the physical movement will rattle the thought from her brain.

It doesn't. The image of the tape in the back of the drawer, hidden and ominous, taps her mind's corners, unrelenting. She draws a weighted breath, pulling it deep into her lungs. She holds. It's a quirk. People do all sorts of things in their sleep. They walk, they talk, they have sex, they eat. Primal desires worked out in unconsciousness.

Maybe her sleeping mind just wanted to fix something. Hadn't she for years asked Dean for various home repairs that always fell ignored? Maybe her brain was striving for unrealized improvements.

She lifts her head a little as she plucks a tomato from a basket to be chopped. It's a nice thought: maybe she's growing.

The front door clicks open and slams again. A rattling clang echoes from the front of the house, Dean dropping his golf bag in the living room. Lily dices faster, finishing the tomato just as he crosses the kitchen's threshold.

"Hey!" she cries, wincing at her voice's excited shrill. She tries to recover, popping up on her toes to kiss his cheek; she pretends she only imagined his body tensing with her touch. A sharp waft of cheap lager wafts from his breath, maybe even his pores. She steps back and waves a Vanna White hand before the spread: spiced chicken, slivers of avocado, bright red chunks of fresh tomato, diced jalapenos and onions, flour tortillas warmed on the stove beside the pot of steaming rice.

"Chicken tacos just for you," Lily chirps, lifting her voice for a more pleasing lilt. It almost works until her natural warble jostles for position at the end, choking the "you."

Dean's eyes fall briefly on the display. His expression doesn't change, forehead lines unmoved. "Me and Lucas grabbed food on the way back," he says. He grabs a stack of mail from the top of the microwave and flips through. "Next time let me know."

Lily's shoulders slip a notch. She glances at the piles of food. It's enough for both their lunches next week. Great. She kneels and begins pulling storage containers from a lower cabinet.

"You check out your camera?" Dean asks, slicing open an envelope with a dirt-caked thumbnail.

Steps

Her voice echoes from inside the cabinet, fingers clawing in the dark for a matching lid. "Yeah." She emerges, clutching a stack of lids, none of them likely to fit. She rocks back on her haunches and looks up to Dean. He scans a bill notification, flipping the paper over before tossing it onto the counter. He goes to the next piece of mail. She drops her eyes and shuffles the lids in her hands. "Just sleeping."

Dean snorts and grabs the stack of opened envelopes. "I told you."

"You did."

"Probably just knocked my phone off the table with your fuckin' sleep flails. I told you you're a nightmare to sleep with."

Lily nods. "You did."

Credits blacken the television screen. Just as white-lettered names begin their rapid scroll, Dean clicks the set off with a decisive jab of the remote. "I'm hitting the hay." He stands and stretches, his t-shirt rising over the sway of a beer belly, exposing a thatched path of hair trailing down his midsection. "You coming?"

Lily glances up from a magazine she'd been too distracted to read. "I'm not tired yet." She flips a page for emphasis, furrowing her brow as she looks back down, her best reading face.

He shrugs and traipses down the hall.

She waits until she no longer hears the nighttime sounds of the toilet flushing, water running, drawers opening and closing. She waits for several moments of silence, her fingertips brushing the glossy sheen of the magazine. When she's certain he's asleep, she tiptoes to the kitchen and brews a pot of coffee. She doesn't want to sleep tonight, but already her tired eyes droop.

The coffee pot groans with percolation. Lily thinks of the camera. She left no evidence, not that Dean offered any more interest beyond gloating. She returned the camera to its place atop the wardrobe. The duct tape—she'd barely wanted to touch it after what she'd seen. Still, she returned it to the kitchen catch-all drawer. Now she slides the drawer open . . . it's still there.

The coffee pot sputters the final throes. It's not like she can never sleep again. How is she supposed to willingly fall into bed after what she's seen, though? Sleepwalking is one thing. Sleep-hiding objects is another, but still relatively tame. The thing that's sticking in her mind, though, the image she can't stop playing, is the look on her doppelganger's face as she'd walked out of shot after doing whatever that was to Dean.

She didn't know her facial muscles made that expression. She was serene. No tension marred the corners of her mouth, no sadness tugged her eyes, no concern knitted her brow, deepening that vertical wrinkle between her eyebrows. It wasn't just the serenity that perplexed Lily. Nearly everyone becomes serene in sleep, even if they're wandering around.

It was more than that. As it walked away from Dean, the sleep twin's mouth twitched. It started slow, growing, expanding, lips stretching wider and wider until she disappeared from the lens.

She'd smiled.

Steps

The lid peels off her lunch container with a damp crack. She gazes into the plastic box and sighs. Two days later and the tomatoes are mush, the avocado nearly black with bruising. She pries open the microwave, caked with the crust of countless employee lunches bursting with no cover. It should've been replaced last year. She hopes the microwave bleeds the ingredients together so she can at least pretend not to know what she's eating.

She leans against the counter and folds her arms, closing her eyes. She could sleep here, a quick rest. By the grace of coffee, she's made it since Saturday without sleep, without incident. Her steps were normal. The sleepless can't sleepwalk. Lily's eyes fall heavier. She doesn't know how long she can do this. Her lunch pops in the microwave. It continues whirring, a clunky mechanical hum. Her head drops a notch. Just a minute. Just a rest. It's all she . . .

"Hey, how'd that—" Marcus stops as her eyes fly open. A fine tension grows, starting at her lips, threading through the tendons of her neck, laces her clavicles and pulls her shoulders sharply down, curling her back. Her exhausted eyes burn, searing Marcus where he stands. Employee and manager freeze in time. Lily remains curled and feral. He can't even remember what he was going to ask her. It ceased to matter the moment her eyes hit him. He felt suddenly small; he didn't like it.

The microwave gives a sickly beep. Her muscles release and she turns, yanking her lunch from the turntable. She shoulders past Marcus, his coffee jostling as he jerks out of her path.

⚬⚬⚬⚬⚬

She feels her eyes close. She allows it. Just for a blink, a brief respite. The television blares with a hunting show Dean follows with religious rapture. He doesn't hunt. Nor does he do the woodworking from the magazines he orders or brew beer from the kit she got him years ago. He doesn't have hobbies—he watches them. Other than golf, and Lily suspects he rarely swings a club for any reason other than the myriad beers that follow. He collects hobbies he doesn't perform and she's meant to support him.

She feels her eyes close, but she doesn't feel her body relax. She doesn't notice the moment she no longer hears the television hunter murmuring dulcet admirations for the white tail he's about to shoot through the heart. The next thing she notices is Dean poking her arm hard, a sharp jab breaking a dreamless sleep. She flies from the couch into a crouch, arms bent rigid for combat. "What the hell are you doing?" she yells.

Dean steps back. A brief smile skitters across his face. He wants her angry. The smile flits away and he furrows his brow. "Don't talk to me that way."

Her arms drop. Lily folds them across her body, drooping into a familiar slump. "You scared me."

"Maybe you just need to be less jumpy." He slaps her elbow. "You need to pull it together, girl. I don't know what's going on with you, but I don't like it." He turns toward the hall. "C'mon. I'm tired."

Steps

She wants to resist. If she was a better person, she would stay up another night. She can't. She can't be better. She can't resist sleep another moment. Even now, she doesn't feel like she can make it to the bedroom. Her left foot drags, her right follows. Step by shambling step, she makes her way down the hall and into bed.

⸙⸙⸙⸙⸙

The next day's footage isn't so different from the first. Her screen sister sits up. It waits. It rises and disappears. Lily doesn't hold her breath this time. She just waits for it to come back and, like a faithful creature, it does. In the same pattern, it checks Dean's feet, her birdlike body crouched over him. She can't muster the horror she did before. Maybe she's still tired. Maybe she's been tired for years.

It holds Dean's ankles in its hands. Slow, methodical movements turn them: left, right. He sighs a little, his shoulders roll, a slight readjustment. It holds deathly still, feet in its grasp, and waits. He collapses back into peacefulness. The night creature nods, then rests his feet gently back into position. Barely moving the mattress, it slinks off the bed and onto the floor, disappearing from the camera.

It reappears a moment later by the nightstand. Silently, it slides the drawer open and begins to dig. It knows where it's going; it doesn't take long to discover the tape is no longer there. It flies up, suddenly erect.

Lily leans closer to the screen. This is different. The screen self turns its shoulder just enough to glare

25

up at the wardrobe. The camera. Quick as a snake, it runs to the end of the bed and disappears for a flash. As fast as it was gone, it reappears, perched on the footboard. It rises, spine ratcheting, until it stands, rigid, in front of the camera. It leans in again, as close as it can. Its lips twist, almost a smirk.

It's not really angry. But it's caught her. It raises a finger. Lily looks at her hands. She didn't realize before how bony her fingers are. She glances up at the screen. It's almost as if it waited for her. The finger wags once, twice. It tuts. Its mouth twists into a grin, the same smile she saw last time: this is a game, and she didn't play fair.

The thing steps off the bed, landing soundlessly off screen. Lily tries to peer around the edge of the television to see where it went. It returns with a bag of items this time. It tucks the bag deep in the drawer, just like before. Closing the door, it turns to the camera one last time. It widens its unblinking eyes in a final warning. With a smirk, it crawls into Lily's place in bed and folds into sleep once again.

Lily lifts the last dish from the sinkful of soapy water and runs it under the faucet. Her sleep self can keep whatever she stashes in the nightstand. Clearly, it's important to it. If that's what it wants, it can have it. Lily's too tired. She can't keep staying up for this; keeping herself awake is hurting her a hell of a lot more than squirreling away nonsense items in her sleep. She runs a towel in circles over the dish, front and back and slips it into the cabinet. It's time to be done. She can't keep going. She nods to herself: this is it.

Dean belches as he crosses into the kitchen. "Hey, next time, you think you could try adding at least *some* seasoning to the food? I mean, I'd love some flavor, but Jesus Christ, at this point I'd settle for a dash of salt." He laughs and opens the refrigerator, bending to peer in. The wet fizz of a beer can cracking open precedes his straightening. He takes a loud slurp, clearing the foam. "Hey, you haven't been yapping about your fit-band-whatever-the-hell lately."

"I wasn't yapping," Lily mutters, not looking at him. She dries her hands on the dish rag.

"Eh? What was that?" He steps closer, mock-tugging his ear like an old man. "You say something?"

She slaps the dish towel on the counter. "I. Wasn't. *Yapping.*" She enunciates each syllable, whirling, standing taller to glare up at him. "I was sharing a concern with my husband. My mistake." She wags her finger between them, once, twice. "I forgot that's not how *this* works."

Dean's tongue works under his lips, running over his canine tooth as he regards her. "This how you talk to me now?" He shakes his head, taking a thin-lipped sip of beer. "I don't know what's going on with you, but I hope you snap out of it real quick."

A vein pulses in her neck. "Snap out of it? *Snap out of it?*" Lily throws her hands before her, claws daggering the air between them. "I have been doing everything I can to *snap out of it.* I've used your stupid camera, I've watched *hours* of us sleeping, I've *stopped* sleeping just so I can *snap out of it.*" Her entire body pulses now, eyes bulging and wild. "And *you*!" She jabs an arrowed finger at him. "*You* sleep like a rock *Every. Single. Night,* nice and rested to freshly harass me every *goddamn* day! The *only* way this has impacted your life is it gives you one more little spike in your boot for kicking me while I'm down. That's *it*."

Lily's chest heaves and she's not sure she's ever said so many words in row. It feels good. Her throat feels open in a way she's not sure it ever has. Breath rushes freely through her windpipe. Her eyes never leave Dean; she doesn't dare blink.

He lifts his chin and stares back down at her. "That's how you see me?" He steals another step between them. Lily forces her feet to stay grounded. "Do you have any idea what people see when they look at us? Do you? *Look at me*."

He straightens his posture, seeming to tower over her now. He spreads his palms to display his magnificence, and maybe he was once. Maybe in a time when his face didn't sag under the weight of regret, when resentment didn't line his skin, when kindness crinkled his eyes more than contempt—if there ever was such a time—maybe then he *was* what he thinks he's showing her now.

"They see some poor sap who settled for the first girl who seemed like she might make a decent wife." He laughs, a sharp clap that shudders her bones. He leans so close she can smell the hops on his breath and she fights the urge to bite the nose right off his smug face. "Guess that was *my* mistake, sweetheart."

He drops back on his heels and shakes his head, a snarl barely curling his lip. She's not even worth the effort of a full sneer. "Look at you. You know what I say when I run into folks from the day? I tell 'em we split up years ago. I tell the guys at work I barely see you. I tell anyone I can find that I got nothing to do with you anymore because the *idea* of being connected with *you* in any fucking way is the worst humiliation I can imagine."

He swigs his beer again, his eyes never leaving hers. He drops the can to his side and swaggers forward. "And you know what people say? They don't say 'sorry.' They don't feel bad for me. You know why they don't? Because they know what a sad fucking *joke* you are. They know I'd be better off without you."

Her chin won't stay up anymore—another moment lifted and the quivering might give way to tears and she will not let him see it. She might cry, but he will not see it. Her head drops and she closes her eyes, willing herself to breathe just steady enough that he won't know. Lily feels his eyes on her, though, and she's ashamed. A few quick gulps, then the sound of metal crunching. He tosses his crushed beer can just past her to the sink, the velocity breezing her hair.

"I'm going to bed." He throws the words behind him on his way out of the kitchen.

She waits until his heavy steps reach the bedroom. Her head snaps up. She draws a long breath through her nose and draws in her shoulder blades. She breathes deep until she is sure she won't cry. Long, soundless strides carry her to their shared bathroom where she flings open the medicine cabinet, scanning for anything with the letters "PM." Her eyes land on a nighttime cold medicine; she smirks and pulls out two pills, quickly dry-swallowing them before her weakness could stop her.

In the bedroom, Dean is already snoring. She changes into pajamas and slips quietly into bed beside him, pulling the blankets to her neck. Under them, she folds her arms over her chest like a corpse and waits for the pills to lull her to sleep.

A muffled bellow startles her awake. Lily blinks. Where is she? She's standing. No . . . she's not. She's crouching. The realization brings gravity with it and she tumbles sidelong onto the mattress. The motion lights her tracker: 9,949. The mattress jolts and Dean yells again, an amalgam of panic and rage pitching his voice. She hasn't heard this before. She looks up from her tracker, her mind still battling to shake her waking confusion. On the mattress beside her, Dean is flat on his back, uncovered, hands over his head.

Lily blinks.

"What are you—" She stops short. He squirms and something at his wrists glint over his head. Duct tape. She scrambles to her feet on the mattress. Under her, Dean is bound like a spitted pig, his wrists taped and lashed to the headboard, his feet similarly trussed to the footboard. His mouth, too, is covered with the silvery tape. She falls to her knees and rips the duct tape off, watering his eyes. "Dean, what is—"

"Don't do it," he yells, damp eyes wide on hers. He drops his voice, pleading, "Don't do it, please, I'm sorry."

"Do wh—" There's something in her hand. What— she understands before she can even lift her hand. A thick plastic bag crinkles in her grip. Lily holds it up. Her sleep sister's offering. She looks back at Dean. Two offerings. She closes her eyes tight. When she opens them, she'll *really* wake up and none of this will be happening.

"Please, I'm telling you, we can talk about this, I can change, I know it hasn't been great lately."

She sighs and unclenches her eyes.

His voice rises again, a fresh wave of panic, "You don't have to do this. You don't have to do this, Lil. Please. I didn't mean what I said, Lil, you're great, everyone knows you're great. I didn't settle for you, Lil, you—you settled for *me*!" He nods, eyes wide and wet, like maybe he's almost believing it. She doubts it. "You settled for me, Lil, and maybe I'm just jealous, maybe if you just let me loose, we can talk this out and really make it right. What do you think?"

If this were a movie, Lily would know he meant it. If this were a movie, she would rip the tape from his limbs and they'd tearfully fall into each other's arms, inextricably bonded by their close call. In their movie, he'd hold her tight and they'd both know this was forever and this was real.

"Come on, Lil. Just let me go. Let me go and we'll talk. That's what you always want, right? To talk? Now we can! We can talk all you want, Lil, I promise, I promise."

She cocks her head to the side. He's a pitiful sight, bare-chested and bound, eyes wild and pleading. A desperate creature who would say anything to get out of the trap it built.

This isn't a movie. It never has been and never will be.

Kari McElroy

Lily looks to the bag in her hands, the plastic gleaming like water in the street lights from the window. She thinks of her sleep sister, and all she went through to bring them here. Her mouth quirks. Her lips draw up, an invisible string pulling the corners from each ear. She crouches over Dean and she smiles.

The Eleventh Hour

Kasey Pierce

May 18, 2000

Welp, the gang is finally moved in! Me, Ang, and our boy Hal.

The new home is really coming together. Ang needs to quit with the church rummage sales, though. This house is beginning to look like a dime store.

Still, I do love the snowy alley picture she picked up. She grabbed it by mistake. Kept saying to throw it out and that it gave her the creeps. Hell, I loved the snowy telephone poles. Reminded me of the burbs I grew up in. But "People get jumped in dark alleys," she said. "Throw it out."

And that's exactly why I put it up. Ain't I a stinker? ;)

✺✺✺✺

"Rob, get up and help me with these groceries."

Angie had had enough of this conspiracy bullshit.

The way she saw it, her husband let some obsessive internet fearmongers take over his entire state of being. His body, an absent husk. She needed him present, to look alive and to pay the mortgage.

Forcing the normal, she avoided eye contact with her Lurch of a husband while she organized the kitchen. Rob was taking a long time, listlessly unloading cans and cereal, when his son interrupted him.

"Dad, can I go to Devin's after church tomorrow?" Daniel asked.

Rob looked over to see a stout child rubbing the window with his meat mittens. "Sure," he replied, entranced by the pig boy.

Angie interrupted. "Not this Sunday, honey. Grandpa's having a spaghetti lunch in the basement after his sermon. Mr. Tulle just lost his job and we're helping out, sweetheart. I—"

She stopped to watch Rob gently stroking their son's cheek. There was something slightly unnerving about the sight.

"Why are you crying, Dad?" Daniel asked.

"I—I don't know, kid . . . " Rob sobbed softly.

"Okay! That's enough!" Angie threw down the rag she was using to wipe down the counters. "Daniel, go outside!"

Daniel stepped back as Angie hauled Rob into the living room.

"Jesus!" she whispered harshly. "Are we going to have to send you to a shrink? I'd send you to my dad for counsel but I don't even want him knowing about this! You're losing it! That blog, and these—these *theories* . . . they aren't real! Your family is!"

The Eleventh Hour

Rob stared at the carpet, as absent as ever. "Leave me."

Angie stood frozen, shaken by the all-too-simple delivery of that statement. "What?" she breathed.

He turned like a frustrated primate, mouth agape. "LEAVE ME, ANG! Enjoy what's left of this peaceful reality!"

"Shhhh." She put her hands on his shoulders to bring his orchestra down. Leaning her forehead against his, she spoke, softly this time. "Rob . . . this is going to stop and *I'm* going to help you. We*'re* going to help you."

"We?"

※※※

Jan 26, 2012

I'm going on day three of touch-and-go sleep. It was last night that I asked my wife to hold me. I know that, to her, it was a strange request. Especially coming from me. To be completely honest, I really wanted my mother. Me, a grown man. I've never been this helpless before.

They're watching me sleep, too. I know it. I feel them breathe. I thought I saw one pass in the hall right before I slipped into sleep. I just threw the blanket over my head. I'm not ready to know what they want with me.

※※※

"Christ has taught us that we show true love through sacrifice."

Reverend Moss had arrived at a brief fermata, like ministers do, the dramatic rest wedged in to let the previous statement soar, for showman's sake.

"First John 2:11: *But he that hateth his brother is in darkness, and walketh in darkness, and knoweth not where he goeth, because that darkness hath blinded his eyes.*"

Angie strayed, letting the current of the crowd take her and Daniel away from Rob. Her father would fish him out, like they'd planned.

Rob felt the callused, heavy hand of Reverend Moss on his shoulder. "Robert, I'd like to speak with you, son."

Rob gave a slight nod. He didn't want to attract any attention.

Moss's office was like that of a small-town dentist: cheesy wallpaper and dated inspirational posters. He motioned to the folding chair opposite his desk. "Have a seat, son."

"I'm sure Angie's told you about my behavior, as of late," Rob mumbled.

"Sure, but I want to hear it from you. Right now, I am not your reverend or your father-in-law," Reverend Moss said, taking a seat behind his desk. He leaned back. "No, right now we are simply two men in this room."

Rob forced every thought he had to the back of his mind. What questions could the old man possibly answer? Unless he could recommend a pill for seeing purple elephants or give him some chicken bones to shake over himself.

Their breath became slightly more laborious as they stewed in the thickening awkward. Rob was hiding himself in plain sight, wishing he were invisible, while Moss was bound and determined to move things along. He pierced the silence with an exhaled prayer, a groaned "Thank you, Jesus."

That's when it occurred to Rob, the way his father-in-law could help. The realization was a stabbing thought that jarred the words out of his mouth. "Why do you read from the KJV?"

Reverend Moss frowned, as if thinking. "Well, the King James Version is a very sacred text, son. We Pentecostals believe that the essence of the blood of Christ resides in this text and we plead it over our lives each day to protect us as we walk amongst evil."

Rob licked his teeth and looked around the room before killing the thought with a bland, "Okay."

Moss squinted, apparently unsure if he was supposed to feel a jab or not. "Is this about your faith, Rob?" he asked gently.

At that, Rob slapped his knees and looked the Reverend straight in his wrinkly-jowled face. "No, Pops. I'm afraid it's about *yours*."

"What do you mean?" Moss studied the frazzled young man in front of him.

"Your KJV is different now," Rob said in a whisper. He leaned toward the desk. "*They* changed it."

Silence bridled them both. Moss knew Rob as a son-in-law, sure. Over the last decade, he'd watched him turn become a loyal husband to his daughter and a doting father to his grandchild. Rob had worn a lot of hats but this was the face that Moss was afraid to see again, a face he hadn't seen in quite some time. The strung-out face of an addict. Moss hoped his glance at Rob's forearms would go undetected, but he was caught instantly.

Rob rolled down his shirt-sleeves and scoffed. "Are you serious right now?"

"Calm down, son," Moss said. "We're all just worried about you."

Rob turned and gave a pleading look to the opposite wall. He looked desperate and unhinged, tossing his hands in the air for no discernible reason.

"Rob," Moss spoke quietly. "Who are *they*?"

Rob whipped his head around to face his father-in-law. "DON'T! Please," he added, his voice shaking. "Don't let them hear you. Or they might do it again."

With that, he made his way to the door.

"Just read it again," he said.

⸝⸜⸝⸜

June 7, 1997

Today, I can proudly say I'm five years clean. It's still hard to say that because five years is just a blink in time. I felt like I was shootin' up yesterday.

But then I met Angie. We all come short of the glory. Even Reverend's daughters, it seems. It was nice to know that the holiest among us could fall. Lucifer fell from Heaven, no? This woman was a beautiful angel and on her path to redemption . . . with me. It feels good and I feel good about the future. Her father is even grooming me for the family business. No, not for the pulpit. Heating and

40

cooling. I complete my journeyman's at the end of this month.

⸎⸎⸎⸎⸎

"HA! Rob, man, you serious?"

Erick stopped by with beers after an SOS from Angie. She only thought her dad's counsel would work because his vice-to-Christ had worked so well before. Or so it seemed. Angie's intentions were pure. She was just sending "the friend" in to talk some sort of sense into him. He'd expect a pal to hold off on the outright mocking. Still, it was nice to have the company. And the beer.

Rob flicked a tin cap across the basement. "What's so funny?" he asked.

"I'm sorry, man." Erick snorted in disbelief. "If the Bible is made up of bullshit, why does it even matter if its changing?"

"It's not just the Bible, Erick." Rob's response was less than passionate. He didn't care much if he won or lost the debate. To him, neither would matter. Rob figured he'd take what he wanted out of this—to feel something other than the thick of the new reality he'd sunk into. He'd really prefer Erick shut the fuck up and just deliver some laughs. But Erick's jokes didn't land at all. They were atheist ideals thinly veiled as mockery.

"So what else is there? Oh, wait," Erick chuckled, leaning forward. "Lemme guess, Christ rode into Nazareth on a unicorn."

Rob tried to drown out his friend's high-pitched laughter by swishing Heineken in his cheeks. That's

41

when Rob saw it. His mouth dropped open and his whole body stiffened, gone cold.

He was staring into the face of Seamore the Seal, a small stuffed animal. The basement's fluorescent lights danced off its blue plastic eyes.

The seal had belonged to Hal.

That's when the wooden paneling began to expand and collapse. The room was breathing and its hot breath made Rob sweat.

"What do you want?" Rob said aloud, scanning the walls and ceiling for any further sign of *them*.

Erick looked around, confused, then back at his friend. He set his beer down. "What's up with you, man? I want you to come back, bro!"

⸎⸎⸎

Feb 1, 2012

I saw Seamore the Seal in the basement.

Well, he saw me.

I know you can read this. I don't feel like I should be scared but I am. You win, okay? You have me terrified. I just need to know what you want. I also want to know why. Why are you doing this and where is he? Where is Hal?

⸎⸎⸎

"It's 8:30, Daniel. Go brush your teeth and tell your dad goodnight."

The child rubbed his plaid sleeve over his eye and yawned. "Goodnight, Dad."

Rob, holding the palm-sized stuffed seal, gave the smile that was expected of him. Daniel went up the stairs and Rob turned to where Angie was washing dishes. He hoped the sound of plates clanking would shift their home's heavy atmosphere. He wanted it to distract him from the weight of the stares from unseen things and bring him back into the present.

He smelled something nearby. Sour. As if something was perspiring on the couch, there and waiting. There was nothing there when he looked, but he could feel it. He had them worried. They didn't like what he was about to do.

Rob tossed Seamore the Seal's lumpy body to the countertop by the sink.

Angie smiled. "Aww, cute. Where'd you get this?"

Crippling regret settled in as soon as Seamore left his hands. What he'd thought was an armed pistol to fire, what he'd thought was evidence, was nothing more than a white flag. He had surrendered to *them,* outed himself. He wasn't some inter-dimensional outlaw. He was clueless. He felt as vulnerable as ever.

Rob rubbed the back of his head and readied himself to deliver what he'd silently rehearsed. It was a soliloquy to get Angie to say the child's name. Not Daniel. But as the words spilled out, he knew he'd made the wrong move. He was only fueling this waking nightmare and he knew it. He also knew that the nightmare had only just begun.

Rob stammered as he spoke, "You . . . you can't tell me you don't remember him."

Angie dried her hands then picked up the small stuffed animal to look at it more closely. "No, not at all," she said. "I feel kind of bad for not knowing, like maybe I should. Did you win this for me in a claw machine?"

Rob sighed hard and looked to the ceiling, hoping the tears would just roll back into his head. "No, Ang," he said hoarsely. "You have to remember him."

They began whispering now. It wasn't very clear what they were saying, but it was clear they were listening. It was clear they weren't happy.

He couldn't be a prisoner of his own life anymore. He refused. Come what may. "Hal."

Angie look perplexed and maybe a little annoyed. "Who?"

And then, all at once, Rob gave up his position. "Hal, our son."

A roar of wind rushed over his ears. He could guess that they were angry but when it came to Angie, there was no guessing. It was all too clear. She became volatile. The wind rushing past his ears wasn't them this time, it was her right hand coming toward his face. That slap sounded across dimensions.

"You insensitive prick!" she cried. "You've always blamed the miscarriage on me!"

※※※

Sept 12, 1998

Thirty-three hours of labor but she did it. My Angie is the strongest woman I know. I'm so blessed to say we welcomed Hal Lee Parker into the world at 11:58PM! He was really racin' to get here before the day ended, I guess! Ha ha!

I can't blog long but I wanted to report that I'm

sober and serene! New baby and a new job! Glad that insurance kicked in before the boy came! I'm living the suburban dream and, yes, it really is all it's cracked up to be. A Pleasant Valley Sunday kind of day EVERY day isn't so bad here in status symbol land. I have status. I'm someone to someone—heck, now I'm someone to two special someones. I'm overjoyed.

✧✧✧

Angie kept on screaming her "how dare yous" and something about divorce papers. Meanwhile, Rob had darted down the hall to Daniel's room. Daniel was the kid who just showed up one day in place of Hal, the boy he'd raised. Angie claimed Daniel was the only child they'd ever had, but Rob had no memories of Daniel being born, of pinching his rubbery baby cheeks.

And now, Daniel was gone, too.

All that was there when he turned the corner was an office. No dinosaur wallpaper. No racecar bed. No traces of youth at all. Something was different, though.

He stood in the hallway and clutched his hair as tightly as he wished he could time.

Angie could slam all the doors she wanted. Nothing could distract him from the glimpse of that picture, the one Ang had gotten from the rummage sale. The photograph of the dimly lit, snow-covered, empty suburban alley.

It now featured a small red car rolling up the way.

Angie wasn't the only one who lost her mind that night.

Kasey Pierce

❦❦❦

Dec 17, 2012

"The end of the world is nigh!" Yes, I admit to being fascinated with that conspiracy and maybe I *did* get a little roped up in it . . . and pissed off the wife.

I have to remember before I was a user, I was quite the scholar. I've studied countless Mayan texts and I don't know if I buy that when this calendar ends, so do we.

Odds are the poor bastard that chiseled it got assaulted by a rock from another savage creeping up behind before he could finish. People forget that primitive shit happens in primitive times. #primitiveshithappens

❦❦❦

Angie stood on the snowy stoop and smoked anxiously. One would have thought she were freezing, the way her hands shook. No one would guess that it could be nerve damage from having smoked a whole pack just this morning. She was out of patience, answers, and feeling in her tongue.

The snowbank in the backyard served as a screen on which she projected life as a divorcee. A sudden "Mrs. Parker?" startled her out of her future life story.

There stood a neighborhood boy she'd often seen but she couldn't place his name. He just registered as "neighborhood chubby kid" in her mind. "Oh, kid!" she said, coughing and laughing. "You scared me!"

46

"I'm sorry," he said with a smile. "I didn't mean to scare you." He stood there with rosy cheeks as if he expected her to continue the conversation. Rude accompanied awkward, and she felt some embarrassment for not knowing his name.

"What can I do for you, kiddo?" she asked, flicking her cigarette into the yard.

"I was just seeing if your son was home to play."

The awkward smile fled her face and made a beeline toward rage. Rob had something to do with this. Never would she have dreamed he'd sink this low. "I don't have a son," she responded in a voice so low, her frosty exhale carried the sound for her.

"Um, oh." The little boy stammered a few times then tried again, correcting himself. "Your stepson, I mean . . . I think. Danny?"

Angie stared daggers at the child and asked, "Did he put you up to this? My husband?"

While Angie was busy with interrogation at the back porch, her father was knocking at the front. Rob answered the door to a man whose every fiber was about to ride the wind like dandelion seeds.

Moss held a Bible in his hand and looked at Rob with pleading, glazed eyes. He tried to speak, "Rob . . . "

Rob rushed at him and pressed his palm to his mouth. "*Shh!*" He shook his head and looked to see if Angie was still preoccupied. He led the older man down to the basement.

Kasey Pierce

Dec 20, 2012

Nothing much to report. Seems dull to say the world is coming to an end, eh? All I'm saying is that if it does, this guy isn't getting his furnace looked at tomorrow. I only mention it because I was told that I'm the third H&C guy he's called out this month. Just replace the damn thing, eh?

 Some people.

Rob trudged his way up the snowy walk of the unkempt bungalow. The siding was stained and there was an old, duct-taped loveseat on the porch. The smell of mildew permeated his senses as he knocked on the door. *This guy's gonna be a troll, I just know it,* he thought to himself.

Just as he guessed, the man who answered the door was a stout, middle-aged creature who wore what was left of his hair like a donut crown. He was wrapped in an olive-colored afghan, no less, with a pencil behind his ear.

"Hello, Mr. London," Rob said. He assumed this was the right guy, though something in him hoped that maybe this was the wrong house. "I'm here from Grace Heating and Cooling. You called someone to look at your furnace?"

The hobgoblin-man poked his head out and swept his eyes across the porch, checking that the coast was clear. "Yes, come on in," he muttered.

Mr. London led Rob through the carpeted sea of soda cans and soiled paper plates. The little man looked all around the room as they walked, paranoid and anxious.

Rob scrunched his nose at the smell of stale potato chips. "Cleaning lady off today?"

Mr. London didn't even turn around. Waddling his way to the study, he murmured something about "them" taking away his family. The living room walls wore layers of pencil sketches of the same woman and child in different poses. Rob opened his mouth to ask about them but part of him didn't really want to know. On a drawing table in the study was a Bible with a homemade cloth book cover. Surely someone's grandmother had crafted it.

"So where's this pain-in-the-ass furnace ya got?" Rob said with an uncomfortable chuckle.

Mr. London did an about-face and motioned to the leather computer chair. "Please, Mr. Parker. Have a seat." Rob settled into the chair and Mr. London stood behind him. "Um . . . so," the little man said, his voice trembling. He opened the Bible in front of Rob. "It's not about the furnace, not so much. I just need an unbiased party, I guess."

Rob looked at him and smirked. "Okey-doke. So . . . what am I lookin' at?"

"I need to know before it changes again." There was panic in Mr. London's voice. "They keep changing the King James on me."

Rob frowned. He wasn't sure what that meant, or who "they" were, but the speed at which Mr. London flipped through the pages had him slightly alarmed. Hell, he couldn't lie. This whole thing was wildly uncomfortable, like a weird dream. He was ready to play along with whatever this guy needed to hear just so long as this whole ordeal was over soon.

"There." Mr. London had stopped flipping pages and was pointing to the book. "Read that—but not out loud . . . please."

Rob squinted at the underlined verse. It was Matthew 1:2-3. "Abraham begat Isaac; and Isaac begat Jacob; and Jacob begat Judas and his brethren." Rob leaned back from the text and gave Mr. London a curious glance. He'd carried out a task and awaited orders for the next step.

There was an uncomfortable pause between them until Mr. London broke it with, "Well?"

"Well, what?" Rob replied, clearly confused.

"Is there anything weird about that to you?"

Rob read it again with a more analytical eye. He stroked his chin a bit before responding. "Well, I do feel like there may be a typo. But that's about it."

Mr. London brought his feet together, raised his head, and inhaled; preparing for the answer to the final question he was about to ask. "What here is misspelled?"

"Well, I think it meant Jud*ah* not Jud*as*. The way this reads, it's like Judas wasn't an apostle but a part of the Christ bloodline." He scoffed and gestured to the page. "I'm no minister, but anyone who's read the Bible can tell you that Judas is synonymous with treason against Jesus."

Mr. London teared up and cleared his throat before whispering, "They've made my Savior the seed of a traitor."

"Aw, c'mon. This is a misprint, sir." Rob tried to calm down the rising drama. "Show me another copy and I'm sure you'll find this is a fluke."

The Eleventh Hour

The little hobgoblin man was practically wheezing. "This is the seventh copy I've looked at and they're all like this. Go into the kitchen and see for yourself."

Rob sighed and made his way to the other end of the house, stepping on every plastic fork in the place along the way. He rolled back the paneled divider to the kitchen and saw open books on both the counter and stove. He was making his way to the Bibles when the sound of a gun rocked his chest.

He ran to the office and found the walls spattered in brain matter. The body of Mr. London lay in a pool of plasma that flowed steadfast from his half skull.

Dec 21, 2012

This is the worst day of my life.

In a fit, Angie slammed clothes into a suitcase. Her aim was to flee to her parents for a while. She'd no idea that her father had just fled to their basement—to Rob.

"Now what did you read, Dad?" Rob asked solemnly. He didn't even take into account whether or not they were listening. He had come to the conclusion that there was nowhere to run or hide.

A mournful but silent reverend sat, bent over at the waist, holding himself. "All of it. It was the words of serpents that said Christ would not defeat Satan . . . and that . . . that his Father would die."

Kasey Pierce

❧❧❧❧

Dec 23, 2012

I'm playing along because they want me to. They watch me all the time now. They took my son, Hal, they took Mr. London's family, left us here to go mad. What they want from me I don't know. My life, like Mr. London's? What are they trying to do? Rip the wings off a moth and watch the ants devour it?

I feel them all around me. I'm surrounded but I don't want to surrender. There's something to this, though—what I'm learning. Maybe if I play ball, they could bring Hal back.

❧❧❧❧

Rob withdrew from everything and, if it not for telling his job he quit, could well have been a missing person. Though more alone than ever before, he felt just the opposite.

They weren't just watching, they were making a lot of noise now. The floor had never creaked so loudly and each time it did, he felt the ceiling drop a little lower. He'd often scream aloud, crying out and asking what they wanted. Forever naked to that he could not see.

He had no routine to speak of anymore for fear that any normalcy would be ripped from him once he obtained it. They weren't done with him, it seemed. There was more to their mission.

It was the drop of ice from the icemaker, as loud

as an M80, that finally scared Rob off. He grabbed his keys and wallet and ran out the door.

He felt as if he were driving through a giant fishbowl. Wherever he went, he couldn't escape the weight of an invisible, collective stare. He sought refuge at Del's Coffee. He'd be sure to make it a decaf.

Rob's unruly beard entered the shop before he did. This being his first day out in a month, he felt like he should be ashamed for walking amongst the living, like he'd escaped the asylum. At first, at least.

His eyes panned around the coffeehouse. It was a serene sight for sore eyes. Heads of dreads sipped Chai with heads of beanie caps. The espresso grinder even seemed to sing instead of scream. For once, he felt like he reached the dell in this nightmare game of tag.

A young, messy-bunned barista made her way to him from the far corner of the café, examining him from top to bottom as she strolled. She smiled and placed a pencil in her hair. "What's the story, morning glory?"

Rob stared at her blankly.

The woman chuckled and extended her hand. "I'm Cora. What's your name, stranger?"

He gripped the handful of mood rings and replied, "Oh. Rob."

She smiled slyly and shifted her weight from one foot to the other as if she were dancing. "Well, Rob." She motioned to a corner table. "We're not strangers here at Del's. We're all friends. I'll introduce you."

Maybe they left, he thought. *I don't feel the heaviness anymore.*

At the table were two thirty-something men, both

of them a cross between hippies and scholars. She provided a linked-arm introduction, "Ben. James. Meet my new friend, Rob."

James readjusted his cardigan and offered a warm hand. "Pleased to meet you, Rob. I'm James. Hey, have a seat."

Ben moved his book bag and tossed his sandy mop to the side to have a closer look at their new table buddy. With a matter-of-fact delivery, he asked, "Do you do drugs?"

Rob burst into laughter. The question was such a welcomed absurdity. It felt good to laugh. It was the first time in months that he'd done so. "Not anymore," he said, still laughing. "A long time ago."

James nodded and took a gulp of his tea. He watched Rob as he asked, "What kind?"

Before Rob could answer, Ben's voice rolled out like molasses. "I have a feeling they were the *wrong* kind of drugs."

James laughed and added, "Yeah, see, we do the right kind. All the right kinds."

Rob chatted with his newfound hippie scholars and closed the café. He collected their contact information and, when he went home, suddenly felt even more naked without them. With Ben and James, *they* weren't around, it seemed.

When he went home, it was right back to being monitored by the hordes of faceless things. This was Saturday and he knew full-well his new liberal liaisons didn't have church in the morning. He invited them over.

The next morning, he tidied up the place. He pointed at corners of the room and warned them that his people were coming over and they better not take his new friends away from him. There was no reason to.

At 10:00 AM the gang was at the door. "Hey!" Rob said loudly, letting them in. Cora held a small rolled rug. "Cora, what is that?"

She smiled and said, "I have my own magic carpet . . . helps me fly when I dance!"

Rob laughed and watched each one of them come inside. They each seemed to slide through the door in the coolest way possible. "We're dancing?"

James held a small brown baggie to Rob's face. "After pancakes."

Dining on psychedelics didn't sound like a great idea to someone as paranoid as Rob. Still, he'd remembered back to when he himself was a scholar. He'd read enough Huxley essays to know that DMT was enlightening. Maybe he'd find answers, his place in all this, or even just peace. Peace would be fine enough. Even if it was only for the twelve-hour stronghold.

While Ben and James lay in the living room listening to Neil Gaiman's *Norse Gods* on audiobook, Cora danced on a Hamadan rug in the office. It seemed to light up every time her feet moved. Rob's eyes found solace in the entrancing sight. He stood in the doorway, looking at the beautiful woman, and then something else caught his eye.

The photo of the snowy alleyway.

Rob watched the picture that Angie had hated so much. The small red car had never gone away, and now . . . it was rolling up the alley.

The small red car was actively rolling up the alley toward the frame.

He was eleven hours into the trip and the whole time he'd felt detached from *them*. He thought they were gone, at least for a little while. Maybe just while his friends were over.

Rob's body began to shake once he saw that red car moving. He knew he'd been mistaken.

He watched the scene through the intermittent tossing of Cora's dark locks. Four dark silhouettes: a driver, a passenger, and two backseat passengers came into view. The passenger got out and started up the gravel alley and closer to the frame. Closer to Rob.

The thing had no face to speak of. Just emptiness. It stopped still for a moment to study Rob, who by this time was clutching the wall farthest from the picture. It was his last voluntary motion. They had him pinned, paralyzed.

The passenger held up a white card with black writing on it that read, "We've been trying to tell you." The card dropped and the next one said, "What we've been up to."

He dropped the third card to reveal another message: "Things have been complicated since it happened."

Rob licked his sweat glazed lips and gulped. "Since what happened?"

"Since God died."

A burlap sack rolled out from the backseat and into the muddy snow of the alley. It was then he heard a voice he hadn't heard for a long time. A voice he had longed to hear for so long, but not like this. Not these cries.

Rob stood cemented to the spot, unable to tune out an eight-year-old's pleas for mercy.

The Eleventh Hour

Feb 13, 2014

Let me ask you a question. What scares you more? God's non-existence? Or that He once existed and now He's dead? The answer may vary based on where you come from, I'm sure.

✼✼✼✼

Something struck Cora. It sent her knees crashing to the Persian fibers of the rug in front of the live-action photograph. Her tongue picked up dancing where her body had ceased. Whatever had struck her, it took over. A spirit—was it *the* spirit?—had invaded her body. Incoherent jabbering ensued.

It was then Ben entered the room. Frozen like he was, Rob could not turn his head from the unholy sights and sounds. Ben, however, came into clear view once he knelt beside Cora. Rob cried out to both of them, "Please! My son! Do something!"

Ben ran his fingers through his sandy locks and turned back to Rob. "The weight of the world is far too much being dethroned from the right hand of my Father." Tears streamed down his cheeks. "Thank you for your sacrifice."

✼✼✼✼

If you answered "A," his non-existence is more frightening, then you must fear some sort of metaphysical vulnerability; that there's no protector or salvation from evil.

If you answered "B," that he once existed and now he's dead . . .

. . . that opens a window to a whole 'nother slew of fears, doesn't it?

⁕⁓⁘⁕

The three of them—Ben, Cora, and Rob—watched the unveiling of a lacerated Hal. His fair limbs and back now raw, his once-soft flesh now mere pomace.

⁕⁓⁘⁕

. . . who plays God now?

⁕⁓⁘⁕

James stepped into view with a moleskin notebook and pen in hand. He took his place beside Ben and put a hand on his friend's shoulder.

Ben looked at him and said, in a gentle voice, "Thank you for following me, son of Zebedee. Your Sainthood lives on and my Father would rejoice in your being at my side for this occasion. Please take account of all you see here." With that, James nodded and began scribbling in the notebook.

"Please help him!" Rob wailed. "Jesus Christ, help him!"

"NO!" Ben whipped around to reply. "One to save the world. One to be the new Savior."

The card-holding shadowman marched from the

foreground of the picture, past Hal. He began to scale one of the many telephone poles lining the alley. The pole stood under direct moonlight.

As the clouds rolled past the moon to light this cathartic and holy event, three other shadowmen pushed the naked and beaten Hal along. Once they reached the foot of the pole, one of them pointed to his shadow brethren at its peak.

A sobbing Hal climbed and his father screamed.

The faceless creature at the top danced a hammer in his right hand and jingled a fistful of nine-inch nails in his left.

I can't tell you who they are. I don't know. But I can tell you something.

I can tell you that things aren't what you think they are.

The second you realize things aren't the way you thought they were, ignore it. Never speak of it.

Don't eat the fruit.

I could tell you I'm God now, but you wouldn't believe me.

Ultimately . . . you should forget you ever read this.

Manifestation

Stefani Manard

H ere it is. The moment I had been actively avoiding ever since my sister was first placed in the care of the mental health system. I arrive wearing nothing remarkable, as my clothing will be taken away and replaced with less ominous apparel and slip-on shoes. No shoe laces on suicide watch. I am cataloguing the staff at the front desk, the calm décor that must be meant to soothe a depressed soul upon entry, and I know that even when the walls around me seem normal, inside there are wars being raged, minds being destroyed, in heads other than my own.

"Come with me. Your room is ready." The woman behind the desk, broad shouldered and lovely in the way that old paintings are, gestures for me to follow her. I oblige. My mind tries to stop my feet, but I have made this decision, so I move down the neutral-colored hallways, the ceiling a boring Tetris of bland, rectangular lighting.

I hear the woman ahead of me talking, but there is no part of me paying attention. I am beginning to question my choice, as nothing strange had happened to me in the last couple of weeks. Maybe there was a gas leak at my house, which caused me to have delusions, and I am here with a sound mind. That has always been a fear of mine. But I signed the paperwork, and at this point, the most important thing is my mental state. I need to know the truth.

✧✦✧✦✧

I had just buried my cat. He was my birthday miracle, my first fur baby, and he changed so many things in my life. I had resented him for waking me in the middle of the night when he was a kitten. I was twenty-one and my life revolved around college and late nights out with my friends.

He made this grating, high-pitched mewling sound, and I would throw my pillow over my head and wonder why I had taken on this responsibility. Eventually I would get up and care for him, but it took time to wash away the annoyance. When I placed him into the hole I had dug next to my house, I heard those sounds again, as echoes of the past, and wept, knowing I would never hear them ever again.

The hole was about three feet deep, and narrow. I didn't understand the weight of this slow dig at first, but when my brain comprehended its completeness, I felt guilty. I just threw him in the ground, as if he no longer mattered simply because his soul had moved on.

I found an empty cat litter bucket, and this seemed appropriate to my grief-stricken mind. I put some of his toys in there, even though at thirteen-years-old he had rarely played with them. I picked the flowers near my house and placed them in his makeshift coffin. One last gift to the little cat who had given me so much. When I could no longer find pretty things to send him off with, I put his hardened body into the container. It was difficult, both physically and mentally, but when I had finished, I felt that I had done my best.

I lowered the bucket into the earth and covered it with dirt, using my hands as a shovel. I felt . . . unbalanced. When I looked up, there was a small black mass sitting at the base of the tree in my yard. I didn't think anything of it. Hell, I barely gave it a second glance. My tears simply must have caused some ocular disturbance befitting my state of mind.

≈≈≈≈≈

"Here's your room. Lunch is at noon. Your roommate will show you around." The Rubenesque woman left me standing in the doorway to a small room, holding my thin sweater and my despair close to my chest.

I set my belongings in the small dresser. The unkempt, empty twin bed next to me oppressively occupies the space. I am not great with meeting new people, and am relieved that my roommate is not present. My body feels heavy, so I sit on the bed and lay back on the thin pillow.

This must have been what my mother felt like, detached and confused and trapped inside herself. Or my sister, on her third or fourth "stay" at whatever hospital would take our insurance. Generations of us, lost girls trying to find their way back to normal.

Stefani Manard

If normal exists, it is not a creature I've encountered. I've always prided myself on how I wasn't like the rest of my family, how I had my head together and no matter what traumas occurred, I always could find my way back.

But here I am (at last, at last), the fluorescent lights painting me jaundiced on a shitty bed in a place that most people never visit, and it feels . . . inevitable. It took so much wear to get me here. At least I can take pride in that.

Weeks had passed, and I had cleansed my home of almost everything that reminded me of him. All the trappings of his simple life, stripped away so that my pain could stay hidden in the dark where it belonged. I couldn't erase him completely. I kept a photo montage of him at the top of my stairs, from young to old, from lively to struggling to eat. A collage of his beautiful life, and my place in it. He would always be alive and a kitten in my mind.

I used the glow from my cell phone to walk up the stairs. The rest of the lights were turned off. I heard what sounded to be little feet scampering to the spare room, the room I had mentally dubbed, "Boo's Bedroom."

My heart dropped and I ran up the last few stairs and into his room for the first time since he died. There was nothing there, just the paintings waiting to be hung and an old TV waiting to be taken to the trash. I looked around anyhow, just to be sure, and that's when I saw it—that shadow thing I had seen at

Manifestation

Boo's funeral, or something very similar, was squatting beneath the window.

It was less of a blob now. In fact, it looked like it was trying to take on a form. I approached it with fear, as any sane person would do, and it vanished before my eyes. This time, I couldn't pretend it was a figment of my imagination.

I ran out of the room and into my bed, where I pulled the covers over my head, and hoped that the moonlight was just being the ever-creative trickster I'd grown to love. It was only a trick of the eyes.

That night I dreamt of Boo. He laid on my chest, as he often did, and I stared into his eyes. They were big and green, aware, and truly lovely. His tail swished, and as I reached to pet him, he leapt off of me, propelled by his strong back legs. He landed on the floor in the middle of the living room and stared at me, his tail still swishing. He talked to me, in that mewling way, the different sounds of a cat trying to tell you about his day. I got up and he led me to the back door. Even though he was never an outdoor cat, I opened it and let him out, following him out of curiosity.

My backyard had been replaced with a graveyard. It didn't look familiar, but it did, in the way of dreams. There were a dozen headstones, all in a row. Boo ran toward them, rubbing against each stone, purring all the while. I was unsure what this meant, and walked closer, curious. He laid down on one of the graves, looking content. I was close enough to read the headstones, but the words had been eroded by time.

A sense of dread came over me and I knew in this moment I needed to get my cat and go, but when I reached for him, he hissed at me. He was to be left alone, among the dead. My fear building, I walked away, but I kept calling Boo. My voice sounded like the sounds he made as a kitten calling for me, his ill-prepared mother.

As much as I didn't want to leave him, I knew I wasn't welcome in that place. Boo watched me; his huge green eyes glowing. I turned away, finally, and that was when something grabbed my ankle . . .

I woke with my chest heaving and my heart racing. I looked over to see if he was there, knowing the answer but hoping anyhow.

Even then, I was able to hold onto my rationality. I shook my head and let the dust settle, allowed my heart to reach a safe beat. I performed the breathing exercises an old shrink taught me to stave off panic.

Once I was still, I could chalk the whole thing up to heightened emotions. Grief. The subconscious manifestation of the worst of those things.

Dreams are nothing more than figments, I told myself. I pulled myself back to sanity because what choice did I have, really?

⸎⸏⸎⸏⸎

A younger girl with long, dark hair shuffles into the room, walking straight past me. I don't exist in her version of the world. She has on a long-sleeved Henley and hospital pants, bland as everything else in this place. She sits down on her bed so lightly, it's like she's a ghost.

When she pulls up her sleeves, baring her forearms, I catch sight of the slashes. It looks like they

66

are well on the way to healing, but they still radiate crimson around the edges, making them look angry. I can't help but wonder how that must have felt, to feel so broken that the only way to fix yourself is to cease to be.

"I'm Melissa." Her words are abrupt, her introduction hanging in the air like a strange cloud. I have nothing to say. She speaks again after several endless moments. "You must be Megan. They write our names on the outsides of the doors, so they don't get confused."

I am still silent.

"You saw my marks." She shrugs. "Suicide attempt number two, this one much more intrusive and accurate. Who knew there was a proper way to throw yourself into the void?"

I am startled by her honesty, but feel compelled to ask, "Why?'

She walks toward the window next to her bed, stopping to gaze out vacantly. "The world is simply too heavy for me to ever be light."

I understand this sentiment perfectly. I feel its weight as my delusions become more tangible.

More weeks had passed since the dream. I was outside tending to the small, pitiful garden I was attempting to grow in my front yard. My skills with plant life mostly involved trying to not kill them. It was hot, and sweat ran into my eyes. I needed a break. I got off my hands and knees, wiped my brow with the back of my hand, and stood for a moment, debating my next move. Intending to go inside and get some water and a blast of air conditioning, I found my feet taking me in the other direction, to the side of the house where my cat was rotting in the ground.

I had avoided this subconsciously, for obvious reasons, but it was as if my body was being drawn there. I rounded the corner of my two-story Tudor and froze, sweat turning to ice on my forehead.

A man was standing there with his back to me, no one I had seen around the neighborhood, and certainly not someone who should be lurking on my property. I was going to speak when he turned to face me. My shock turned into doubt and my head buzzed with ways to explain this impossibility. It was my grandfather. He had died many years ago, but now he was standing there, grinning at me as if this were a routine visit.

The vision of a dead loved one might be comforting, for some. Or disturbing. But when that dead loved one had been, in life, a man who had instilled fear and sadness inside of you, a person who had planted a seed of dread that quietly grew until you turned seventeen and found yourself having panic attacks for the first time in your life, feelings leaned toward anger.

And fear. Fear of the man who was there, but never *really* there, for my mother and grandmother. The man whose idea of support and love was playing cards and calling names, the man whom I held responsible for the decline of my mother's mental health. This man had no place here, even though he lived on, in the dark place inside me.

I was never one to shy away from the

supernatural, and my fear of my grandfather had turned to hate a long time ago, so I moved toward him, almost as if a hook had found its home in my guts and was dragging me there. As I came closer, I saw that his features were not fully formed, almost as if a child had drawn him.

His clothes, brown velvet shirt and brown pants, appeared as if they were made of hundreds of small animals, crawling all over his body. This was not my grandfather, not in the physical sense of the word.

No. This was an abomination, a version of him that appeared as his insides must have looked. His features continued to melt away, and when I was just a few feet from him, he exploded into a few dozen black birds, as indistinct as they could be while still recognizably avian. They flew in every direction, including at me.

I broke free from the paralysis and ran around to the front yard, into the house, and locked the door. I headed to the window to see if there was any lingering evidence of what I had just witnessed.

There was nothing, save the cry of distant birds.

I had many questions following that encounter, and much that I felt I needed to research, but there was no substantial answer that could set me at ease. In all my years of dealing with strange happenings, with death and the ways it can manipulate every facet of life, I had never experienced something so powerful, so utterly insane, as the phenomenon that had occurred in the vision of my grandfather.

There was a wealth of books on the supernatural available, as well as irreputable shamans on the internet claiming to be able to see spirits, all for the low cost of your dignity. I called in sick to work and spent the next several days at the library, huddled in the back corner of the study area, hoping no one would disrupt me.

My bag was filled with notebooks and pens, as well as my camera, just in case I was put into a supernatural situation again. After a week of studying and notetaking, I learned that if I could recreate the scenarios where the sightings had occurred, I could make them happen again.

I searched out these experiences, wondering if something was being shown to me that others hadn't had the chance to see. As if the universe decided that I, in my grief, was worthy of a glimpse behind the curtain. I never put myself in harm's way, but I attempted to recreate scenarios I thought would bring about another vision of my cat, another visitation by a spirit, however malevolent . . . anything to prove those two brief but jarring situations were real, and not just in my mind. The scientist in me wouldn't let me truly believe until I had experimented.

Never once, during this descent into abnormality that had become my life, did I see death as a way out. If anything, it made me want to live so that I might uncover something new, to look beyond the curtain and touch the other side.

My roommate Melissa has so little life in her it is a wonder she just doesn't disappear. Sensing that she doesn't want to talk anymore, I get up and go for a walk along the halls. Getting the feel of the place makes me more comfortable, and I need to move so I don't get lost in thought.

I am peering into the craft room when an orderly taps me on the shoulder. "Lunch time. Follow me."

I grab a wrapped sandwich and an apple, pocketing them as I head back to my room. After so much time spent alone, it is overwhelming to be surrounded by so many people, even in such a large space. I eat, go into the bathroom and wash my face, and lay back in bed. I'm not scheduled for anything today other than eating, and so far, this day has been exhausting.

All I want is quiet, and rest, things I have had so little of recently.

❧❧❧❧❧

My sleep patterns changed. I stayed up from dusk until dawn, sitting near the tree where I had first seen the darkness. Some nights I sat in Boo's room, ever so quietly, so that maybe the darkness would try to manifest there once more. At dawn, when the sun rose gracefully in the East, I sat by Boo's grave, waiting for my grandfather, for anything, to show itself to me.

It became quite the obsession, and my life suffered. I lost my job after calling in too many times, and I barely left the house. I lived off strange, random canned goods left over from bygone shopping trips, not caring if I ate much or even at all. My friends stopped coming by, and I turned off my cell phone. The most important thing was to find a way to see the ones I had lost, one last time, and to be sure that my mind was still intact.

Stefani Manard

My mother came by one afternoon since she hadn't heard from me in several weeks and was concerned. After seeing my living conditions, she got groceries and decided to stay with me for a few days. We had always been close, so I didn't mind much, just so long as I could still seek the truth.

I was careful to stop my experimentation until she was asleep, and thus she didn't witness any odd behavior. I slept in small spurts during the day. She worried that I was depressed, as that runs in our family, and when I was awake with her during those few days, I assured her I was fine. I made sure to eat everything she cooked, to laugh at her jokes, and pretend, for a time, that everything was the same as it had ever been.

She needed a patsy to blame my odd behavior on. I never told her I saw her dead father burst into birds. She would think me mad! She would have recognized it, having lived it herself, and I wasn't ready to give up the ghost yet. The day before she left, I gave her something.

"The insomnia is back."

My mother was chopping carrots for stew in the kitchen when I blurted this out. She turned to look at me, large knife gleaming in her hand. "Have you tried taking meds for it?" She returned to butchering that night's meal.

"You know I hate taking them. I have a prescription, but those pills make me feel groggy."

She plopped the carrot chunks into the crockpot and turned back to me. "If they are prescribed, take them. How long have you had issues with this? Fifteen years?"

Manifestation

"It's been much better, Mom, and I'm still seeing my therapist. It just threw me for a bit. I'll survive, like always." I leaned in to hug her. Our height difference made it awkward, but in that moment, our hearts so close together, I could sense that she trusted me. This made me feel guilty, but sometimes we lie to the ones we love to ease their minds. She left the next day, and I returned to what was becoming my new life.

I thought of giving up when nothing happened for another month. I was tired of being in solitude and my bills were piling up, an eviction notice probably not far off. I started to think my grief had left me weak, that when facing something so heartbreaking I had just snapped, and what I was doing was futile and harmful.

In that moment of clarity, I called my mother and had her take me to a mental health care facility. There was nothing else I could think of to do.

There was no secret out there, no truth, just sadness and loss.

It's my first day in a place that I've actively fought against ending up in my entire life, and I came willingly. I am cognizant of behaviors, and mine had become so poor that I could see no other option, so I gave in to the family curse. I guess we were all mad.

I fell asleep trying to cling to moments of happiness instead of the pain, trauma, and familial uncertainty that peppered my entire life. I sleep through dinner, and through the night, my dreams vapid and forgettable.

Day two, and I meet my doctor. We do a medical history, and he puts me on a cocktail of drugs that I am vaguely familiar with. They make me tired, my days foggy and unintelligible from each other. I go to group, eat, sleep, and then repeat the cycle over again.

I don't talk much outside of the group therapy sessions, and even then, it is limited. No discussion of the bizarre sightings, no mention of bird grandfather. Instead, I use this platform to tell my favorite stories about Boo, but only when I feel up to it. The others give me looks, as if my loss is nothing in a place so filled with horrors. I don't care.

"Megan, what is on your mind today?" The group leader, Mr. Chambers, is a squat man, with wire-rimmed glasses and ugly brown shoes. He is good at his job, but even I can tell he isn't excited to hear me rehash the same thoughts.

"Can we just skip her? Some of us have real problems." Some of the others have no issue speaking up in group, especially when it involves me.

"If I ever see a damn cat again, I'm going to kick it." Charla is borderline personality and loves to incite infighting at group.

Mr. Chambers, per the usual, must interfere and regain dominance. "This group is for everyone, Jamie, Charla . . . let's keep our opinions to ourselves and let Megan have the floor."

"I think I understand now." That's all I say. Everyone gets quiet fast, looking at me like I'm a conjoined twin at a carnival.

"What is it that you understand?" Mr. Chambers asks.

I hesitate. "I know that you can't understand why

Manifestation

I put myself here, why I keep talking about the life and death of a cat, but I think I understand now."

No one speaks, so I continue.

"So much of my life has been heartbreak, sadness, and uncertainty. I never thought I was going to experience the kind of love that I craved, that I needed to grow into a stronger person. My cat was the only one I ever felt loved me enough. As much as I loved him. Others have tried, but they let me slip through their fingers after promising to hold me forever." I pause and shift in my seat. "My cat loved me enough, and now he is gone. He took my hope with him. How can I live happily if I have no hope?"

Mr. Chambers nods, still looking a little confused. "Animals can be a great comfort in our lives, Megan. I understand your feeling of loss, but hope only goes away when you abandon it." He clears his throat. "We'll touch on this more in our private session. Who's next? Charles, what do you have to share today?"

But I am not finished. "Grief is a powerful thing, Mr. Chambers. I need to know if grief can cause grand delusions, delusions so real that you can feel the flutter of wings against your skin?"

He pauses for a moment before answering. "Grief can cause many things. Dreams of those we have lost are very common, as are illusions that you feel them around you. It is how the mind copes." He turns to look at me, a very serious gaze flashing across his face. It chills me to the bone. "Time is running out. We must move on."

Admission has not been the catharsis I imagined. I have been at the facility for a couple of weeks now.

The medications make me feel worn out, and I sleep most of the time that isn't occupied with food and group. Those weird experiences I had feel like a dream. I consider signing myself out. Maybe I've reached a place where I can function again, minus the mind-numbing meds. I think this, but then it happens again.

It is nighttime, and Melissa is snoring in her bed. I can't sleep, since I slept ten hours today, so I lie there, watching the lights from the parking lot through the blinds. Melissa is between me and the window, and while I am staring off, I notice something stir beneath her bed.

I assume it is a shadow, but stay vigilant, my body reacting of its own volition. When it moves again, I get up to get a closer look. As I reach within a foot of the bed, a shadow darts from underneath, slipping past me, and continuing toward the door to our room. I follow it as it leaves the room, skitters down the hallway, and disappears underneath a door.

Looking around for orderlies, I follow its path, opening the door slowly. It is not a patient's room, as I had guessed. It contains abandoned furniture and other discarded items. The window is wide open. Walking toward it, I am careful to keep watch for the shadow thing that led me here, but I reach the window without any confrontation. When I look out, I feel something put its hands over my eyes, changing the view from an empty parking lot surrounded by office buildings and fast food restaurants, to something strange.

I am transported to a place filled with what I sense are people, but they appear to me as buzzing balls of energy. They move about from one place to another, and they all seem to have a purpose. I feel no fear, no sadness, just existence. The vision shifts, and I watch the balls of energy, some joining together and some separate, enter tubes all heading in different directions. When they enter, they are taken to a place that I feel eager to see, but don't get the chance to.

Instead, the vision changes to the graveyard from my previous dream, but this time there is no sense of impending doom. The sun is shining, flowers bloom around the headstones, and a feeling of calm washes over me. While there is no one to be seen, an androgynous voice speaks soothingly from somewhere.

"The ones who suffer are those among the living. It is a sad state of things, really, when there is such a fear of death among those above ground. That is part of the suffering, like a snake eating its own tail. The living want to escape the only inevitable thing that comes from life, and mourn those who have died. They want to move on to a place where none of the doubtful, painful feelings that plague them can follow. Your grief is only important to you. It is a torture you inflict upon yourself, because you see how brief life can be and, in that moment . . . the feeling of dread is inescapable.

"You fill every moment of the day with mindless activities to forget that dread, even for a brief time. But you . . . you didn't try to forget the dread, you dove *into* it. Death is the reward for living, not a punishment. Living is where darkness hides; people are covered with it and filled with it. Death is the release of all sorrow. You have been allowed this brief glimpse of knowledge, which of course, you will remember as nothing more than a dream when you wake. No one should know that life is essentially Hell. That would cause quite a problem. But remember, your suffering is all a show, and does nothing for the ones who have left this mortal coil. They were loved, and that is all that matters. Your tears do nothing but sully that."

A bright light blinds me, and I wake up in bed. The window is open and the sunlight pours onto my face. Melissa has already gone to breakfast, and I get out of bed, brush my teeth, and head to the nurse's station. I am not sure why, but I am certain that it is time to move on.

I take one last look at my room and say my goodbyes to Melissa on the way out. I send what positive energy I can spare her way, knowing that her brokenness is a state she may never recover from.

Me, I am ready. For what, I am still not sure, but I know that living is a part of it, and no one can truly flourish in a place filled with such sadness. I walk out the front door, ignoring the staff, the decor, focusing only on what is ahead of me.

It took some time, but I regained myself. I found a new job, moved to a small apartment in the city, and left my ghoulish obsession behind. There is a bliss to be found in simplicity, and it was that feeling that saved me.

I took little from my old place, as it was a reminder of an old skin I wore, a sadness that almost destroyed me. I did take the photo montage of Boo, because there was no forgetting him. It hangs on the wall across from my painting table. I look at it from time to time, and one day an urge rolls over me. I walk over, pull the frame from the wall, and begin to attack it with tools and paint, with a fervor I haven't felt in a long time.

I hang it back up after it has dried. It now looks complete. I have attached a small wooden piece to the bottom, hanging by two thick yellow ribbons.

It is a small sign, simply stating, "You were loved."

jinnofar
2019

Beating a Dead Dog

Scarlet Driscoll

Sandy dances expectantly as I pull into the parking lot. I hear the jaunty, metallic jangle of her tags, and the muted tap of her toenails on the pleather back seat. Gravel crunches underfoot as I step out. Sandy's nose smudges across the window before she hops down nimbly and sniffs the early morning breeze. I take a moment to watch clouds moving across the overcast sky. The trees remain bare but the air carries the muddy smell of springtime thaw.

Sandy sniffs about the gravel lot and the trailhead. These areas always have the most foot traffic of both humans and dogs and so demand her utmost attention. I attach her leash to her fraying red harness, but wait her out as she noses about the garbage bin. Gradually, she pulls toward our usual trail. It loops around a meadow before cresting a steep hill, where the path opens up to a wondrous view of sky, treetops, and a glistening river at the bottom of a deep ravine.

At this hour, a hazy mist hangs over the still brown

brambles of the unmowed meadow. The dew drips from sad-looking raspberry bracken. Spring is still so young that it's easy to overlook the first tender shoots nudging up through last year's sodden leaves.

After about a half mile, the path intersects with the park's main road. This is where the trail begins its ascent up the hill. The summit is probably not much more than a mile straight up in front of me. But the path zigs and zags back and forth up the hill in a series of cutbacks that ease the angle of ascent just enough to make it passably accessible to the casual hiker. The park's brochure recommends a walking stick and warns against use during inclement weather. In a downpour, a washout could render this steep climb a real danger.

I readjust the straps of my backpack and we begin to climb. Sandy wags her tail. I watch her shoulders hunker down as she shifts into her more concerted stride; these hikes are serious business to her. She is always keenly alert, enthused to explore the scents and eager for the exercise. We walk briskly. We breathe deeply.

As part of our ritual, we pause at several strategic spots for brief rests. There is one bench I particularly love. It is dedicated to the memory of Noretta Tisch, but a vandal's blade gouged the "T" into an emphatic "B." The inscription now reads, "Noretta Bisch." I envision an elderly woman swaying as she leans over her sloshing wine glass and leers, "Ha! She really was susch a bisch, Noretta, but gawd I misch her!"

The bench is a soggy gray today. In my pack I have a mat—one side is a square of old vinyl tablecloth, the other is an upcycled, felted sweater—sewn together

Beating a Dead Dog

by my daughter during her brief stint in some off-brand Girl Scout troop. At the end of summer, after soccer camp and her annual visit with her dad, I hope to bring her hiking with me. Having her along would definitely change the mood of these excursions. Compared with Sandy, she'll need me to engage with her much more. But it'll be good to get her off the beaten paths, give her an escape from the hustle and bustle of the typical suburban preteen schedule.

The next traditional stopping spot is a rocky outcrop nestled into a curve of the path. We sit in contemplative silence. Sandy thumps her tail on the ground, while I peer down on a muddy trickle of run-off that joins the roaring and swollen trout stream at the foot of the ridge. Though the gusty breeze still hurries clouds across the sky, the sun shines down strongly enough to feel warm and comforting on my back.

At the crest of the hill there is an observation deck, right where the trail loops back down. I don't spend very long at the summit. It was never today's goal. Just out of view from the scenic overlook deck, fifty yards or so, is a service track. Paved with gravel rather than mulch, the route is wide and straight rather than rambling. It is intended for park personnel and allows vehicles up the steep grade for trail maintenance. I turn down this track and Sandy trots along beside me.

After a few minutes walking, I leave the trail altogether and venture straight into the woods. Fallen leaves coat the forest floor. They are slick and black with water, mucky even, and our footsteps make squelching noises as we stroll deeper into the trees. Where the trees grow closer together, I spot trillium growing among the tree roots.

Scarlet Driscoll

At a fallen log, I spread my mat and sit down. We are far out of view from the unfrequented road. From my pack, I bring out two water bottles and a dog bowl. I pour some water into it. I also locate several cheese sticks. Nominally, these are for school lunches. The reality is the dog eats at least a quarter of each stick, fed to her under the table every afternoon after school. There are giggles as she licks fingers; her thumping tail betrays the deed. Nobody verbally acknowledges the transaction. I buy more cheese sticks on every grocery trip.

She whines and her tail now swishes over the soggy leaves. I grab an old pill bottle from my pack. Advil PM, more than two years out of date. I fit one blue pill after another into a cube of cheese broken off from the marbled yellow and white sticks. She gulps them, one by one, from my cupped palm. Only eighteen pills. I had thought there were more than that left. I feel her breath and the soft, gentle wetness of her tongue with each gratefully greedy lick.

When there are no more pills and no more cheese sticks, I wipe my hands together and she understands. Her tongue lolls out and she breathes open mouthed, her eyes partially closed; she is content. A stray beam of sun glints on her reddish-brown fur and I scratch behind her ear.

She lies down. I stand up. From the bag, I take a foldable metal spade that our family has used on many camping trips over the years. I use the point to mark out a rectangle roughly two feet by three. I dig, carefully piling the damp dirt in a mound off to one side. As I work, my back is toward her. I hear her take a drink. Her tags clink against the bowl. Then she settles down into the leaves, panting.

I take off my jacket and set it down by the backpack, which leans still unzipped against the log. Soon the hole is two and a half, maybe three feet deep, gauging the depth against the length of the shovel. The sides are mostly straight but the bottom is waterlogged. I walk back to the log and tap the shovel against it to knock off the mud. I sit down on the log, dog sprawled at my feet. Trillium surrounds us.

I wait a long time, judging by the shift of sun and shadow. I listen to the sound of the breeze through the branches and the tentative twitter of birds. The full spring frenzy and symphony of mating and nesting has yet to begin. Breathing is what I hear, deep and slow. I focus on its changing. I had wondered about side effects—either the awful sound of dog ralphing or worse, diarrhea. But her panting grows to deep, long breaths which gradually taper to become almost inaudible.

Then I draw out a nearly new knife from my pack. It came from Kroger two weeks ago. Our kitchen knives have been dull long enough to justify a new one, especially one on sale. I lay my hand firmly on her flank. I debate options momentarily: one deep plunge or one quick stroke?

I pat her head, petting down the back of her neck, and then under her chin. One hand pulls back the soft, loose skin, the other quickly, firmly swipes across her neck with the sale-priced Kroger knife. The blood flashes Christmas red on the blade and against her fur. But the gush and flow are dark against the dank leaves. I wait, watching, unable not to.

I wipe the flat of the knife off against her flank. I rinse it by pouring water over it, then dry it along the back of my pant leg. The knife goes back into the bag.

Next, I finagle the tags off the ring on the harness and tuck them into the front pocket of my jeans. I shift the dog into the hole, easing her down head first. I want the blood to drain into the dark mud. Then I scrape the heavy mucky pile back over the hole. I stamp it down and make broad, sweeping motions with one leg to spread leaves over the bare dirt.

My mat is still on the log. I give it a shake, then add it into my backpack along with the collapsible camping spade. I squat down and half lift, half grapple the log over the fresh mound. I wipe my hands together and pour water over them to rinse away most of the grime. I brush off my clothes as well, looking for traces of blood. My nails are deeply dirty but nothing else is out of the ordinary for a long day spent hiking. I dump out the water bowl and repack it, then take a last swig from my water bottle and add it to the bag. With one last parting look, I double check that I have left nothing out.

The downhill trek to my car is faster than the arduous climb. It's always easier for those coming down to smile at the hikers going up. As I drive out of the park and onto the rural highway, I check my rearview mirror. Far down the lane is another car, but my finger finds the window lever. The window whirs down and I fling Sandy's tags into the ditch along the roadside.

I call my daughter. It isn't hard for her to understand that the dog died. I had already told her how worried I was about Sandy and that I was taking her to the vet this weekend.

Beating a Dead Dog

"Honey, I'm so sorry. I know it's such a bummer. It hurts, but I think it's better this way. I'm just glad she didn't suffer."

"No. I carried her ashes up our trail, you know how she always loved our walks."

"Definitely. We could still get a rock or a brick and paint her name on it real nice and put it under the tree in the back yard."

"No, she won't really be in Heaven, but you know, babe, she'll always be with you, if you remember her."

"Maybe, when you feel up to it . . . we could get a kitten."

When I get home, I post Sandy's picture on Facebook with the comment, "We had to put our dog down today."

My feed is filled with sympathy. Everyone knows how hard it is to lose your dog.

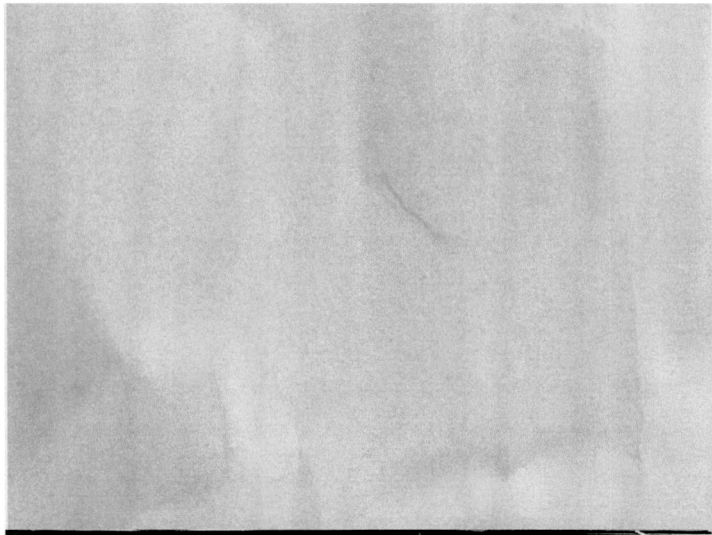

Red Woman

Michelle Joy Gallagher

I t was the sound of singing that woke her. Fragile and familiar voices. Hokte Cate smiled softly, then winced. The taste of blood, the rush of memory, everything flooded in all at once, as it always did after the merciful amnesia of an exhaustion-fueled collapse. The gaping wound above her right brow immediately began to throb. And then there was the raw and shameful pain between her legs. That was familiar, too.

They'd put two hundred miles between her home in Otciapofa and here, here in the dark with the taste of iron and fear, here where they'd take you whenever they wanted, dragging you like a rag doll behind the big stones or in the deep woods. If you were lucky, you'd return with only minor bruises. Torn skin. Another piece of your soul stolen.

Some of them didn't bother to hide your shame; they didn't take you behind the big stones or into the deep wood. They'd strip you down to nothing right in front of your betrothed, right in front of the elders. Your own blood.

The price for disobedience was death.

Her kin were only half the number they started with on what seemed like an endless journey. The men who led them on this death-filled path only ever stopped to spell their horses. The comfort of the horses took priority over the human lives they'd been charged with herding like cattle from the sacred earth to—well, she really didn't know if there was an end, or if it was simply a slow means of torture and execution.

On the first day out, still following the path that straddled the Ocmulgee river, one of the guards had grabbed her by the hair. "Guess I'm choosing this one. She's fairly clean. Little thick, but ain't nothing to fuss over"

The missionaries had taught them basic English; she didn't follow all of his words, but the intent was clear. He spoke about her to the others as though she were a hunting trophy. A carcass. To be fair, that was how she felt. Just another corpse left alongside the trail with empty eyes and rotting insides.

Surrounded by the guards, her head yanked back by a cruel hand, her heart began to stutter in fear. She could feel the breath leave her lungs. She didn't notice as Efv, her brother, snuck up behind her assailant and struck him on the back of the head. This instinctive, protective move immediately signed Efv's death warrant.

Stunned, the guard released his grasp on her and she fell backward. He then swung around, incensed, to see who had dared perpetrate such an act upon him. He was one of the untouchables, after all. He laughed heartily when he saw the boy standing before him.

Red Woman

Thirteen years old and wiry, Efv was a good athlete. He could keep up with the grown men at stick ball. But he was no match for the guards and their guns. While the white man was still sizing up Efv, Hokte Cate broke free from his grasp and scrambled toward her brother. She embraced Efv tightly, screaming. Knowing.

Efv buried his face in her neck, hiding his fear, his tears, kissed her cheek gently. "*Ecenokecis*," he whispered: "I love you." They ripped him from her grasp and dragged him to the water's edge. He thrashed against them, fighting to the last. The cowards—four of them—held his head under and kept him from fighting back. Finally, he was still.

Her heart died with him. The shell of her stumbled now through the muck and the horse shit and the vomit and waited for the next indignity. Every particle that comprised her, forged and fortified in the crucible of survival, had turned its sharpened edges toward the tender necks of those who had thrown her and her clan into this torturous void.

Last she could recall, she'd fallen asleep curled up with the shredded remains of Efv's pack. She recovered it after they'd let the dogs at his body. They'd left him at the water's edge and wouldn't let her near him. He'd lain there on his back, blue and swelling, staring lifeless at the swirling dance of stars. She had gazed at the same stars that night, breathing, heart beating, but just as dead in so many ways.

The acrid smell washed over her first. Then the

sounds, metallic and foreign. There was an odd, incessant chirp, like no bird she'd ever heard before. She was cold, but felt layers of cloth brush against her skin with each movement. The feel of the smooth leather straps from her brother's pack was missing from her fingertips.

This jolted her awake in a way the other details could not. It was her last shred of comfort, that bag, and it had been taken from her. Today, someone would pay, even if it meant her own life. Was this life? Not the way they had been forced to live it.

A calming voice drew her attention. "Rebecca? Rebecca, it's okay. This is Nancy, your night nurse. Do you remember me?"

The nurse was a woman with golden hair and eyes of cornflower. Her brilliantly white clothing matched the wall behind her. She was looking down at Hokte Cate. *Nancy? Nancy.*

As Hokte Cate's eyes focused, she could make out a frightening tower of metal and glass emitting a strange light (the source of the *chirp, chirp, chirp*). To her horror, she realized there were wires leading from the accursed tower into her skin. It stung where they bit her. Instinctively, she reached over to pull them out. The woman Nancy was there in a flash, having grown accustomed to this nightly ritual.

"Rebecca, you know you can't do that, hon. Hey, can you tell me what day of the week it is?"

Rebecca. The name felt like rolling through thorns. It pricked her. She could still smell the smoke in her hair, the ash, the leather from her brother's pack.

She opened her mouth to speak but nothing came

out. She couldn't take the choking smell of the room; it burned her nose and her eyes. She hated the sounds, the lights, most of all Nancy and her mewling condescension.

Hokte Cate didn't know the day of the week because the day of the week meant nothing. She knew she was sore, she was thirsty, she was tired, she was weak, and she was alone, and that her mind had finally been broken.

This had to be some sort of illusion created by a sanity that had been unwound. Where were her kin? Where were the guards? What had they done? The hollowness swallowed her whole, the empty terror of not knowing the answers to any of these questions, the ones that mattered. She fell backward inside of herself, a bottomless well of darkness and fear.

"Rebecca, open your eyes! Can you remember the name of the president of the United States?"

Hokte Cate closed her eyes against the violence of Nancy and this world full of confusing words and sounds and smells. She bit her lip until it bled, trying to wake herself . . .

But for what reason? To be transported from one hell to the next? The rage built in her until she shook. What manner of curse had brought her here? Her confusion and fear and hatred for the world caused her body to thrum like one of the taut drumskins after the men had stopped their chanting. She wanted more than anything to be locked in that last embrace with Efv. She wanted to be there for all eternity.

The blood within her veins begged her across the centuries for comfort. For vengeance. For a pound of flesh.

What was a president? What was the United States? What did those things matter to her? A prisoner to the Hvtke.

"*Owv*," Hokte Cate whispered. *Water.*

Nancy grimaced and mumbled, writing notes in the patient chart as she did. *Patient is again using native phrases, will not answer simple prompts for mentation.*

"One step forward and two steps back, eh Rebecca?" Nancy sighed.

"*Esketv Owv*," Hokte Cate croaked again, this time prompting Nancy to storm out of the room. A sly grin crawled across Hokte Cate's face as if this were her goal.

A drink of water.

In Nancy's absence, she scratched again where the wires from the metallic tower bit her. She scratched until the tape holding them down came loose and then she pulled the wires slowly from her skin, biting her cotton gown against the pain. She thought she was in the clear, except the tower started making a hellacious alarm once the wires were disconnected.

Instead of panic, she had the countenance of a woman who'd made up her mind long before the alarms and Nancy in white. She held the wires loosely in her hand, waiting for the nurse's return. The sheets bloomed red from the wounds where the metal had punctured her, and she marveled at the sight of it. She did not fear it. After all, blood had become most familiar to her.

Nancy came running in with the glass of water she'd forgotten she was holding, sloshing it around the room as she went. She was cursing under her breath and lecturing her patient about the medications and how they were there to help her, not harm her.

Hokte Cate saw all of this as if in slow motion and heard none of the words. She watched Nancy's lips move and her hands work to silence the alarms, the cup flying from her hand as she did so. Nancy, queen of the metal tower. She was frazzled and she was tired and she wouldn't have to worry about any of that after tonight. Hokte Cate would make sure of it.

She laid still in the bed until Nancy came alongside her to reinsert the IV, the new kit arranged before her on a metal tray, everything so cold and sterile, so removed from the earth here. Where was her small cabin she shared with her mother and grandmother, with the dirt floor? Where was her grandfather with the gruff voice and the corners of his mouth pulled down into an infinite frown? Where was her wild brother with the fire in his eyes? Hokte Cate craved the firelight and the stars, even the dirt.

It was early morning, with the sun still slung low on the horizon, when the men with guns arrived. There were only two watchmen out with their horses and they sped back to warn the Mekko. Before the watchmen had even arrived, the gunmen had pulled most of them out of their cabins and into the center of the village where they kept the fires. The pit was dark and full of ash, never to be lit again. One by one, the gunmen took the leaders of the tribe to the edge of the river, made them kneel, and shot them in the back of their heads.

It was their belief that the red clay of the river had formed the first people. That they were molded from the earth itself. For her to see the sacred water become a place of death was worse than death itself. She could see the same emptiness fill the others. Slowly at first, then all at once. A black smoke that choked out all light.

She was *Hokte Cate*. Red Woman. But she was darkened now by the devastation the strangers had wrought with their guns and their horses and their neverending need to pleasure themselves.

Hokte Cate's grandfather was last. Kin-Ke-Hee was in his eighties and his knees were bad. He knew her by her voice, and when she greeted him, his face would light up. She always brought him *sofke*. Although her grandmother didn't like him drinking, Hokte Cate loved making him happy. She watched from the circle as he knelt bravely before the Ocmulgee, that sacred water, now running red with blood. The river had power, and he whispered to it as he knelt, words that only he and the river would ever know. She called for him at the last second, but her voice was drowned out by the gunfire that took the back of his skull.

It was these visions she conjured, now drowning in rage and fear and grief, when she wrapped the IV cords around Nancy's porcelain neck and pulled as tight as she could. She didn't know why, really, or what she was planning, she just kept winding the ends tighter and tighter with each memory.

Fair Nancy with the golden hair, she'd done no harm really, but she had to pay. She was not one of Hokte Cate's kin, and that meant she was one of *them*. And she would pay dearly for it.

Nancy flailed and she scratched and got a couple

of hits on her attacker, but if there was one thing Hokte Cate could do, it was tolerate pain. Nancy's bloodshot eyes were open wide in shock and she groaned at Rebecca, a mute sort of sad moan, like a buffalo that'd been run to exhaustion. She had fought valiantly, but now Nancy was going blue in the face. Her days of mumbling over notepads, barking commands, and pushing pills down the throats of helpless patients like sick cats were over.

The tower had toppled in their struggle, and Hokte Cate took a small satisfaction in that. She released the IV tubes embedded in Nancy's neck and took the first deep breath she had since being forced from her tribal town that unknowably long time ago.

The white men were more obscene than anything she'd ever seen, and she had seen all manner of animals born and killed. She had been near death from illness and she had carried the dead to their resting places, but all of those things were natural and therefore carried their own sense of grace.

This was pure profanity. All of it. The enforcers and their grunting and their curses and their spitting and their fighting and drinking and their weapons, while the mothers and grandmothers and babies huddled together freezing, waiting to be used, and the men were stripped naked and starved.

None of them would look her in the eye anymore. Not since her Efv died. Not since the guard returned, soaking wet from the struggle of drowning her baby brother, to rape her at gunpoint in front of them.

Now she was alone, even amongst her own people. And she was damned. She feared her body's whispers that she was with child. She vowed to die before she saw the end of the trail, especially if she carried the child of such profanity.

Hokte Cate started gathering stones. Absentmindedly at first, she'd pick them up as they walked the endless walk toward nothing. She kept the ones that glinted in the sunlight. The granite and the quartz. She kept them in a strip of her dress she'd torn and lovingly made into a sack. It distracted her from the monotony.

As the days wore on and her thoughts became structured plans, she began to more carefully select the ones she knew were easy to shape. Shale and basalt. Stones she'd watched the hunters use to clean the buckskin.

Her entire body was a bruise, and she suspected she had a broken foot, but she would pay penance for her shame by taking the brunt of the abuse meant for the others. She kept gathering the stones.

The struggle between Nancy and Hokte Cate and the ensuing noise did not go without notice, regardless of the fact that Hokte Cate had gotten the jump on the nurse before she could sound any alarms. There was the matter of the spilled water, the toppled IV tower, the blood on Hokte Cate's face and arm, and Nancy's dead body. Hokte Cate searched the room for anything that could provide protection from the orderlies bounding down the hall in a rushed confusion.

Red Woman

There it was—the silver prep tray Nancy had rolled in to replace her IV. Various tubes, tapes, things sealed in strange packaging, all laid out neatly on the steel tray. There in the center was a thick steel needle that would have to do. She didn't know how far she could get with it, but she wasn't worried for her safety anymore. She was already dead. It wasn't a matter of "if" anymore. It was a matter of how and when.

The orderlies burst through the door like fevered, hungry dogs on the trail of a wild rabbit, one of them yelling, "Rebecca!"

Hokte Cate played dead. The orderlies stood in disbelief at the scene. Spotting Nancy's sensible shoes sticking out at the far side of the bed, one of them went running over, and promptly slipped on the spilled water. Hokte Cate couldn't help but laugh to herself. It was unreal and stupid and silly and frightening all at once.

Who had she become? What was happening? It was as if she was outside of herself, hearing her own mirth, feeling the humanity in her being slowly replaced with the cold need for revenge. But it was already too late. She intended to make them pay as dearly as she had. Her laughter melted away.

While the second orderly struggled to help the first, Hokte Cate made her move, jumping onto his back and jamming the IV needle deep into his eye. She dug as deeply as she could against his thrashing and screaming, then she twisted the needle and pulled. The unfortunate orderly's eyeball was attached to it like skewered meat. She laughed and squealed as she waved it in the air triumphantly.

The man screamed incoherently while the other

orderly slid around in a mixture of what was now water and blood, trying to gain traction and get a hold of Hokte Cate. She had entered into a sort of ecstatic state, riding the back of the one-eyed orderly as he begged for help until he slowly collapsed onto the tile floor, unconscious, his head resting on Nancy's shoes.

The second orderly soon gained traction enough to grab a hold of the laughing Hokte Cate, still holding the IV needle resplendently ornamented with the unconscious orderly's green left eye. He was holding her arm in his hand but he was unable to move. He stood there and stared at her, covered in the blood of his coworker and her own blood from the struggle with Nancy. He watched as she laughed hysterically.

He assured himself that this was the last straw at this god-forsaken hospital. Once he was sure his ass was safe from having an eyeball plucked from his face, he was going to quit. He called for backup on his walkie and tried to subdue the patient as well as he could on his own, but she now occupied another state of being. At this point, she was built more of revenge and memory than flesh. She was no longer the patient he had known as Rebecca.

She scratched at his face with her free hand until he was able to pin both hands behind her. Wresting the needle from her grasp proved to be easier than he expected, given the amount of blood covering her. He threw her to the ground, hitting her face against the tile and chipping one of her teeth, then put a knee in the middle of her back.

Hokte Cate managed to turn her head to an angle where she could see the unconscious orderly's head propped up on dead Nancy's shoes, his left eye a mess of coagulated blood soaking into Nancy's once bright white socks. Hokte Cate laughed at the sight of all of this, blood spitting from her broken gums.

A tromp of footfalls came down the hall. Backup was here. Hokte Cate closed her eyes and surrendered herself to the inevitability of her death. She welcomed it.

The others arrived and descended upon her like a murder of crows. The world spun and grew cloudy as the sedation set in and she imagined this was the view of the world her grandfather had as he aged. She smiled at the thought of him before finally giving over to the dark.

After many nights, she was finally able to fashion one of the stones into a knife sharp enough to cut. It would taste flesh. Either hers or theirs. Whatever came first.

She was his favorite now, the guard who had killed her brother, if for no other reason but to remind him of his deed and her of her grief. He forced her by gunpoint to the bank of the river down below the encampment that had been made for the night. She gazed down at the river and smiled softly. She knew the routine. He hardly needed the gun anymore. She started to disrobe without saying a word.

"Why ain't you cryin'? I'm not sure I like it if you ain't cryin'."

"*Cuntv Hvke,*" she said, laughing.

"What'd you say to me in that savage speak, girl? You know better."

He raised the gun up to her forehead, but she stood meek and naked in front of him and he forgave the transgression. He was always violent. He meant to harm her every time and he succeeded. She was afraid she was pregnant but she also feared she may never be able to become pregnant after he was done with her. Soon, it wouldn't matter either way.

When he finished, she started to laugh hysterically, reaching for her clothing.

"*Cuntv Hvke.*" She laughed again. Blood ran down the insides of her legs and she shook violently from shock and from the derangement that had set in since the terrible trip began. She also shook in excitement. For her, it was almost at an end.

He pulled the gun from his pile of clothing, both of them naked in the moonlight at the river's edge, and held it against her forehead for the second time that night. Her laughter only became more ecstatic. The commotion started to draw a crowd. *Good.*

"*Cuntv Hvke!*" She spat on the ground. "WHITE WORM."

She pointed at his groin and laughed. He pressed the gun harder into her forehead, turning bright red.

"Shut. Your. Mou—" the end of the sentence was lost in his red hot pain. She grabbed his penis and slashed hard at it with the rock she had carefully sharpened. Reflexively, his finger pulled the trigger and she fell backward into the rushing river, where her blood and brain matter mixed with the water.

That is how Red Woman was reunited with the clay that made her.

Red Woman

꙳꙳꙳

Rebecca McIntosh, 37
Schizophrenia, dissociative identity disorder
Hospitalized 7/27/03 for self-injury and possible hallucinations.
At times refers to herself as "Hokte Cate" or Red Woman.
Aggressive, especially toward males.
Use caution, even when sedated.
To be under 24-hour suicide watch.
Inform Detective Bartlett of any change in mentation.

Hokte Cate sat straight up from a sedated state, screaming. She reached for her forehead but found that her hands were bound to the rails of the bed. She screamed louder, thrashing against her restraints.

Outside of her room, two policemen stood guard. A detective stood to the side, waiting to question her about what she'd done to Nancy and the orderly. Now was not the time, obviously, but it was progress. She was awake.

She continued to scream until a nurse arrived with a new dose of sedative. Everything was new to her again. The smells, the sounds, the metal tower, the wires that bit her skin like a snake. It was one continuous, hellish loop.

She had forgotten her name was Rebecca. She had forgotten what she'd done to the unfortunates before. She had been raped and then killed beside the

Ocmulgee river and now she was here. This couldn't be the afterlife. The creator wouldn't be so cruel.

"THE RED CLAY, THE RED CLAY, I AM THE RED CLAY!" She thrashed against the restraints until the sedative hit her blood stream and she fell back against the pillow, defeated. Her eyes half open, she gazed slowly over at that tower. It seemed to be the source of all of her troubles in this incarnation. With her arms bound in this way, what could she do?

A man in a suit and tie entered the room and she sneered. She'd grown feral. She had no idea where or when she was anymore. She just wanted all of this to end. The medications didn't help. She spat, and thick glistening mucus ran down the corners of her mouth, down her chin, and onto her hospital gown.

She was the living embodiment of contempt. Her eyes wild and her hair a matted mess of sweat and blood they hadn't bothered to wash away, she threw herself against the restraints. All she wanted was to wrap her hands around the man's throat. She went from wailing incoherently to an inexplicably disconcerting titter. They wanted a savage, and they were going to get one.

The man glanced at her, his expression one of complete apathy. This was just another day on the job. "Hello, Rebecca. I'm Detective Bartlett with the Oklahoma State Police."

Hokte Cate pushed against her restraints and tried to turn her head away from him. She didn't like the smell of him. He smelled like wood and sweat and alcohol. An all too familiar combination.

"I understand there was an incident involving several staff members here last night. I'd like to ask you a few questions about your involvement in that."

She growled.

"Rebecca . . . "

"I AM NOT REBECCA. I AM RED WOMAN OF THE CLAY AND I AM DEAD."

Detective Bartlett sighed. "Obviously you aren't dead if we are here speaking. So, can we just cut the bullshit and get on with this?"

She quieted, then stared at her restraints.

"I don't think it would be wise to let you out of those just yet, Miss McIntosh. Now, tell me about last night. What compelled you to harm those people in such a way?"

Detective Bartlett knew he would get nowhere. This was a clear case of "reason of insanity" if there ever was one. He was just jumping through hoops. She'd end up locked up in a padded cage where everything was gray, including the food, and that would be that. He could think of better ways to spend his time, but alas, here he was face to face with his hot date, Rebecca, the latest strange and smelly fruit shaken out of the local rez tree.

He grimaced, wrinkling his nose, and wondered if she could read his mind because she had started up wailing again. He watched her pull harder on her restraints and, even though she was sedated, he felt a tickle of fear.

It was as if he was witnessing a possession of sorts. He was a man of logic and reason and would never believe in that sort of thing, but he couldn't deny the fear sitting at the pit of his stomach like hot lead. Exactly how harmless was she, he wondered. She'd strangled a nurse to death and used an IV needle to gouge out the eye of a man twice her size.

Bartlett flipped his notebook closed and sat down in a chair at the foot of her bed. He watched her until her writhing and screaming stopped. The rest was paperwork, really. Unfortunately for the friends and family of one Mrs. Nancy Baker who wanted justice, not much was going to change for Rebecca McIntosh.

Her punishment, in a twisted way, was her continued existence.

Shutting the door quietly behind him as he left, Bartlett took one last look at the deranged Miss McIntosh for his mental inventory. He'd covered a lot of cases in fifteen years, but never one so raw.

The woman slept. It was a deep and blessedly dreamless sleep. The next day, she answered every one of their questions correctly.

Her name was Rebecca McIntosh.

She was born on November 16, 1979.

The President of the United States was an asshole.

They took that as a correct answer, even though they weren't in a laughing mood. It meant she at least knew there was a president and a United States.

Rebecca smiled at a familiar doctor who had come to speak with her. She had no memory of her actions and learning about what she'd done had been emotionally traumatic. She sobbed for hours, unable to believe she'd harmed another human being in that way.

Did she know of anyone named "Hokte Cate?"

Red Woman

Rebecca felt something inside of herself flinch and frowned. She did know the name, it tickled some far-off memory, but she knew, very clearly, that she must not tell these people. The name, whoever's it was, needed protection.

When she said she was hungry, an orderly brought her food. A nurse unchained both of her arms once she realized she'd have to be spoon fed her soup and Jell-O.

Nobody noticed a couple of items were missing from the dinner tray when they took it away, or the calm that came over Rebecca even after they'd returned her to her wrist restraints.

When night fell, Rebecca asked for her curtains to be opened and for the lights to be lowered. They obliged, even if grudgingly. The entire staff had a great disdain for the venomous woman. This new reverence and respect act wasn't really passing muster for them.

They'd dealt with violent patients before, but not one that had harmed their own. They wanted their own piece of Rebecca, but there were laws with words like "cruel" and "unusual" and they needed their jobs more than they needed revenge. Still, her IV might have been administered a bit more roughly than usual, and her water jug filled a little less frequently and possibly spat in.

The nurse who had opened the curtains for her, though, couldn't contain her animosity. She'd been friends with Nancy. "I hope you jump out this window, you bitch," she muttered as she left the room. Hokte Cate pretended not to hear her. She had much better plans in mind.

Michelle Joy Gallagher

The night nurses were lazy dolts. All of them. She'd hear patients screaming in the night and the staff remained kicked back in their chairs, reading magazines or chatting giddily about the latest television show. Hokte Cate knew she would remain unbothered for long stretches of time. She began her tedious work.

The night nurses were all but neglectful of her. One of them brought her an extra blanket when requested and Rebecca thanked her even when she dropped it onto her lap and turned briskly to leave. Hokte Cate soon found it had been passed under a water faucet and soaked the blankets underneath, leaving her colder than she was before. It hardly registered.

The Red Woman smiled broadly. The nurse hadn't cared enough to notice the strong smell of iron in the room, or the darkened spot on the blankets near her right wrist. No one questioned why she'd need another blanket because no one wanted to notice anything about Rebecca ever again, and that worked to her advantage.

She worked through the night, occasionally gazing through the window at the stars. At one point she fainted, but no one noticed. When she came to, all the stars were aligned. She had been waiting for this moment.

It was her time.

*

The morning nurse, checking Hokte Cate's room on her morning rounds, found an empty, bloody bed.

Red Woman

Pools of thick blood and bits of skin lined each side of the bed and rail.

The curtain remained open as the patient had requested the night before, the morning light betraying her night's activities. A trail of blood led to the window and then to the door of her room and then stopped. Apparently, she had put the extra blanket to use after all.

There was a palpable panic. The facility was locked down and guards dispatched to search each floor while administrators reviewed the security tapes.

They knew she had to be inside the building. Any window or door open or broken would have sounded an alarm. So where was she hiding? She was turning out to be the Red Woman after all, just not in the way that she wished to be—her signature in blood, not clay.

A stray guard had almost given up searching when he heard a faint moan come from a utility closet. He alerted the other guards and began to open the door slowly. Inside, he found the patient Rebecca McIntosh hunched over in a sorry heap. The blanket on her lap was stained almost entirely red.

She had suffered massive blood loss, that was certain. She was pale and weak, her hair hung over her face in a greasy matted clump that made the guard almost sympathetic through his fear. She was a miserable specimen, curled up in a utility closet like a wounded animal.

He approached her quietly, whispering, "Miss? It's okay now, miss. We're here to help you. Stay calm, okay? Help is coming."

Hokte Cate lifted her head slightly. Her eyes, wide and black and almost lovely if it hadn't been for current circumstances, gazed up at him pleadingly.

He brushed her hair behind her ears and soothed her.

"Please," she said.

"It's okay, ma'am. I can hear them coming down the hall now. It won't be much longer."

She held out the blanket like an offering.

Reluctantly, the guard reached for the blanket and pulled it from her hands.

Beneath the blanket were her mangled hands. She'd taken chunks of flesh off of them using a plastic kitchen knife and slipped out of the restraints. In some places, he could see bone. Clumps of skin still clung in torn fragments here and there, and she still held the knife that did the damage. The smell of blood was cloistering in this small closet and the guard wondered how he hadn't noticed until now. He retched involuntarily.

She started to laugh. At first a giggle, then a full laugh and at last a hysterical high-pitched laugh that was nearly a scream. The incoming guards and nurses heard this and began running down the hall.

"I AM RED! I AM THE RED WOMAN!" She shoved the plastic knife deep into the soft part of guard's neck. He screamed a squelched scream and urinated on himself as blood flooded his throat.

She leaned in close and whispered, "I am the clay. I have taken what was taken from me."

When the other guards and nurses arrived, they surveyed the bloody scene in shock. The patient was still. She was spent. She had done what she'd set out to do. She stood with her arms out, the torn skin of her hands swinging from the muscle and tendon. Her hair was matted with sweat, her own blood, and the blood of the unfortunate guard who found her.

She reached down to retrieve the knife from the guard's neck but a heavyset guard rushed toward her and gave her an angry shove. She stumbled slightly but persisted. A shot rang out from one of the armed guards, the bullet striking her directly in the forehead.

Hokte Cate flew back against one of the utility shelves, knocking several bottles of cleaning agents on top of her when she fell forward. Solvents and cleansers flooded around her, mixing with the blood and urine in the small closet.

That was how Rebecca McIntosh was reunited with the clay that made her.

Lover to the Unknown

Isabella Christiana

October 5

I don't understand how I should write in this. Am I supposed to act like I am talking to someone? As if someone is actually listening? Mom said writing would help my depression and anxiety. We all know that counseling is a joke and my parents refuse to put me on medication. They say it will make me lose my motivation and drive. But I seriously do not have time for writing. With my AP classes, being class president, and trying to maintain somewhat of a social life, I cannot specify a time slot each day just for writing down feelings that do not even matter. We'll see what happens.

January 13

Mom just yelled at me for not writing in here. She spent two dollars on some cheap journal that is supposed to "help" me. Whatever. So, second semester just started. I ended first semester with a 4.2

grade point average based on a 4.5 scale. Still at fifth in my class, but mom expects me to do better than that.

At this point I am tired of being so stressed out. I just want to be happy for me. Being an only child makes me have all the pressure of being their "perfect little girl." Yet, I feel like I am failing everyone. I barely have friends and relationships just come and go.

My parents think writing my feelings out in some journal will give me some answers that I have never found before. Little do they know, the pressure they put on me is what gives me the anxiety. The only answer I know is I need to get out of the same cycle and do something that makes me happy for me and no one else.

January 30

Today at school, Mrs. Milton took a tumble down the stairs. I am not sure what exactly happened because I was in the art room in the basement. Carol told me that Mrs. Milton simply tripped, but the other low-life jerks are trying to tell people that they shoved her, which I know is definitely not true.

Mrs. Milton is the English teacher everyone hates. She glorifies the nerds at the school while everyone else means nothing. I am kinda stuck in between, I guess. I'm smart, but I'm not afraid to speak my mind and stand up for my ideas, which most of the time she hated about me. Let me just say I am not terribly sad that she took a tumble down a flight of stairs and will be out for the rest of the school year. English has been my lowest grade, so now with a permanent substitute hopefully I can raise my grade and get my mom off my back.

February 5

My friends Alex and Carol say I go from guy to guy and I am not relationship material. Jokes on them, I have been in more longer relationships than them. Well, I should mention I am not the greatest with relationships, either with boys or friends.

Alex and Carol are just jealous. I have never been able to surround myself with people that truly understand me for *me*. Either girls are too catty or they are not adventurous.

So they were goofing off and started messaging Dean during English class. School still hasn't found "the right fit" for a permanent substitute, so we're stuck with Mr. White who just sits at his desk and reads. Basically it's just another study hall. I hate it though because I am just trying to raise my grade and become a better student. Whatever. At least it's giving me time to study for other classes. I use it as time to write to Dean sometimes, too.

Anyway, Alex goes behind my back and tells Dean that I'm talking to multiple dudes. I mean, I am but . . . I like to live my life spontaneously and some people do not understand that concept. We're in high school nothing is meant to be serious.

At least that's what I have always felt but, with Dean I was starting to feel like there is something different. My friends do not understand. They just see him as another guy that I hookup with in the middle of the night.

Isabella Christiana

I don't have anywhere to turn, between the lack of supportive friends in my life and the stress my parents put on me. I feel like I should always please people if I want them to love me.

February 20

It's been a few days and things are starting to be a little rough. Dean kinda blocked me out of his life. I mean, I didn't do anything wrong . . . He claims that I was being "too clingy" and "cared too much."

They say that's what happens when a guy takes a girl's virginity. I should've known what I was getting into, with his body count in the double digits and we're only teenagers.

Losing my virginity made me lose a piece of me. I feel like I have changed. I am not the same person I was just a few months ago.

Honestly, I'm not mad at him totally about how he left. Yes, I'm hurt. He didn't cheat on me or anything, he just got annoyed by me. I thought I would be tolerable to be around, even if he just wanted to have sex with me.

That's what the last few months were, the same old routine. I would sneak out of my house in the middle of the night just so he could just park in the empty parking lot behind the school and get his hard on. It wasn't even good! I had to do all the work, and then he would drop me off at my home like I was nothing. I was not complaining because at least I felt close to someone and I had true feelings for him. I thought I loved him.

Honestly, I knew he was going to ghost me. I saw

it from a mile away. He started acting weird and disconnected, like he didn't care anymore. Then, he blames me and says I am the problem, makes me feel like I am the fuck up.

I haven't told Alex or Carol or my parents how I am feeling about this situation. They don't need to know. It doesn't affect them. How I feel doesn't matter to them. Even if he used me or neglected me. I will just move on to the next.

February 28

Finally, after nearly a month of dealing with Mr. White, our school found a permanent substitute for English class. His name is Mr. Jahns.

Once he stepped into the school, the air actually changed because he took all the girls breath away. Who can blame them? Mr. Jahns is older but not a "teacher looking" old. He looks like he just walked off the runway right into Mercer High School. With his tanned skin and muscular body, he had all the girls drooling over him. Besides him looking about 21 years old, there's something different about him compared to all of the other teachers—and all the other guys— at my school. He walks around as if he has no cares in the world, with his chin up and shoulders back Mr. Jahns almost knows he has power . . . especially over the ladies.

He had us read Old English literature in class today. I have to say, the old stuff is definitely not my favorite to read or even talk about, but Mr. Jahns made the old books not so boring. When he was reading Beowulf out loud to the class, he was able to mesmerize us. No one was sleeping or hiding on their phones. Everyone was in a trance when he spoke, almost as if he cast a spell just with his voice.

I kept staring at his lips while he was reading . . . there were so full and firm. He has a way of reading that makes me just sink into my seat. His voice sounds like he's trying to seduce the whole class.

March 4

Yeah, karma is a bitch. Today in class, I saw Alex and Carol whispering together and when I walked over to take my seat behind them, they stopped talking. They have always been their own best friends and I have been the third wheel but, this seemed different. It was like they were talking about me.

After the bell dismissed us, they got up and left the room in a hurry. I tried to catch up to them but they were moving too quickly and I was not going to chase them down the hall. At that moment I knew something was wrong. I did not stress about that situation for the rest of the day. I decided to move forward and since the only class I had left was English, I had to keep my attitude high for Mr. Jahns.

In class today, Mr. Jahns assigned the class a project based off the story we have been reading in class, Beowulf. There are multiple parts such as multiple essays and a presentation, and random mini projects within it. Overall, I am not complaining. A project to finish out the class? Sounds easy enough and low stress to me. Just how I like it.

March 11

Being so focused on Mr. Jahns had almost distracted me from everything else that is going on in my life. I really want to impress him with this project. I have almost forgot about Alex and Carol being stupid and whispering behind my back. I have never been good with confrontation so I just left it alone. Well, it has now come to my attention that my friends have totally gone behind my back.

Today in class, I noticed that Alex was wearing a maroon colored sweatshirt, and Alex never wears sweats. When I went up to her after class, I saw that it was from Harrison High. At first I was slightly annoyed that she didn't tell me that she was finally talking to someone, but then I realized that sweatshirt looked a little too familiar . . . because it used to be mine! She was wearing Dean's shirt! I am not one for confrontation but, I could not let this slide. I could not let her get away with this.

In the moment, I wasn't thinking . . . I just acted. I have never felt this way before. I felt betrayed, alone, and enraged all in one feeling. I didn't know whether I should scream or cry, and I ended up doing a little bit of both. Alex was only a short distance in front of me when I came up and yanked the hood and stopped her in her tracks. She turns around and says "what was that for?!?!?"

Everyone around us slowly starts backing up, knowing as if something was going to happen. Even Alex's sidekick, Carol, got out of the way. I started frantically crying, my lip was quivering, I could barely speak. Yet, I had the rage roaring up inside of me that

I could not just be left speechless. I was as snarky as I could be when I said, "Oh, nice sweatshirt. How could you possibly walk around knowing that Dean gave that me after we fucked? You never were my friend!"

I was about to run off because I had said my two-cents, but I stopped. What Alex came back with, and her attitude, hurt more than ever. She told me the nights he was too busy to be with me he was with her. She actually said, "I was the one who had his attention, not you. You are an A typical girl. No one would ever want to be with you. You're just a loose whore and you gave him what he wanted. Now, he wants a real relationship, something you could never give him."

I tried to be strong and stand up for myself but, I could not get any words out of my mouth. I hate that when I am upset that I just sob and my lip begins to quiver so much that words cannot even come out. I just walked to English, knowing that I made a fool of myself in the hallway.

In class, Mr. Jahns acted in his typical ways. He didn't seem to notice my smudged mascara and red swollen face.

I just really need someone to comfort me. I need some reliable people in my life that won't betray me. I want to feel loved again, because at this point I feel all alone.

March 15

For years, I have dreaded going to last period. Now, having Mr. Jahns as my last period teacher, makes the school day much better. These last few days have gone by so slow not having my friends. After the incident in the hallway no one took my side. I am kinda all alone now. I try to keep to myself and lay low.

After class today, Mr. Jahns asked me if I was understanding the stories because, as he said it, "You look lost while I'm reading the story."

I wanted to tell him "I am lost because I am focused on you." But I played it cool and said "Yeah, I am a little lost. I have been going through a lot with people in my grade and I am distracted."

I was surprised when he told me he'd heard people talking through the hallways. "Just know that you can always come to talk to me whenever you need someone."

I realized that was my in so I said, "I'll take you up on that offer. For now, maybe you should tutor me on the subject to better help me understand."

I was able to confide in him a little about the drama with Alex and Dean and he comforted me so much. I think he is someone I can rely on. He gave me his number to set up study sessions and in general for comfort. Just a disclaimer, I have a few teacher's numbers. At my school it's not that big of a deal because the teachers and students have pretty close relationships. Still, usually my teachers don't text me about personal matters. It's strictly about school.

Having Mr. Jahns's number feels different. I think it will be different between us. He told me he could get in trouble, since he is a substitute. I won't tell anyone. I mean, I am telling you of course, journal, but no one else. I know I can't. They would just be jealous and probably tell on him, anyway. It feels good to write it down, though.

Hey, journal, at least you're finally proving to be good for something!

March 17

Finally, today I am going to text Mr. Jahns. I am thinking about asking him to meet up at the downtown library so he will help me with the Beowulf project. The project is actually very simple and easy, but I feel like I almost need to see him every second of the day.

Mr. Jahns is able to comfort me. When I am with him, I feel . . . wanted. It's like nothing else in the world matters.

This text has to be good, a perfect mixture of flirty and serious. I cannot just send him a "hey" or "whatcha doin later?" He is not like any other guy I have talked to. Also, do my texts have to be grammatically correct since he's my english teacher?

(later)

I did it. I texted him. The text said, "Hello, Mr. Jahns I am working on my English project at the moment, but I am stuck at a few parts. Could you take the time out of your day to help me? I would love to meet up and see you. Library at 7?"

I was anxiously waiting for a reply. Yet, I did not have to wait too long. He replied almost instantly. His text was simple and hard to read, just like how he acts in class: "See you then. Let's sit away from everyone else so you can focus on your work."

I guess I should come up with some questions

about the project, but I am not planning on talking about the project the whole time . . . I think he and I are on the same page.

(later)

Tonight with Mr. Jahns went amazing! We barely covered the English project, which I expected. We mostly just joked around and laughed . . . a lot. The study room became our little escape in the moment, it was only us. My focus was only on him. That is, until the librarians came in our study room to tell us to quiet down. Jokingly I suggested that maybe next time we should go somewhere more private to work. Mr. Jahns did not seem too opposed to that idea. Hopefully I will be able to see him again soon . . . and not just at school.

March 20

I have some very exciting news to share! Mom and Dad are going out of town tonight and leaving me home all by myself. I texted Mr. Jahns after school and asked him if he wants to come over to help me with the homework he gave us. Not so surprisingly he said he would. This time we don't have to worry about keeping quiet and disrupting others around us.

If it was any other guy I would probably wear some typical black leggings with whatever sweatshirt looks not so baggy or worn out. For tonight, I'll stick with the black leggings but wear them with a tight long sleeve V-neck.

I've never worried about how I dress at school but with Mr. Jahns teaching now I at least try to look somewhat cute for him. I am not a 'curvy' girl compared to other girls in my grade, but I have to try to impress him somehow with what I have.

So, I am not sure what Mr. Jahns is expecting to do tonight. I mean does he really want to just study? I am going to be prepared either way. When I was with Dean, I never had to worry about if my bra or underwear matched because all he cared about was my body. Finally, I am going to wear a black lacy set for Mr. Jahns. I don't feel insecure about myself or silly because he is older. I just hope that I am up to his standards. I have never been with an older man or a good-looking man like him. Anyways, I need to get into the shower and get ready for him to come over ASAP. Will update you on the details later.

March 21

Last night was the absolute best night of my life! When Mr. Jahns came over we headed into my room and we laid on my bed and just talked about old english literature. This may sound boring but, the way he talks about it just makes me sink and melt. He can make the most boring subjects so romantic. His voice soothed me and laying there with him made the world around me nonexistent. In that moment it was just us.

I felt comforted by him, even though we were studying. After a while, we just stopped studying. Then, I was able to open up to him and tell him everything about me. From my favorite color to why I have this journal. I let him know my weaknesses, which I have never shared before. He mentioned that next time we were alone he wanted me to show him my journal so he could get know me more.

Lover to the Unknown

I just . . . feel a connection! It's unlike any of the other guys I have been with before. Yet, while I was opening up about my life, feelings, and likes Mr. Jahns was just acknowledging me like he was taking note of everything about me. I appreciated having someone actually listen to me.

Mr. Jahns was being stubborn on his side. He did not open up to me about anything. He wouldn't even tell me his first name and we laughed about him being unfair. I don't know anything about this man that I shared a bed with and all my feelings with, but it doesn't worry me. Mr. Jahns is always hard to read but I know for sure he cares for me. He wouldn't bother about asking all those questions and getting to know me unless he didn't care a little bit.

When we were done studying, we didn't do much talking for the rest of the night. We were laying in my bed just looking at each other. We were gazing into each other's eyes (his eyes are emerald green!) and waiting to see who would make the first move. I mean, he is my teacher. I didn't know what his limits were. I didn't know what he wanted out of all this. I soon learned that he wanted so much of me. No boundaries, just us being people. In the moment I was not a high school student and he was not my substitute teacher.

Eventually, Mr. Jahns made the first move. He caressed my waist and brought me in even closer, as if we were connected. He grasped me so that there was not room in between us. He gazed into my eyes and took control of me.

Mr. Jahns did not take advantage of me. I knew what was happening and I wanted it to happen. Every second with him was intimate and the connection between us just became even stronger. The love we made fulfilled all my needs. It was not about the sex with him, it was so much deeper than that. He made my night amazing and I do not regret anything I did.

All I am thinking about is how I feel almost addicted to him. Mr. Jahns is all I ever need in my life.

March 28

Not so happy Monday . . . Since Mr. Jahns took my attention that last weekend I was not able to focus on my schoolwork. All weekend, I have been having flashbacks about the weekend. Every time I try studying, I think about being connected with Mr. Jahns. I miss his touch and our bodies being intertwined together. Yeah, it was great and all but now it is a major distraction from my work, haha. In class, I have zero energy to complete any work. Lately, I have been slipping on my studying. My grades on the last few exams have not been too great. I am blaming it on my mental health. I do not have friends to motivate me anymore . . . at least I have Mr. Jahns. He can help me out on more than just my school needs.

Today, Mrs. Reed, my counselor ran into me in the hallway when I was walking to one of my classes. She pulled me aside and asked me if I am handling everything okay. I guess that word gets around the teachers pretty quickly, as it does with the students. She heard about the drama in the hallway with Alex and Carol. She tried saying that she noticed the incidence has affected my grades. I guess that could be a part of it.

Luckily she does not know about Mr. Jahns and I. That we are . . . dating? I don't know what I would call it. We are definitely more than just acquaintances, more than just student and teacher. I won't rush into labels. Let's just see how things go together.

April 7

Since Mr. Jahns came over that night a few weeks ago, class is the same it always has been. There has been no acknowledgement of our sensual night together. It was killing me. Finally, today, he was able to give me a little more attention. During study hall, Mr. Jahns sent me a text message. The text message said, "Come up to my room, urgent."

Again, a simple text but, I did not think I just did. I was in study hall and in an instant I got out of my seat and asked Miss Neill if I could use the bathroom. She didn't need to know I was going to Mr. Jahns's room. I don't want people to start assuming and ruin his reputation. I am keeping us a secret for him.

I quickly walked out of study hall and walked up the stairs. While I was walking, my palms were sweating, I was so eager and excited to see why he wanted me. I wasn't missing anything in study hall because I couldn't focus anyways. He was on my mind, like always. These days he's all I can think about. When I walked into his room there was no one in the room. So, I just took at a seat at his desk and waited for him. I assumed that it was his planning period since no one was in the room.

A few minutes later Mr. Jahns walked in. All of a sudden without any hesitation he picked me up out of the chair and sat me on the desk. The feel of us together was magnetic. He pulled my hair to the side and started kissing me down my neck. In my head at the time I knew it was not right, but it felt right because it was with Mr. Jahns. He started kissing me down to my chest, then—ever so nonchalantly, he pulled out a note out of his back pocket of his dress pants. He placed the note in my bra and told me to get back to class.

I didn't want to read the note in front of anyone, so I waited until the end of the day to open up the note. It was a simple typed note that read, "Meet me at the Marina alone at ten o'clock if you want more than just a tease." A little dirty for a teacher to be writing to a student, but I will let it slide for him, of course.

(later)

I just finished getting ready. I cannot wait to see Mr. Jahns at the marina. I know we are going to create many more memories tonight—the best ones yet, I think! I'm going to bring this journal too, because last time he said he wanted to read it to get closer to me. I cannot wait to grow even closer to him and share more with him. This journal shows so much about me and my feelings. I'm not a little girl any more.

This journal is my closest friend, my only friend at this point. I would not consider Mr. Jahns a friend . . . he is my lover and I need him. Without him I am lost and empty. I cannot wait to meet up with him and have another intimate night together, just us together.

???

Whoever is reading this . . . help me.

I drove down to the pier to meet up with Mr. Jahns. His back was facing me. I walked up to him and tapped him on the shoulder. He turned around and said, "Go."

That was when two strong men came running down the pier and grabbed me like I was some cattle in a rodeo. I could not escape their tight grip. I was helpless. The men put a rag over my face and then I felt myself fall over and pass out. The last thing I saw was Mr. Jahns glance back at me. He didn't have the look of love that he had before. Almost, it was like he was grinning as if he'd won in a game he was playing.

Currently, I am in an unfamiliar place. The people here are speaking a whole different language I have never heard before. Being fluent in Spanish does not help me, I have never heard this type of language. I am locked in cell with six other women, none of them understand me when I try to speak to them. The woman look so skinny and they have bruises all over their body. I can tell this because we got our clothing taken away. I managed to hide my journal and pencil behind a loose brick. Then the men who grabbed me at the pier have taken control of me like they own me and there is nothing I can do.

Every day a middle eastern man that I have never seen before wakes us up by shouting at us. I assume he is saying "get up," but I am not exactly sure. He dresses in high-end clothing with gold jewelry. Once everyone in my cell is up, different men come in and handcuff us and take us to tents. There I am separated from the other girls in my cell.

For the rest of the day through most of the night I am not the high school class president I once was with good grades and caring parents.

All I wanted was to be a part of something and to be loved.

I used to crave adventure and try new things. I was a lover of the unknown . . . but now I am a slave to love.

Hardly a Scratch

Leah McNaughton Lederman

This was the last thing she needed to deal with today. It couldn't be that hard to make a breakfast sandwich. When the order on the slip says "with egg," why must the sandwich inevitably come wrapped in its greasy sheath *without egg?* The peachfuzz-lipped employee behind the counter—Mike, his nametag said—wiped his nose on the back of his hand and gave a noncommittal holler, "Need sausage breakfast slider with egg, please!"

The incompetence nauseated her. Or maybe it was the eight vapor tons of grease hanging in the air. Why Marty insisted on eating at a place like this boggled her. More than that, it worried her. She knew his health was failing, and if he kept it up with these meals . . .

Just stop, Cathleen.

She steadied herself on the counter and took a deep breath. In through the nose, out through the mouth. Yoga breaths.

"Sorry for your trouble, ma'am." Nametag Mike nearly had to shout over the noise. She managed a

smile, or at least a grimace. Probably more than his surely single, drug-addict mother ever offered him. She'd consider it her good deed for the day.

Somewhere in the kitchen she could hear construction. The sound of the drill reminded her she had a headache.

Probably violating about thirty different health codes, Cathleen thought to herself as she took the bag from him, fresh grease stains already seeping through. Presumably it contained the correct sandwich this time. She held it by a corner and managed a cold smile. "Yes, well, I'm sure I'll be seeing you again soon, Mike."

She grabbed a handful of napkins at the condiment counter, then collided with a bulbous woman who stood staring at the traffic through the front window.

"I'm so sorry," Cathleen said. "I didn't see you there." She really hadn't. When she'd stalked in wielding the bag with the wrong sandwich, the dining room was empty.

The woman turned and simply stared at Cathleen with pink, watery eyes. Or, near Cathleen. It was hard to tell. She didn't seem to be focused on anything. The skin of her face was thin and loose, like it had been stretched and had since gone slack. There was no definable color to it, either. She simply washed away into the dishwater gray sweatshirt she wore.

Cathleen looked over her shoulder, maybe to see if there was something behind her the old woman was staring at. Maybe she just needed to feel like she was doing something. Obviously, there was nothing there. Just an oversized hamburger plastered on the oversized window.

Hardly a Scratch

The woman's stare turned into a leer. "Hardly a scratch." She started to snicker, then held a shaking hand up to her face, giggling. Spittle collected at the corners of her mouth and she roared with laughter. Cathleen watched and let out an uncomfortable "Heh," at which point the woman stopped abruptly. Her pale, thin skin pinched into a glare and her eyes blazed. "Hardly a scratch," she whispered. She made a sound that was a cross between a sniff and clearing her throat, then walked toward the counter to place her order.

Cathleen offered a polite laugh and re-shouldered her purse. "Well, uh, have a good one." She lifted her coffee in a weak salute. "See you."

When the woman still didn't move or make any motion whatsoever to acknowledge the executive vice president in front of her, Cathleen gathered her unnerved wits and stalked out of the restaurant. *Whole world's gone mad. Or just stupid.*

✌︎℘℘℘℘

Walking through the lobby, Cathleen made a mental note of necklines and skirt lengths. Marty was holding interviews today, and if he wasn't careful, he was going to wind up with a lawsuit.

She had to wait to be buzzed in. New office protocol. The building was expanding and the new neighbors were building some sort of medical suite. She'd seen construction workers and medical staff alike wandering through the community break rooms.

Jacey, the flustered girl at the front desk, managed to open the door only after Cathleen had buzzed it twice. "Sorry, I was—"

Cathleen's cold, raised eyebrow cut her off and Jacey shrunk behind her computer until the older woman had reached the boss's office.

"Am I allowed to promote you twice?" Marty said when Cathleen handed him the grease-stained paper bag. His oxygen canister greeted her with its familiar click and whistle.

"Only if I get another raise." Cathleen set her purse down and started taking off her gloves. "Marty, did your ad say that the candidate needed to be a teenager? I have hemorrhoids older than some of those girls out there. And once we're done with this, we're going to need to do something about that useless creature at the front desk."

The old man just waved a hand. He was holding the sandwich in the other and his mouth was full.

"You planning to get started on them?" She didn't know why she bothered asking.

Marty swallowed hard then grinned at her. "I double booked—*that girl up there*—double booked me. I'm due to meet Mr. Hildebrandt and . . . "

"Just stop." Cathleen rolled her eyes.

He waved again and said, "Don't worry. I'll give you another promotion."

"Another promotion and I'm going to make you my assistant!"

Marty took another mouthful of sandwich and used his waving hand to give a thumbs-up, then pointed to a stack of files on his desk. Cathleen grabbed them and started thumbing through them on the way to her adjoining office.

So, who was the ideal candidate?

Hardly a Scratch

The interviews went as well as Cathleen could hope for with a wall-to-wall hiring fiasco. It was the only way Marty did things—the most difficult and inconvenient way possible. She'd been hired in the same way, sort of. She'd hardly gotten through the interview before she was in a trial run. Two of the office assistants had quit and the interviewer, obviously overwhelmed, had to take calls while he was asking her the typical "Where do you see yourself in five years" crap. Finally, when a third line started ringing, he asked if she didn't mind picking it up.

That was nearly fifteen years ago. Since then, Cathleen had completely taken over the run of the office. She had streamlined every process, created templates for every communique, oral and written; she'd created the operation. It worked so well that Marty entrusted every part of the process to her, so long as his name was on the marquee.

She and Marty saw eye to eye on a lot of things. When she'd caught the budgeting snafu, the way the Horster account had been overcharged, Marty brought her into a line of thinking she easily understood—more money in her pocket. For several years, she had simply turned a blind eye, until she found out there was more in it for her if she helped with the numbers. They never got greedy, really, just enough for . . . well, Marty liked to call it a "gratuity."

Clearly, she thought, watching another pair of knees strut out of her office, she was going to have to revisit the conversation where they delineated candidate expectations. The first five interviews offered maybe one potential employee. Cathleen had little hope for the last one of the day.

She checked the file in front of her as a smartly dressed woman walked into the room—modestly dressed, Cathleen noticed with relief. Plaid pants with a gray blazer over a maroon turtleneck. Not the typical "interview suit" option, but it looked sharp, even if the blazer was a bit faded. "Heather?"

"Yes ma'am. Heather Conzen. It's nice to meet you." The woman had a firm handshake, too. Cathleen dared to hope.

Mrs. Conzen had done her homework. She breezed through the preliminary "what would you do" scenario questions, and seemed to know the job requirements and the flavor of the company without Cathleen having to offer much explanation. This was going to work out quite nicely, Cathleen thought. She stood up to retrieve her clipboard from her desk.

"Your resume has some really interesting items listed under your previous employer . . . that was Synergy Corp, correct? You strike me as someone who—" *Ouch.* Walking back to her desk, Cathleen knocked her knee against the mobile cart that stupid intern Jacey must have parked there.

She tried really hard not to swear and held up her finger to indicate she would need a minute. With a long exhale she smiled and straightened herself, looking again for the clipboard she'd set down earlier. "Sorry about that."

Mrs. Conzen waved her off. "Oh please, don't apologize. Though I suspect in a place like this, you can't let them see you falter. Not even for a second."

Hardly a Scratch

"Excuse me?"

The interview had been going well—so well it almost seemed scripted, Cathleen thought to herself—but what Mrs. Conzen just said was inappropriately presumptuous and borderline contemptuous. Cathleen didn't take well to people overstepping their bounds.

But overstep this interviewee had. And then she had the nerve to stand up and take a step closer, even. She leaned closer toward Cathleen, who bristled, and gave a stage whisper, "Hardly a scratch, right?"

Cathleen felt her hand jerk, but she didn't drop the clipboard she'd located. Very aware of the pacing of the turn of her neck, she turned to face Mrs. Heather Conzen.

The woman looked taller, somehow, and more filled out around the midsection. The gray blazer Cathleen had admired when she first came in had somehow changed. It was a blander gray, if that were possible, somehow nondescript, like a white t-shirt that had mixed too often with darker laundry and finally resulted in a watery, charcoal color. Mrs. Conzen's ashen face wasn't a far shade off, now that she was standing closer. Standing closer and looking at Cathleen, but not quite focused on her.

"Is there something wrong, Cathleen?" the woman asked. It definitely wasn't Mrs. Conzen anymore. Her face looked like it didn't have enough skin to cover it, and she was pale. She looked familiar, like—

Cathleen's breath caught in her chest. It was the woman she'd seen earlier. The woman from the restaurant.

Cathleen stuttered something wordlike and half-stumbled to the door. Marty was standing by the window, studying a file when she spilled out of her office into his. He offered her half a glance before placing the file down and giving his bonsai tree a disinterested poke.

"What's the good word, toots?"

A dry squeak came out where her words should have been. Cathleen cleared her throat and tried again.

"Mm hmm." Marty wasn't listening. He grunted, fiddling with his oxygen canister, then spritzed some water onto the bonsai tree. "You think that man here to see you has anything to do with it?"

"I told Jacey not to—" Cathleen stopped. "I'm sorry, who?"

"Out there, in reception." Marty sprayed some water over his shoulder toward the door.

Cathleen followed the trail of water droplets with her eyes and found the man. Blue jeans and a faded black blazer, elbow pads. A professor? His salt-and-pepper hair was spiked by a pair of reading glasses shoved back from his forehead. "What the hell does he want, Marty?"

"How should I know? He said he'd wait till we were finished, but he wanted a chance to talk to you, if one turned up. Just don't give away all our secrets, eh?" What was supposed to be a wry laugh turned into a series of choked coughs.

Cathleen watched Marty dab away spittle with his handkerchief, then turned back to the man in the lobby. "This oughta be good."

The man looked up when Cathleen pushed open the main door to the office. It was typically noisy in the communal area, though today things were worse than usual with the grinding and pounding sounds coming from the construction down the hall. She offered a dry smile and took a seat across from him in one of the lobby chairs. *Jesus, these things are uncomfortable.*

"Cathleen Williams, I presume?"

"You presume correctly. And you are . . . ?" She tried to keep her tone light, but the fact that she was a busy woman with more to do than anyone else in the building wafted off of her designer shoes and tailored jacket. And her head had just started to ache.

"Mrs. Willi—"

"'Ms.', if you don't mind."

"Of course. Ms. Williams." He inhaled deeply and grinned. "Like the Ms. Dior you're wearing."

Cathleen leveled her gaze at him, taking him in from his eyeglass-spiked hair to his cheap wingtips. "Is that a come on?"

His smile flattened. "It seems you've had an interesting few days, *Ms. Williams*. Care to tell me about them?"

She did not have time for this. Not today. "I'm sure I don't know what you mean."

"I'm sure you don't." The man stretched and pulled his pants up around his waist, then drew a business card from his coat pocket. "But in case anything comes to mind about the last few days— anything strange you can recall . . . you just get ahold of me."

"Fine, fine. Thanks for the card. I have no idea what the hell you're talking about, but I have had a weird day, so yeah, maybe something will shake out.

Oh, and the perfume is 'Miss.' *Miss* Dior." She looked at the card in her hand. "Enjoy your day, Detective Putnam."

"Yeah . . . sure thing." He took the glasses from the top of his head and slid them onto his face. Of course, then he had to look over them to study her. He gave her a long, hard look. "You sure you're feeling all right, Ms. Williams?"

Cathleen brushed her hair from her face with a huff. "I'm just fine, Detective. And I have a lot to do, so if you'd please . . . " She motioned toward the building's exit.

The man stared at her for another long moment, running his tongue along the inside of his cheek. He was thinking something, and he seemed to be laughing at some running joke she didn't get. She turned and walked toward her office, stopping momentarily to watch him amble away, whistling a tune, his hands stuffed in his pockets. Something about the man bothered her, deeply.

"Cathleen?"

The voice snapped her from her thoughts and an involuntary glare contorted her face. *Who the hell wanted what NOW?*

It was one of the scrubs from the medical facility they were putting in next door. A flour sack with a mop of curly hair. Only an idiot would have that hair. He was holding his stethoscope in the air like a surrender flag, approaching her like she was a rabid dog. How the hell did he know her name, anyway?

"It's Ms. Williams, thank you. What do you want? You're not interrupting my work enough with that incessant hammering over there? I thought you guys would be finished by now."

Hardly a Scratch

The pathetic little man shrank back a bit more with each sentence she spat out. Another man, this one in a white jacket, walked over and put a reassuring hand on the scrub's forearm, nodding silently. "I think that's enough, James. Why don't you let me speak to Ms. Williams?"

Cathleen was walking into her office by that point, grinding her teeth against the stabbing pain in her head. She had no time for any of this. The whole day was gone, it seemed, and she'd only had blown interviews by too-tight skirts. She still needed to finish that damned insurance policy Marty was hounding her about.

Another lightning strike to the temple. She let go of the door and grabbed the sides of her head. The man in the white coat was at her side, immediately.

"Ms. Williams, please. Sit." He led her to one of the lobby chairs. "You've been through a lot today."

Cathleen let him sit next to her while she caught her breath. The stabbing in her temple hadn't gone away, but she had found its rhythm. "I'm sorry . . . do I know you?"

"I'm Doctor Thomas. We met this morning. Do you remember our conversation?"

She tried to look him in the eye, study his face. His eyes were a twinkly green. Did she recognize him? He had a salt and pepper beard and receding hairline. When was this morning? The room blurred and the sound of his voice rose to an echo. "Cathleen? Can you hear me?"

The only sound she heard was the plastic clatter of her phone when she hit the floor.

It took a few blinks for things to come into focus, and even then, Cathleen was only aware of her throbbing skull. It looked like she was in her bedroom, at least. What day was it, Wednesday? She had been drinking pretty hard lately, though it had been a long time since she'd blacked out on a weeknight.

Someone started hammering next door and Cathleen threw the pillow over her head to protect her aching temples. *Who the hell is hammering at—oh, shit. What time is it?*

She threw an arm out from under the covers and pawed at the nightstand. Eventually she followed the charging cord to where the phone had landed behind the bed. *At least I plugged it in*, she thought. Then her eyes bugged out when she saw it was nine in the morning. She hadn't been late in six years.

Part of her wanted to spring out of bed and make the coffee-spilling, mad dash for the office. That's what they always did on TV and movies when the hungover main character was late. Cathleen knew herself. The mad dash didn't suit her.

She pressed a few buttons on her phone then held it to her ear. "Yeah, Marty? Uh huh . . . I know, can you believe it? Yeah, I'm a mess over here. I'll stay at the home office today . . . yup, I'll email them over in time for your two o'clock. Right. All right, see you tomorrow."

The hammering was right above her bed on the other side of the wall. She gave the wall a few kicks before rolling out of bed for a shower and some aspirin.

Hardly a Scratch

It was going to be an easy day, Cathleen told herself. After those interviews yesterday . . . were they really that bad? She had blacked out not long after. Something must have gotten her going, if she was that far gone on a Tuesday afternoon. She wasn't a drunk by business standards, but she would be if she didn't dial it back. Maybe she'd go for a run later.

Coffee in hand, she snuggled down in front of the computer to send some emails, check a few documents, then hit snooze on that new project. The truth was, Marty hadn't been doing so well these last few years, and the numbers at the office had been suffering as a result. There was an audit coming up and so she might as well get a relaxing day in while she still could. And he wouldn't stop bugging her about the insurance updates.

A stab of pain seared through her temples. *Damn it,* she thought. *Why did I remind myself of the insurance bullshit?* She punched a few keys on the laptop, then wiggled the mouse. *And why isn't this loading?* After a couple of restarts and a few dozen clicks, she realized the wi-fi was down. A power drill groaning through the walls was all she needed. She picked up her keys, shouldered her laptop bag, and walked out of the apartment.

Ten years ago, she might have powered through her headache and gone for a run. Not today. She had no one to impress. Her laptop bag kept her from bothering with a jog and besides, she was comfortable enough in her own skin to put running in the "Things Not Going to Happen Today" column.

Everything in her life ran in columns and tables. There was a file for each thought, idea, project; a deadline and a budget. This was how she operated. It was the only way to get things done.

Cathleen didn't feel the need to impress anyone, but she could also hear her doctor's voice chiding her that if she couldn't fit in a run, she could at least try some brisk walking. A face flashed in her mind, a man with green eyes and a beard, wearing a white coat. Doctor . . . ?

She worked through her memory while she walked, trying to put a name with the face. A hot lance pierced through her skull then, and she doubled over from the pain. *This is no ordinary headache*, she thought to herself.

She took a seat on the stoop of an antique store to catch her breath. It was closed for remodeling so at least she wouldn't be in anyone's way. But remodel meant more hammering and drilling, and Cathleen found herself stomping away from yet another construction site. *Seriously, what the hell?*

Just a coffee, that's all she needed, and she was almost there. Up ahead, she saw a bulldozer and a front loader in the coffeeshop's parking lot. Cathleen figured she'd try to set up her laptop at the cafe but was already mentally preparing to hike to the library instead. She sighed. The whole goddamn city couldn't be under construction.

Cathleen waited at the intersection for the light to turn. The coffee house was just across the street. Waiting beside her, a few students tapped their thumbs on the screens of their phones, and a homeless woman sat despondent at their feet, her cardboard sign propped up against her knees.

Got Fired. Spare Change Appreciated, it read.

Hardly a Scratch

The woman held out a cup with a shaking hand. Cathleen's lip curled reflexively, and she thought to herself that it was no surprise the woman had been fired. She could hardly hold a cup. What use could she be? Then Cathleen's eyes traveled from the greasy cardboard sign to the shaking hand to the woman's face.

She dropped her laptop bag and took a step backward. It was the woman she'd bumped into at McDonald's yesterday morning, and again at the interview, somehow. But her face . . . her face was gone wrong. It had been singed horribly on the one side, and blackened skin flaked at the edges of red, exposed muscle and a row of naked teeth. Something like what came from a hot glue gun oozed from the woman's left eye, straight out of the pupil. The words on her sign had changed, too: *Burned by Fire. Hardly a Scratch.*

Seeing Cathleen's reaction, the woman's mangled face broke into a grin. "Spare change?"

Cathleen tried to turn; her plan was simply to run—fast, and far away. Instead, the heel of her shoe caught in the strap of the laptop bag she'd dropped. She tripped sideways, tumbling directly into the traffic streaming by. One of the college students screamed and Cathleen heard a car horn somewhere off in the distance.

All of the sounds were drowned out, though, by the sound of the homeless woman laughing, shrieking, choking on her words *"Spare change?"* and then falling into her mindless cackle once again.

Cathleen wasn't sure if it was the beeping or the roar of the power drill that woke her up. She was in a hospital bed. Jesus, she must have hit the sidewalk harder than she'd thought. That stupid old store manager. How many times had Cathleen warned her she needed to salt the sidewalk in front of the store?

"Ah, look who's awake!" A young man in green scrubs walked into the room and made a beeline for her IV. He had curly brown hair and a pudgy, sweet-looking face. Not unlike a hobbit, she supposed. "How's the head, Ms. Williams?"

Cathleen frowned. "Now that you mention it, though—yeah. My head is pounding. What is that, power of suggestion?"

"No suggesting at all. You're pretty severely concussed, Ms. Williams." The young man had her follow his pen light, then his finger. "Do you remember how you got here?"

"Well yeah, it was that stupid dope at the corner store. Her gutters drain right onto the sidewalk and when they freeze—what? What's that look for?"

He gave a noncommittal shrug. "Sorry. Didn't realize I was looking any way. So, you slipped on the ice, then?"

"Yeah, and I'm pretty sure I want to file a suit. I mean, I *warned* her about that stupid sidewalk!"

The young man folded his arms and stared at her intently. "Sidewalk? Not stairs?"

"Yeah. Right in front of her store." Cathleen frowned at him. "Why are you looking at me like that? What stairs?"

Hardly a Scratch

Another voice interrupted their conversation. "Is everything all right, Ms. Williams?" A balding man wearing a white coat over his scrubs had entered the room. He peered over the top of a chart, studying her.

At the sight of him, Cathleen felt a stab of pain in her temple. He looked familiar. "Ow," she breathed. "No, not all right. My head is killing me."

"Yes, the headache is a concern. We want to get you back to feeling better. Dr. Fortin here has arranged for you to have a CAT scan later today. Can you tell me what you remem—" The grinding whine of a power drill cut him off.

"God DAMN it! What is wrong with you people?"

The man in the white coat ignored her outburst. He took a pen light from his pocket and shined it in her eye. She slapped it away. "Get that stupid thing away from me! Dr. Frodo over here already shined his flashlight in my face. My head hurts and no one is making me feel *better!* It's all flashlights and construction!"

"My dear, I'm so sorry." The older doctor exchanged a look with the younger.

"You don't seem sorry. Isn't it a bit ridiculous to have construction going on where there are patients trying to recover? It's goddamn cruel!" She gripped the hair on the sides of her head. "My head is *killing* me!"

The older doctor paused for a moment, studying her, then wiped his nose with a handkerchief. "I quite agree. Construction zones and hospitals don't mix. But you're quite a special case. There wasn't really anywhere else to put you. For now, at least. No matter. Dr. Fortin will administer some pain medication to help you sleep."

149

Dr. Fortin followed him into the hallway. Cathleen did her best to eavesdrop on the conversation they had at the nurse's station across the hall, but the construction sounds chopped up their words. Still, she managed to piece together something about falling down an elevator shaft, a car accident, slipping on ice. The older doctor's droning voice cut through the construction. " . . . It's something different every day . . . "

Sounds like a busy patient roster, she thought. *God, my head is killing me.*

Dr. Fortin came back in, a small syringe in his hand. "Ms. Williams, this is going to help you sleep. I'll be back this afternoon to take you in for your scan." He tinkered with her IV while he spoke. "Sweet dreams."

It must have been Jackson's clipboard smacking down on the table that jarred Cathleen awake. No one seemed to notice she'd dozed off. Too many long days this month. It was starting to catch up to her. Then again, another board meeting? Even on her best day she would have slept through it. Besides, Jackson and the other grunts could shoulder some of the weight for once.

C-Click. C-Click.

Cathleen glared in the office manager's direction. Floppy blonde hair with an arrogant smile, Jackson always brought a pen that he wouldn't stop clicking. She was up to her ears in renewing the office insurance policy and could hardly keep up with prepping for the audit on top of that, and all she could think about was the irregular rhythm of his pen. *C-c-click. Click. C-click.*

Down the conference room table, none of them did anything to make Cathleen's job easier. All they had to contribute was noise. Knuckles on the table, whining chairs, shuffling feet, cleared nasal passages.

Marty was hashing out some details on a subparagraph of the mission statement, opening another piece of candy. It squeaked and crinkled as he twisted the metallic paper. Wasn't he supposed to be in for another round of treatments? The old man leaned over to review the notes Jackson had taken down, his oxygen machine clicking and whistling as he breathed. That goddamn pen wouldn't let up, either. Cathleen squeezed her eyes shut to block out the noise, as if that would work. *Stupid, Cathleen. Stupid!*

Then a rhythmic whirring grew louder, the vacuum cleaner edging its way up the hallway. It didn't help things. Esther must be working early tonight—or was the board meeting just running late? Cathleen checked her watch. 9:17. *Jesus, Marty.*

She stood up and made her way to the door. Maybe some more coffee was in order if the old man was going to have her running more quotes once he'd finished up with Jackson.

Cathleen nodded a greeting at the cleaning lady as she passed her in the hallway. The older woman couldn't hear a damn thing anyone said, vacuum or no. And apparently having the top executives meeting in the conference room didn't deter her from shutting down and cleaning out the coffee machine.

Son of a bitch, Cathleen muttered to herself. She turned on her heel to head back to the meeting and slipped on the break room's linoleum instead, hitting her elbow on the "wet floor" sign on the way down.

"Miss Cathleen!" Esther called over the sweeper. She ran over to Cathleen, crouching beside her. "Are you all right?"

Cathleen rubbed her insulted elbow and jerked away from Esther. Just what she needed, that derelict woman breathing on her. "Yes, Esther, I'm fine. Other than my wounded pride." The vacuum whirred in a blaring panel of white noise. Esther hadn't turned it off.

Marty peeked his head out from the conference room and hurried over when he saw the two women sitting on the ground. His oxygen tank clattered behind him.

Esther looked like she would cry. "Oh, Miss Cathleen, I am so sorry! I didn't mean for anyone to get hurt. I should have waited until you were all out of the building—"

He held out his hand to the older woman to help her to her feet. "None of that, Esther." He grinned and pointed. "See look, the wet floor sign is up and everything. Nothing to mark down on an insurance form, eh Cathleen? No harm done." His oxygen tank clicked and whistled under the broad hum of the vacuum.

Cathleen was eyeing her shirt, noting the small white blotches showing up on the fabric. She sniffed at her sleeve. There must have been some bleach mixed in with the mop water. Mixed with her Miss Dior perfume, it was nauseating. *Son of a bitch, this was a nice shirt.* She gave him a glare but accepted his outstretched hand. "My hero," she said, rolling her eyes.

Marty let out one of his belly laughs, too loud for the occasion, and patted her on the back. "Oh, Cathleen. You are the best." He turned to share the laugh with Esther, but found the cleaning lady wringing her hands, practically falling over again. "That's enough of that, young lady! Don't worry about Cathleen, she's cranky by nature. I mean, hell, she'd complain if you hit her with a new car." He laughed at his own joke, and his oxygen tank rattled and hissed in errant harmony with the vacuum.

Cathleen wheeled on Esther and spat, "Would you *please* turn off that sweeper?"

Esther jumped visibly and clambered toward her vacuum cleaner. The empty space the lack of sound made was louder than the space it had filled. Cathleen's temples throbbed.

Marty exhaled loudly, satisfied. Always the smug satisfaction. "There now, isn't that better? And look at Cathleen, here." He grinned. "Hardly a scratch."

Cathleen punched the wall, upsetting the framed posters hanging there. "Hardly a scratch? Hardly . . . a *scratch?* This is a three-hundred-dollar shirt that I'll never wear again! God *damn* it, Marty! I need to get out of here."

On her way back to the conference room she heard Marty speaking softly with Esther, followed by the tell-tale crinkle of a toffee candy as he gave one to the bewildered woman, who really did look like she might throw up or pass out. Cathleen knew he wouldn't get back to work until he'd sufficiently consoled her. As ruthless as he was, the man couldn't resist a vulnerable woman.

Cathleen packed up to leave. She wasn't going to get much done stinking like bleach, especially not with Esther's sniveling noises added to the office mix. In the hopes she might get something done after her head cleared, she threw the files she needed into a box to take home. She scrunched her lips and threw her glare out the office window when she heard the familiar click and whistle coming down the hall.

"I thought I might find you sneaking away."

He leaned on the doorway, loosening his tie. He was trying to catch his breath without being obvious about it, but she knew.

"Yeah, Mart. It's been a hell of a day. And I'm just about finished—"

"Honestly . . . " Marty put up a hand to stop her. "I know you'll get it done. You always do. It's why I like having you around."

Cathleen smiled. God, he could deflate her. She hated that he could make her smile when she was so angry. "The tight ass doesn't hurt either, though, does it?"

He responded with a wheezy chuckle and then stepped into the office, shutting the door behind him. "You've been with me since the very beginning, toots. When we were still working out of a broom closet. Hard to imagine we'd be pulling a two-million-dollar policy on these digs, huh?" He eyeballed the walls and ceiling as he spoke.

Hardly a Scratch

It had been what, seventeen years? Twice they very nearly shut down. This latest was just a small scare, and a few well-timed settlements would keep them afloat. But it wasn't like Marty to wax sentimental. And why now, when all she wanted to do was get in the tub?

"What I'm trying to say is, I know I can count on your loyalty. Right, Cathleen?"

There it was. He wasn't being sentimental. She met the old man's eyes and they were focused, blazing cobalt. The only sound was the click and hiss of the oxygen.

"Marty, what—?"

"Things aren't going well. You have to know it."

"Oh, but the Bickford settlement is going to help, and—"

"It's more than just the overhead. Cathleen, I've gotten into . . . some trouble. I . . . " he trailed off.

"Marty, what is it?" Cathleen set her things down and gave him a hard stare. "C'mon, there's nothing we haven't dealt with before. We survived 2008, didn't we?"

The old man gave a wheezy exhale that might have been a laugh, but he was shaking his head. "There's more to it than that. Really, the less you know on that end, the better. The fact is, I'm going to need to ask for your help if any of us want to keep our retirement." He coughed a phlegmy cough. "Or stay out of prison."

≈≈≈≈≈

≈≈≈≈≈

The streetlights made stripes of light in the car as Cathleen rode home. She'd been biking to and from the office lately, but given the long day and the atom bomb Marty had dropped on her at the end of it, she opted for the cab.

He was going to torch the place. Wait till everyone was out of the building, and boom. But he couldn't do it, not on his own. He tried to blame it on the oxygen, saying, "I just can't move fast enough, Cathleen," but the both of them knew that wasn't it. He didn't lack the speed, he lacked the cunning.

Cathleen and Marty both knew the reason they'd stayed afloat as long as they had was because of her creative thinking. So here it was, the ultimate test. And it wasn't just loyalty. If they couldn't recover some of their losses through the insurance, Cathleen was likely to lose it all.

Son of a bitch, Marty.

It was going to be a double Ambien evening, looked like. There was too much work to do and too much worrying, but it would have to wait until the next day. She was going to need her strength.

⁓ℓℓℓℓ⁓

"Rise and shine, pumpkin pie."

Cathleen's eyes snapped open at the sound of a strange voice in her room. When she looked around her, she was even more bewildered. She'd fallen asleep in her bedroom, but here she was in a hospital gown, lying in a hospital room. The machine next to her beeped and she could hear construction pounding away down the hall.

156

Hardly a Scratch

She looked for where the voice had come from. A dark-haired man was grinning at her, seated close to her on the bed. Too close. *Who the hell*—then she remembered. She'd met him before. It was that smarmy detective. What was his name again? Putnam.

Holy hell, her head hurt. Each beep out of the machine bounced around the inside of her skull.

"What the—why are you here? Why am *I* here? Isn't this a private—" Cathleen's thoughts whirled into a fury until she stopped herself. *Focus, Cathleen.* Questions later. She wanted this man removed immediately. "*Hello?* Somebody help me, please!"

An orderly came in and stopped short, looking from the detective to Cathleen. "Yes, Miss Williams?"

Another man was right on his heels, the doctor in green scrubs . . . the hobbit-looking one, Dr. Fortin. When he spoke to her, his voice was cold. "What seems to be the problem, Cathleen?"

She rubbed her temples, trying to ease the throbbing and clear her head. *Who the hell were these people and why did she know them?*

Detective Putnam spoke up. "There's no problem, Doc. Just paying a visit and taking a precaution, is all." He took Cathleen's wrist and gently pulled it away from her face.

"Don't you touch me!" Cathleen spat at him. She used her free arm to land a few slaps against his arms, trying to push him away.

"Easy now, easy. I don't want to add 'assaulting an officer.'" He latched her wrist to her bed with a pair of handcuffs.

The orderly and Dr. Fortin had rushed forward to

restrain their patient, but Cathleen fell back against the pillows when she felt the handcuffs. She stared at the detective in a daze. "I—I'm sorry. I don't understand . . . "

"Really, sir, is this necessary?" the orderly looked from the doctor to the detective, flustered.

Detective Putnam snorted. "Someone was trying to pay our esteemed executive a visit in the office . . . before the whole thing went *kapow*." He held up a square glass bottle with a metal bow at the top. Cathleen squinted with vague recollection. It was her perfume bottle.

"Where did you . . . ? That was in my desk."

"No, not anymore. You've got a cleaning lady with sticky fingers. They found it on her when she was admitted. After she told me you'd rigged the place." He opened the bottle and spritzed some into the air, then grinned. On his way out of the room, he stopped by the doctor. "I'd say our little arsonist here could use some extra supervision."

⸾⸾⸾⸾⸾

The sound of her breathing woke her, a ragged pant. She squinted from side to side, instinctively looking for a light source, but she couldn't see a thing. Were her eyes even open? It was too dark for anything to register. And then the pain came creeping, tiptoeing around from the back of her ears to the sides and front of her skull. The first throb landed like a blunt object.

What the hell happened?

Lights were blaring across her field of vision now,

shattering the dark into shards. There was yelling. Footsteps, tromping boots running past her.

"Ma'am. Ma'am? Can you hear me?"

Cathleen let out a croak and the blunt object smashed against her skull again. *Jesus God, it hurts.* "Yes . . . yes. I'm here . . . "

But the man hadn't been speaking to Cathleen. Another voice answered, this one more clearly than she'd been able to. "I'm okay, sir. You see to that lady over there."

Esther.

It was Esther's voice.

Cathleen managed to open her eyes, finally, squinting against the lights. Emergency vehicles, everywhere. She saw the man make a gesture to another group of paramedics, who came running to the spot holding a stretcher.

"You just stay still, ma'am. These guys are going to get you help. Don't move. You hear me?"

"I'm just f-fine, sir . . . " Esther said.

He didn't respond to the older woman, or even hear her. He was already running off toward the flaming structure. Esther's eyes landed on Cathleen's, and her singed face wrinkled. Was it a smile? A glare? Her voice came out as a choked rasp.

"Hardly a—hardly a scratch."

Cathleen let out a groan and rolled to her back. The flaming structure in front of her was the building she'd worked in for nearly twenty years; the building she'd just torched. A little tinkering with the gas and a well-timed spark from the microwave in the staff kitchen. Too easy.

Flames licked out of the faux-Victorian

windowsills, wafting heat into the black sky. A team of emergency workers leaned over Esther, working gently and quickly to get her onto a stretcher.

The EMTs waved off a group of police officers wanting to ask questions, but Cathleen watched as a grumpy-looking man in a cheap suit sidled up to Esther. The old woman's voice was like an old frog's as she spoke with him. Cathleen couldn't make out the words. The man gestured toward the building, standing lonely behind a wall of flames.

No one was supposed to be in the building. *Goddammit, Esther.*

As if she'd heard Cathleen's thoughts, the old cleaning woman moved her head slowly to the side and met Cathleen's eyes. A soot-stained finger rose up and pointed directly at her.

Cathleen's stomach went cold and panic rose up into her throat, ejecting onto the concrete as a load of bile. The man pulled a pad of paper from his pocket and began walking toward her.

"I'm so sorry! I didn't mean to frighten you, Miss Williams."

Cathleen had nearly shrieked when she heard Esther's voice. No one was supposed to be here. No one.

The old woman was trembling. "I hoped to catch you—I-I just wanted to . . . to tell you again how bad I felt about your blouse.

"Oh, Christ, Esther." Cathleen reminded herself to smile. The woman already looked like she might melt straight into the floor. "Remember? Hardly a scratch." Cathleen put her hand on Esther's back, leading her away from the break room, away from the timer on the microwave.

"I-I know it's not as fancy as the clothes you usually wear, Miss Williams, but I hoped m-maybe you could find yourself something nice with this coupon. I felt so bad about the bleach on your blouse." Esther had stopped in the hallway and pulled a crinkled coupon from her pocket.

Cathleen took the paper and looked down at it. There was a JCPenney logo on it. *Oh, hell.* She fought to keep her lip from curling in disgust. Trying to fix the problem, the old lady had insulted her more than anything else. And then Cathleen caught a hint of a familiar scent coming from the paper. It was her own perfume. Cathleen looked hard at Esther. Had she . . . ?

This was not the time or place to worry about theft. How long had Esther been there, and what had she seen? Why was she even in the building?

It didn't matter. They needed to get out of there. "It's late, Esther, and everyone in the building is gone. This couldn't have waited?"

The woman looked down at her hands, her face flushed. "I'm so sorry, Ms. Williams. I-I was going to leave it in your mailbox but then I saw you walking in. I—well, I just followed you." She squirmed underneath Cathleen's hard stare. Finally, she shrugged and tried to sound breezy with a higher-pitched voice. "Working late again?"

Cathleen's mouth broke into a forced grin. "You got it, Esther. All kinds of paperwork to fill out. Audits really are a bitch." She put a firm hand on the cleaning woman's shoulder, walking her down the hall. "It's been a long day, Esther. We need to get out of here if we know what's good for us."

※♪♪♪♪

The jangle of the handcuffs against the bed's metal railing startled Cathleen, but at least she remembered where she was.

A whining drill cut through her thoughts and confirmed her memory.

The hospital. She was safe. Aside from the same stupid headache she'd had for what, a week now? She couldn't have been in the hospital for that long. She'd gone home, hadn't she, and to work . . . she'd been going about her business like nothing had happened.

But something had happened. She'd done something terrible. Her brain ran in circles chasing the thought, trying to peg down what she was missing. That's when she heard the familiar click and whistle.

"You in there, Cathleen?"

God damn it, Marty.

"What are you doing here, Marty?" Her words came out as a hiss.

"Aw, c'mon now! Of course I'm here!"

"What the hell time is it?" The darkness bewildered her. Just as she said these words, a razor-sharp beam of light jolted the room awake. Marty was grinning in front of the blinds, having just ripped them open.

"Damn things must be industrial grade for blocking out light," she muttered.

Hardly a Scratch

"It's been a hell of a few days, Cathleen." *Click. Whistle.*

She waited for him to say more, to explain what was going on, but he just sat there, squinting and grinning at her.

Click. "They're going to burn us to the ground, you know." *Whistle.*

Cathleen grunted and tried to shift her weight in the bed. The handcuff clanged against the railing. "Marty. What the hell is going on?"

"What do you remember, toots?"

The darkness creeped in again at the edge of her vision. Something was scurrying into the dark corners in her mind, trying to get away. "I don't know, Marty. I don't understand what's happening. I'm going in circles and I keep waking up here." She raised her voice with each sentence to drown out the hammering noises coming from down the hall.

"Yeah." Marty cleared his throat and rubbed his knees. "The doctors can't tell me much, but they did let me know you're not real clear on how you ended up in here. That true? Can you remember anything, Cathleen?"

She twisted in the bed a bit. She was in the hospital because she had a concussion. The concussion was from . . . she'd fallen on the ice in front of—no, that wasn't it. Was it an elevator shaft? A car crash?

"Cathleen . . . " Marty's voice was thick. "Cathleen, honey. They're just keeping you for observation because, well, because they're worried about you." His words shook as they fell from his mouth. Cathleen couldn't wrap her head around them. "Something about trauma . . . the doctors are saying there's nothing wrong with you, not a scratch on—"

"That's *it*." Cathleen's words came out as a hiss. "Not a scratch, hardly a scratch—it was *Esther*. She's been following me, harassing me. What's she want with me? Still pissed I walked on her wet floor?"

"Sweetie." Marty squeezed his eyes closed and pinched the bridge of his nose. "I don't suppose you remember talking to me . . . before."

"Before what?" Cathleen squinted at him, studying his face. Her head was starting to hurt again. Faint alarm bells were coming at her from the sides of her mind.

"Just . . . before. Before now. Do you remember having this conversation?"

"I don't understand what the hell you're talking about, Mart. Just tell me what you're trying to say."

"Cleaning lady was walking out of the building with you when it blasted. You know, Esther. She was tore up pretty bad. Landed hard on the concrete and smashed herself up. She uh . . . shit, Cathleen. Esther died last night."

Cathleen blinked a few times as his words landed, each one like a raindrop in a pile of ash. Her thoughts spilled out every which way but she kept shaking her head, back and forth, back and forth. He wasn't making sense. They must have changed his medicine. Esther wasn't dead. She'd walked out of the building . . . Cathleen clanged her handcuffed wrist against the metal railing. "What the *hell* are you saying, Marty? This doesn't make any sense."

Marty shook his head and leaned in closer to her. He smelled like one of those stupid toffees. "Cathleen, you rigged up the office. I don't know what the hell made you do it. Gas and everything. Esther was there, too. Says she saw you in there." His face was right by hers. "She talked to that sumbitch detective right before she—Jesus, Cathleen. You don't remember anything?"

The machines answered for her, the beeps and tones swirling into a frenzy and joining mid-twirl with the roar of a jackhammer. The concerned look on the nurse's face was the last thing Cathleen saw.

This dark, it was different. It was deeper than ink. This dark was sinister. *This dark has legs.* It tugged at the corners of her eyes when she turned her head. Something fearful scurried against the walls, something that didn't want to be seen. Something she didn't want to see.

Holy hell, I've got to stop drinking with the Ambien.

Cathleen rolled from her bed and shuffled about in her usual morning blur, preparing for the day. Once she'd dressed and put on her face, she spritzed some Miss Dior on her wrists.

She'd have to leave early again because Marty was really on a kick for those greasy breakfast sliders. They'd be the death of him, for sure. And goddammit, no doubt he was going to stick her with those interviews today.

Send in the Clowns

Harlow West

Where am I?

Rune tried to move her arms but they were too heavy to lift. *Useless,* she thought to herself. She clutched at the ground, trying to grasp anything for leverage. Handfuls of moss and dead leaves were all that she could get ahold of. They oozed a dampness into her hands as she tried to right herself.

This isn't going to happen.

Rune collapsed back, defeated. The strength just wasn't there. The bark of a rotted log seeped moisture into her threadbare denim jacket. A slow shiver crawled along the full length of her body. It was going to be a long, cold night.

The sound of twigs snapping and leaves rustling in the woods behind her jolted her out of her thoughts and away from the questions of how she had gotten there and who put her there. Everything from the past few days was gone. *At least I hope it's just the last few days,* Rune thought.

More rustling sounded around her. Closer this time.

Goose flesh crawled its way up her arms and a panic began to settle in. Her chest tightened as she held her breath, struggling to hear anything over the sound of her own blood storming through her veins. There was something in the woods behind her and it was getting closer.

About a dozen curse words that would have warranted Rune getting beat with "the switch" were swimming through her head when she saw, in her peripheral vision, what was making the noise.

A squirrel. It must have been caught up in preparing for winter because it paid no mind to her. She would have laughed if she had the energy.

The sun had almost disappeared beyond the tree line when Rune realized she had been engulfed by an eerie fog. A desolate, lonely feeling started to creep into the back of her mind.

Has anyone even noticed that I'm gone? It was more a plea than a question.

Tiny points of light appeared among the trees that lined the clearing. Dozens of glowing orbs grew in size until the outlines of bodies became visible through the mist.

People.

People? Rune felt a tiny swell of hope.

The shadowy figures came closer. It was like they were being ushered in by some sort of unearthly storm. The wind picked up, and with it the dead leaves and dirt surrounding her.

Rune winced as tiny bits of earth slashed at her cheek. It stung. She tried to cover her face with her arms but still couldn't move.

The air was being sucked from her lungs. She gasped.

Send in the Clowns

I'm going to die.

Rune looked around frantically. The world around her transformed before her eyes. The trees danced and swayed. Her vision twisted and contorted around her as she faded in and out of consciousness. The lack of oxygen was getting to her.

Her head felt light and spun with a ferocity she had never known before. She was convinced she would float away if she let go of the moss clutched between her fingers. It was the only thing anchoring her to the ground, she just knew it.

To the left of the clearing the ground cracked and trembled as an outcropping of boulders started to move and change before her eyes. *That can't be right*, Rune thought. She blinked frantically, convinced she wasn't seeing what she was seeing. The boulders, once solid, stretched and morphed into two massive granite elephants, moss and vines clinging to their backs. Their trumpeting reverberated off the trees and thundered against her chest.

Had she not been so distracted by the sudden appearance of the elephants, Rune would have noticed the sickly pale and frail-looking hands reaching toward her through the maelstrom. Over-long, bony fingers latched onto her. That was the last thing she remembered before she lost consciousness.

Rune woke with a start. The windstorm was gone and she could breathe again. Her head throbbed, but she had otherwise regained her faculties and was right back where she had started. Alone again. The hands that had grabbed her were gone; the figures had vanished and the stone elephants were nowhere in sight.

However, what was once an empty field had transformed into a hauntingly beautiful scene. Velvet tents outstretched before her, faded and thread-bare in certain spots, but still standing. Brightly painted wagons lined the perimeter of the field, creating a caravan of whimsy. Doves cooed softly as they perched on their colorful roosts. Their contented songs made Rune feel oddly calm.

As she lay motionless, taking in the scene before her, Rune caught notice of a particularly nasty-looking fly circling her. It landed on her nose and before she knew it, she had swatted herself square in the face. *Shit. Well, at least I can move my arms again.* Slowly, Rune managed to right herself, though every muscle ached as she moved.

It was a fight, but well worth it once Rune managed to get to her feet. A shiver crawled its way across her skin. The night had turned frigid. Dusk surrounded her but Rune had no idea what day it was, or how long she had been . . . wherever she was. The smell of boiled peanuts and cotton candy wafted through the air. A gurgle in her stomach protested the hunger growing inside her.

Rune sized up her surroundings. Strands of lights dangled between temporary posts throughout the fairgrounds. Calliope music from a yet-to-be-discovered organ played a tune that Rune couldn't quite put her finger on, but the music called to her, taking her back to a memory just beyond her reach.

There was nothing else to do, so Rune wandered.

Send in the Clowns

Around her, empty popcorn boxes and half-full drink cups lay scattered on the ground, leaking syrup into the grass and leaving the place looking like everyone had suddenly disappeared and left everything behind. Posters depicting sideshow freaks seemed out of place and time, but nonetheless hung from a dilapidated marquis at the entrance of the fairgrounds.

The music grew, drawing her toward the midway.

Where have I heard that song before? She couldn't quite place her finger on it, but she knew it meant something to her. She just didn't know what.

As she explored, she noticed the bulbs only blinked to life when she was looking directly at them. *Weird,* Rune thought. She followed the flickering bulbs through the now-filled field. She passed all sorts of booths and games. Tattered teddy bears and other stuffed animals adorned the carnival walls. Toys of bygone eras served as what she could only assume were prizes. By the time Rune reached the end of the midway, she realized where the lights had been leading her all along. The sight of it made the hairs of her arms stand on end.

Why did it have to be a funhouse?

From the outside, the building looked happy and relatively harmless. The word "funhouse," in brightly-colored graffiti, adorned both sides of a giant clown head whose gaping maw served as the entrance. Blinking lights flashed in time with the music that had been gradually getting louder as Rune approached.

I know I've heard that song somewhere.

Rune started to take a step toward the clown, then stopped dead in her tracks. Clowns made her uneasy. Something about "always too happy," and "probably a serial killer" rolled around her head whenever she got too close to one. But the music . . . it was coming from there, no doubt about it, and she needed to figure out why she felt so drawn to it.

A rusted gate stood in the place where the clown's teeth should have been. She gave it a nudge and it let out a metallic whine that chilled her to the bone. A few feet beyond the gate stood a doorway, draped in black velvet.

Rune entered, and as she did the curtains closed behind her and shrouded her in darkness. There were no visible windows but all sorts of dangling lights made up for the darkness as one by one, they flickered to life. Toward the end of the hallway stood a set of incredibly steep stairs, the kind that make you feel like you are climbing a rock face rather than a staircase.

Rune squared up to the rock-wall stairs; they didn't look too tough. The first step was fine, but as she continued to climb the steps, they started to rock from side to side. First gently, and then violently. It took all the strength she had to keep from falling off and onto the floor which was getting further and further away. By the time Rune pulled herself up to the platform above, she was exhausted. She sat there for several minutes, rubbing the soreness from her palms and trying to regain her composure.

That wasn't too bad.

About six feet away from Rune was what looked like a hanging bridge. It was made of wood and looked like a stiff wind could knock it down. Two tattered and twisted ropes ran parallel to the boardwalk and served as makeshift railings. Rune wasn't too keen on crossing it, but the thought of climbing back down those stairs—if you could call them that—was even more daunting.

With her first step, the bridge started to sway. Just enough to make Rune acutely aware she couldn't see anything below her, and that she really shouldn't be looking down, either. The second step made a creaking sound; the boards beneath her feet sounded far off, distant.

Another step and Rune noticed the darkness creeping in. By the time she took her fourth step she could hear voices coming closer. Crystal, Alex, and Heidi—or "the bobble-head girls" as Rune would later call them, but only behind their backs—were known to make life hell for anyone outside of their clique, and no one knew it better than Rune. In fact, the first day of middle school was the day she'd learned that important lesson.

"You're such a frickin' loser, Rune. Why did you even come?" Crystal said, walking behind her on the rope bridge.

Rune looked around. She was no longer in the funhouse. With her fifth step, Rune was now back on her eighth-grade field trip, on that nature hike Mr. Doscher arranged for earth sciences, Rune's favorite class.

"She's right, you know. Nobody wants you here," Alex spat over her shoulder. She was walking ahead of Rune.

Rune looked around for a chaperone but none were close enough to help. Just a long line of bored teens and preteens that would rather watch a girl-fight than mess up the status quo. It looked like she was stuck on the rope bridge between the bobble-heads for a little bit longer.

"You should just kill yourself and do us all a favor . . . I mean . . . no one wants you, not even your parents," Heidi said over Crystal's slight frame. Every word Heidi spoke was venom. She had no other setting.

Tears pricked at Rune's eyes as she fought to take control of her emotions. Before she could do anything, or respond in any way, she felt her feet swiped out from under her. She dropped three feet into the stream below and knocked her head on the board on the way down. When she finally emerged from the water, everything was red, literally—her forehead stung from an inch-wide gash on her forehead and she was covered in blood from her scalp to the water line.

"Ugh . . . you're so gross, Rune," Alex said. There was a permanent sneer on her face.

Rune's head throbbed and there was two of everything for a moment. Before she realized what was going on, globs of mud flew through the air and connected squarely with her jaw. The girls weren't trying to hide their disdain, nor the rocks inside the mud balls. They just wanted her to know her place in the world, according to them. By the time a chaperone had realized something had happened, Rune had two new cuts and several lumps on her face and head.

Rune squeezed her eyes shut as tight as she could get them, hoping that if she willed it hard enough, she wouldn't have to be there anymore. It worked. When she opened them, she was right back in the funhouse, in the dimly lit room, standing in the middle of the same rope bridge, gripping the ropes so tight her knuckles were turning white. She couldn't get her legs to move. They just wouldn't listen.

Softly, as if being played in the distance, Rune heard the calliope music once again. It was a haunting, sweet tune. For some reason it made her feel nostalgic. She'd heard it before, she knew. It pulled at her, called to her. She knew she needed to find where it was coming from. Little by little, Rune's legs didn't feel quite so heavy or quite so frozen in fear. She could move again and she knew she had to keep going.

When Rune finally cleared the rope bridge, she found herself staring at the opening of what seemed to be an enclosed slide. She didn't know how long it was or where it went but she didn't care. She knew the only way out now was to keep moving.

Rune jumped. The slide was remarkably smooth and splinter-free. She went far faster than she was expecting to go, which meant she flew straight off the end of the slide and tumbled a bit. When she stood back up, she was ten years old again. The trash bag she clutched in her hand contained everything she held dear in life. Well, everything she'd been allowed to take with her when she was kicked out of her last foster home, which wasn't much. Even less than before, considering the items the older kids took from her at the group home. It was the cost of living there.

When the door opened, a short, portly, middle-aged woman appeared and greeted Rune and her social worker with an almost cruel, vacant smile. It was Karen, the new foster mother.

She's so fake. Rune thought. *I wonder if the social worker sees it, too?*

It didn't take long before Karen showed her true colors. She spent the allowance the state gave her for the foster children on her own kids, while Rune and the others were forced to wear ill-fitting and stained hand-me-downs, eat table scraps, and wonder what new form of torture they would have to endure every night.

What money didn't go to her own children usually went toward the booze that soured Karen's breath and caused her to be abusive in new and imaginative ways. For Rune, most nights involved fighting to get something to eat. They were given one meal a day if they were lucky. You had to be quick in that house or you'd go hungry.

Rune learned quick. You don't talk back. You keep your head down. You do what you are told. If you don't you may just end up kneeling on frozen peas until they thawed, or walking a gauntlet of Legos that you weren't allowed to play with.

Rune had only been there for a short time when she made a friend. Her name was Chloe and she had been in the system almost as long as Rune. She was small for her size. Large, chocolate brown eyes, too large for her face, welled up with the fat tears streaming down her face. Rune had taken to looking at her like a little sister and seeing her like this tore at her heart.

"What did you do?" Rune asked, trying to keep her voice to a whisper. Rune didn't want Karen to hear them. She wiped a tear from her friend's cheek.

"I fell asleep and didn't finish the chores. She's mad, Rune. So mad." Chloe sobbed quietly. "The last time this happened I had to sleep in the bath tub for a week with no blankets."

"That's bull-crap," Rune said. "She is such a bitch."

The sound of plates smashing onto the tile floor shook the two girls from their conversation. *How had she heard them*?

"So I'm a bitch, am I?" Karen screeched, redness filling her over-round face. "I'll show you a bitch."

Karen grabbed both girls by their earlobes and pulled them to a standing position, directing them to the back yard. She twisted their lobes so hard Rune was sure she was going to rip them off.

In the back yard stood an old, beat-up doghouse. Two thick leather dog collars hung on a spike attached to the side of the doghouse. Each collar came equipped with its own padlock.

Karen shoved the two girls in the dirt in front of the doghouse. The rocks protruding from the ground cut into their hands and knees, leaving them wincing in pain. She grabbed the girls each in turn and strapped the collars to their necks, locking them in. The doghouse was their new home . . . at least for the foreseeable future.

Two days passed. Two days before Karen even checked to see if the girls were still alive. No food, no water. Rune pulled a hard roll out of her pocket and tore it in half, giving the larger piece to Chloe when her stomach gave out a startling roar. Two biting cold nights passed. The girls slept in the doghouse, huddled together for warmth, crying. The smell of their own waste stuck with them longer than the memory of the cold.

On the third night, the portly woman came out of the house and woke the girls.

"Get out of there, you ungrateful little shits!" She turned the hose on them. "You ain't coming in the house smellin' like that."

Karen shoved the hose into Rune's face. Rune coughed and spluttered. The water was freezing and tasted like rust.

"Who's the bitch now, little girl? As far as I can see, there are the only two little girls wearing collars around here." Rune and Chloe shivered uncontrollably, gasping for air.

"Say it," she ordered.

"I am," Rune said, her broken voice barely a whisper. "I'm the bitch."

Rune sobbed as Karen unlocked the collar around her neck. Once Chloe was free, Rune shoved Karen as hard as she could, grabbed Chloe's hand, and took off running. The darkness seemed like their only escape.

After a few steps, Rune felt Chloe's hand slip from her grip. *Oh no, she fell.* Rune stopped to help her up but when she did her heart dropped out of her chest.

Rune looked back just in time to see Chloe hanging like a rag doll off of Karen's hip as the evil woman dragged her back toward the house. She was sobbing and reaching out for Rune in a fruitless attempt to break free. She was in for another bad night.

Poor Chloe, she'll never forgive me, Rune thought. *But I'll never save her if I can't save myself.*

"If you leave, you ain't ever coming back. Don't expect your crap to be here, either!" Karen spat at her before the screen door slammed shut behind her.

Send in the Clowns

Rune turned and kept running, pushing through the wooded area behind Karen's house as it got darker and darker. She knew she was going the right direction. She ran as hard as she could, until her lungs burned, until spots flickered into her vision. She ran until she couldn't anymore. A door appeared before her. It stood directly opposite the slide. She was back. The funhouse had more tricks to play on her.

An uneasy feeling grew in the pit of Rune's stomach as she opened the door that seemed to appear out of nowhere. Maybe she simply hadn't noticed it before, but there it was. The handle was ice cold, and the door let out a squeak. Rune's heart jumped into her throat. She stood in the doorway for what seemed like an eternity.

"The hall of mirrors." Rune's voice was barely audible as she covered her mouth with her hand. It was like she was trying to catch the words before they got away from her but it didn't work. The second the words left her lips, a light sprang to life in the distance. She remembered this place from her childhood, and she hadn't liked it then, either. This hall of mirrors was different than the one she recalled from her childhood trips to the county fair with Granny.

Granny! That's it!

Rune practically screamed her name when she finally figured out where she had heard the music before. The same melancholy tune that had been calling out to her through this whole mess was the same tune Granny hummed all the time. A bittersweet feeling passed through Rune when she thought of the old woman.

Focus, Rune told herself, peering down the hall.

Instead of several topsy-turvy, misshapen mirrors that looked fun but were actually creepy, this hall was simply a maze lined with mirrors. They reached from floor to ceiling, looked ancient, and almost seemed to float because of a thick layer of smoke curling across the floor. The single light that had drawn her attention gave way to strobing lights as Rune came closer to the first turn. The flashing lights reflected off of every possible surface. Rune's head spun. Every move she made was a mocking staccato visage reflecting back at her. Nausea blanketed her. The deeper into the maze she explored, the sicker she felt.

She turned to go back. At least the slide room didn't make her sick. She traced her steps back and realized the door she had come through was no longer there. She froze and the hair on her arms stood on edge as the gentle calliope music swelled behind her in the distance. She was reluctant to turn around but there was no choice, she had to keep going.

Rune's hands shook as she followed the music into the hall of mirrors. She found herself moving at a snail's pace. Rune thought back to all the horror films that she had seen in her life. Normally, following disembodied music was a bad idea. She'd seen those horror films. It never ended well for the main characters. But this wasn't a movie and she wasn't a big-boobed co-ed following a noise off into the woods. It was Granny's song.

Her nose crinkled. An unpleasant but familiar odor filled the room as she stepped deeper into the maze of mirrors. Cheap beer and gas station cologne.

Send in the Clowns

Rune knew the smell better than she ever wanted to. Her skin crawled at the memory.

Out of the corner of her eye, Rune saw something move but she kept walking. Turn after turn, it was always just far enough behind her that she couldn't make out what was there, but there was no way she was going to stop and go looking for it. It looked like the outline of something, like a sentient shadow following her from a distance.

Rune pushed herself to keep going, turn after turn. She moved as fast as she could, desperate to reach the end. All the heartache and torment that had followed her throughout her life led her to wherever this place was, and to this moment.

One last turn left her standing face to face with a mirrored dead end and nowhere to go. Dozens of her own reflections surrounded her. The embodiment of exhaustion stared back at her. Her shoulders slumped, her skin was clammy and pale with large dark circles resting below her eyes. She felt how she looked.

Rune sighed. But her reflection didn't. Instead, it transformed before her eyes. The eyes staring back at her turned a brighter shade of the steel gray they had always been. Her skin looked softer and her cheeks filled with color. She looked almost . . . happy.

Granny's song filled the air around Rune. It wrapped around her like a warm hug. Rune looked around to see where it was coming from but couldn't find a source.

Distracted by the funhouse mirror in front of her and the flashing lights, Rune didn't have a chance to notice the shadow creeping closer until she could feel the breath, hot and sticky, in her ear.

Rune's skin crawled again.

Keith.

She could smell him before she saw him. He smelled like cigarettes and bad choices and he was standing right behind her. Rune forced herself to look into the mirror. When her eyes met Keith's in the reflection, she was eight years old again and standing in the middle of her childhood home.

"What the fuck do you think you're doing, fat ass?" His voice boomed in her ear.

Keith was a piece of shit. He was the third stepdad Rune had had in almost as many years. Each one was as worse than the one before . . . but Mommy liked them mean.

"I said . . . what the fuck do you think you are doing, fat ass?"

Rune tossed the doughnut back into the box and took off in a dead run. If she could make it to the crawlspace before he could catch her, she'd be safe. One night with the spiders and roaches and Keith would have forgotten everything. Well, if there was enough beer in the house he would, but Rune wasn't so lucky this time.

Her little face twisted as dirty fingernails punctured the delicate skin on her shoulder and yanked her down to the floor. Blood had already started to drip from the little half-moon shaped cuts by the time she had landed. Too stunned to cry, she flinched and tried to not make eye contact.

"Answer me, you little bitch." It wasn't a question any more. Keith's face was so close to Rune's that his breath burned against her cheek. It smelled like an ashtray soaked in cheap beer and made Rune sick to her stomach.

"I'm hungry." Rune's voice cracked as she spoke and, as if on cue, her stomach responded with a roaring grumble. If he hadn't been so drunk he would have realized he hadn't fed her in two days, but pointing that out would have been useless.

"Hungry? You want some food, you little shit? You want to steal food from me?" His voice, teeming with anger, reached volumes Rune had never heard before. "I'll feed you," he bellowed. "Now open your fucking mouth."

Keith's hand twisted into the hair at the back of Rune's head and gave it a harsh yank. His eyes burned with hate as he started shoving the doughnuts into her mouth. Rune gasped for breath but every time she opened her mouth he crammed in another doughnut.

Rune came to with her lungs feeling like they were on fire. She didn't remember passing out or coming back to the present, but somehow, she found herself back in front of the mirror, gazing at her own reflection again. Fury coursed through her veins liked fire. Her cheeks flushed. Her fists clenched. The anger and hate spread throughout her entire body until she felt like she was going to explode.

And then she did.

Rune didn't realize that she had punched the mirror where Keith's reflection last stood until she saw the shards of glass flying through the air. Within seconds, it was as if she set off a chain reaction in the room. One by one, the other mirrors surrounding her shattered to pieces.

Rune collapsed on the ground. Tiny shards of glass cut into her flesh, but she didn't have the energy to care anymore. She was ready to give up. She couldn't go on any further, not knowing if there was ever going to be an end. When Rune heard the calliope music once more, it was closing in on her like a hot bath.

Looking at the shattered pieces of mirror that surrounded her, Rune no longer saw her own reflection. She didn't see Keith, either. She just saw Granny.

Granny wasn't actually her real grandmother; both of them had died well before she was born. No, Granny was just a sweet old lady who had taken a liking to Rune when she was a child, before Rune had been put into the system. She was an older woman, in her mid-seventies. Her husband had passed a few years before Rune had moved to the neighborhood with her mother.

Granny never had kids. Rune asked her about it once but the sadness in Granny's face kept her from pushing the topic. That was okay, Rune didn't really need to know. To Rune she was just a sweet old woman who would keep an eye on her while her mother was out trawling for a new man. Granny fed her when she could and made her feel loved when no one else did . . . that was all that mattered.

As Rune focused on the music that had returned, and the images of Granny on the mirror shards surrounding her, she remembered the last time she had seen the old woman.

"What's wrong, doll? Why you hidin' back there behind my lilac bush?" Her voice was sweet and genteel, with a slight southern twang.

"I've been bad," Rune answered through the tears, wiping her runny nose on her sleeve.

"Whaddaya mean you been bad? You couldn't've been that bad. You're just a little bit of a thing. Step out here and let Granny see you."

Rune did as Granny said and stepped out from behind the bush. Her clothes were tattered and torn. Her hair sat in a messy bun at the top of her head, and tears left behind streaks in the dirt on her cheeks.

"Tell Granny what you're up to, hiding in my lilac bushes."

"I'm running away." Rune sobbed.

"Is that so?"

"Yeah, I don't like Mommy and Keith anymore. They say I've been bad and they hurt me for it." Rune's sniffles came harder and faster as she started to cry. "I'm gonna run away and join the circus . . . then they won't be able to hurt me anymore."

Granny outstretched her hand to comfort Rune.

"Now don't go saying that, sweet pea. There ain't nothing in this world that's been solved by running away with the circus. Plus, you really want to go and leave Granny all alone? That would make me real sad. Do you want that?"

Rune sniffed and went to wipe her runny nose with her sleeve, cringing when she made contact with her arm.

Granny was watching her carefully. "You okay, doll? Let me take a look at that arm."

Rune hesitated. She remembered what Keith had done to her and didn't want Granny to see it, but there was no point in fighting with the old woman, that much Rune knew.

As Granny tugged at Rune's slightly soggy sleeve, she noticed them—cigarette burns. Fresh ones.

Rune's bloodied skin was already sticking to her sleeve, causing the wounds to reopen when Granny investigated. Right beside the burns was a bruise in the shape of a large hand. Too big to be from Rune's mother.

Granny was pissed.

"If it's the last thing I do, baby doll, this will be the last time that man ever hurts you."

Granny took Rune's hand and walked her back home. Rune slowed her pace and lagged behind until Granny was practically pulling her along.

The old woman slowed to a stop. "It's going to be okay, Rune. Everything is going to be okay. When we get to your house, I want you to run up to your room and lock the door. I'll take care of everything else."

As the two of them approached the house, Rune gave Granny a quick hug and bolted for her room. Since her door didn't come with a lock she ran directly to her closet and hid behind a pile of dirty clothes. It was dark and it smelled bad, but at least she was hidden, and she could hear everything that was going on in the yard below her bedroom window.

"Do you feel like a big man?" Granny yelled. "Does hurting poor defenseless little children make you feel big? What's wrong with you?"

Rune could hear the hurt and pure anger in Granny's voice followed by the smashing of what could only be one of Keith's beer bottles.

Rune burst out of the closet and ran to the window to see if Granny was all right. Her heart beat in her throat as she peeked over the window sill.

"Get out of here, you old bat, before I make you leave." Keith was practically snarling.

"I'd like to see you try," Granny said. "I ain't leaving until that little girl is free of you."

Another bottle went flying at Granny's head, missing her by just an inch.

"I swear to God, you drunk son of a bitch! You throw one more bottle at me and I'm gonna call the cops."

"I'm not going back to jail, you old bitch!" Keith bellowed, and stomped down the porch stairs until he reached Granny.

"And you definitely ain't gonna be the one sending me there." Every word that came out of Keith's mouth was punctuated by the poke of his boney fingers against Granny's slender, frail shoulder.

"We'll go and see about that."

Granny turned away from Keith, pulled out her phone, and dialed.

"Hello, yes, I'd like to report a case of child abuse. One-hundred-fifty Smi—" Granny's voice cut off suddenly as Keith, trying to grab the phone from her hand, made direct contact with the side of her head and sent Granny flying to the ground.

Rune gasped as she watched Granny fly backward and land—hard—hitting her head against the muted flagstone in the front yard.

Granny was right. That was the last time Keith had hurt her.

Rune heard a heart-wrenching scream, not realizing that she was the one making the sound. She screamed with everything she had. She screamed until there was no breath left in her lungs. The pain was more than she could handle, coming from somewhere adjacent to the left side of her soul.

Heaving breaths took control of Rune's small body. She doubled over and placed her hands on her knees. She couldn't stop. She gasped even harder for air and when it didn't happen, spots filled her vision. She looked to the ceiling, anywhere but out the window, but it didn't help. Her bedroom began to swirl around and before she knew it, she was out cold.

Rune was back in the darkness again. Back in the funhouse. This time there were no blinking lights, no shadows, just the shattered pieces of glass surrounding her. She didn't know what to do, or if there was anything she could do, so she just sat there slowly rocking and staring into the darkness.

This is it. I'm trapped. I'm never getting out of here.

Rune started to hum that same old tune Granny used to hum, hoping to gain some sort of comfort from it. What else could she do? As she hummed, Rune could hear the music again. It was getting louder and stronger. What started off as calliope music melted into something that sounded more and more like Granny's voice.

A calm feeling passed over Rune. A slender set of hands rested on her shoulders and she could hear Granny like she was kneeling down right behind her, humming her favorite song.

Rune glanced over her shoulder and jumped at the mirage standing behind her.

"Is that . . . ?" Rune asked. "It can't be. You're dead. I watched you die."

"I know, doll. That's why we have to have a chat."

Granny reached down and helped Rune off the floor. Now that Rune had a proper look at her she realized that it was Granny, but things were different. She wasn't the older, frail woman Rune remembered. She had rich chestnut-brown hair and looked at least thirty years younger.

"I don't understand," Rune said.

"I would be shocked if you did, " Granny chuckled. "Walk with me and I'll clue you in."

Granny hooked her arm with Rune's and started walking into the darkness. To Rune, she was like a beacon of light in more ways than one. As they walked, the room brightened until an exit door was in plain sight.

"I bet you've been looking for this for a while, haven't you?"

Rune nodded. "Yeah. This funhouse wasn't so much fun."

Granny shook her head and let out a noise that let Rune know she knew exactly what she was talking about.

As the two left the funhouse, Rune noticed that things had changed. The carnival still stood square in the middle of the field but this time it was full. People wandered around, performers performed, and animals—well, they did animal things.

Where were we before? Rune wondered.

"I know what you're thinking, Rune. You're confused. Trying to process everything you just went through and you have no idea what on God's green earth you are going to do with it all. I get it . . . But I need to show you something."

Rune felt a pit open in the bottom of her stomach as they meandered through the field.

This doesn't feel right.

189

After a few moments they had made their way back to the spot where she had woken up. Rune couldn't breathe. The cacophony of buzzing flies overwhelmed her, but the sight of her lifeless body propped up against the rotted log knocked the wind out of her. No amount of popcorn or cotton candy could ever cover up the smell of decomposition. Nothing would ever be able to erase the image of the gun resting in the grass beside her.

What have I done?

Rune collapsed onto the ground next to her own corpse, sobbing.

"I told you that nothin' was ever so bad that you would need to run off to the circus." Granny tousled Rune's hair in an effort to comfort her. "I'm sorry that you thought that this was your only way out. I'm sorry that I couldn't save you then."

Rune took a moment to try and compose herself.

"Where are we? Is . . . is this heaven?"

"No, doll. Think of it as a staging area for the other side. No matter how they pass, the lost souls end up here. Some go into the funhouse and never come back out. They get trapped in their memories, good or bad, and they just can't find the exit."

"What about me, Granny? Did you cheat to get me out?"

"No, love. Some unfortunate souls have no light left inside, no inner compass. So many bad things happened to them there just ain't nothin' left. I've been with you since the day I died, sweet pea, keeping an eye on you . . . and those . . . people." Granny had a look on her face like she just ate something that went bad. "I—I'm just sorry you were left all alone. I'm sorry that you . . . "

Send in the Clowns

Rune jumped to her feet and wrapped her arms around Granny. "It's okay, Granny. I'm home now."

Queen of the Waves

Amy Hunter

Three Days Remained

Like flames to dry leaves, dementia burned through Olivia Coyle's mind. She was a fighter, but no measure of watered-down faith could stall mental oblivion.

"Nana?" A redheaded woman hurried into the room, struggling with a fire extinguisher. With her empty hand, she turned a knob on the range and yanked open the oven door. Thick smoke curled toward the ceiling.

"Stay back!" She sprayed inside the stove with a sweeping motion.

Olivia coughed so violently, she dropped the laundry basket and stumbled sideways, her curved spine colliding with the refrigerator. Homemade magnets cracked as they fell to the floor. She glanced up from the broken pieces. "Who are you? Why are you in my house?"

As a lady, she took no satisfaction in raising her voice, but she did not abide strangers in her home uninvited.

The redhead's expression deflated. She placed the extinguisher on the counter and covered her face with her hands. After a moment, she wiped runny mascara onto her sleeve, forcing a smile through the tears that had carved premature wrinkles in her skin.

"I'm Mara, your granddaughter," she said.

Olivia's breathing hitched. The granddaughter she knew was eight years old, played with dolls, and wore pink ribbons. The woman calling her "Nana" was grown.

Something's wrong with me, she thought.

"Who . . . who am I?" She touched her throat, her frail voice foreign to her.

Mara smiled and rested both hands on her grandmother's shoulders, guiding her to the dining table where a worn deck of cards lay spread. "Your name is Olivia, and you're the youngest ninety-six-year-old I know. You love animals, morning walks on the beach, and you think I don't know you cheat at poker."

Olivia's shoulders hunched over her chest as she reached for Mara's hand. She couldn't remember much, but she wanted to make the best of a bad situation. *You'll get through this. You must.* Then, her heart melted when her new-old grandchild planted a kiss on her forehead.

Mara dragged a chair over the floor, and the protest of wood scraping along vinyl funneled awareness to Olivia's senses. A wave of familiarity washed over her. Her granddaughter had sacrificed her job and personal life to move in. The girl took care of her, cooked dinner, and kept house without complaint.

Olivia's eyes watered at memories of Mara spoon-feeding her oatmeal and wiping her mouth. Clear as day, she recalled many times when she had either thrown tantrums or forgotten how to eat altogether. As painful as those visions were, they came second to being cleaned and changed like an infant. Tears stung her cheeks. She gripped the table so tight the routed edge left indentations in her paper-like skin. *I'm a burden, more trouble than I'm worth.*

"I'm sorry," she whispered. She wanted to go back to bed.

"Nana, don't," Mara said, reaching for her grandmother's hand, but Olivia walked away before they touched. "It's—"

"Just let me go, child."

Mara watched with both hands on her hips, prepared for her nana to fall.

The girl had good intentions. Olivia could tell that much within five seconds. All her life she had hidden an uncanny ability to read—and sometimes even shape—people's emotions; it was as if she had a sixth sense. Long ago, she swore she wouldn't use her power on her family because she wanted a life of normalcy. Nevertheless, though she didn't recognize Mara at the time, she wasn't upset about her being in the house. She knew a pure soul when she met one.

The walk to the bedroom was like climbing uphill. At Mara's insistence, Olivia wore rubber-soled socks to keep her from slipping, but they offered little support against gravity when she had a dizzy spell. Holding on to the wall helped, but she was wheezing, so she stopped in the doorway to rest. *Just a few more steps.*

She looked up, startled. A large shadow had emerged from her periphery, swept along her path, and was disappearing through the oak door. Shivering, she clutched her chest to keep her heart still. *You're seeing things.*

Olivia reached for the doorknob. She couldn't duck into her room before she was seen—compromised speed was another injustice of growing old.

"Let me help," Mara said, guiding her by the elbow.

Olivia sighed, relieved to see that sitting on the chaise lounge was Sister Mary Clare, the spirit of a young nun who had followed her all her life. Poised as ever in a late-Victorian habit, the sister studied her charge, for whom the aging process had continued without mercy. Sister Mary Clare regarded Olivia with the warmth and awe one would show a child.

Unaware of the apparition's presence, Mara continued her business, lowering the bed's guardrails. Olivia hated the bed because she knew it was where she would spend her final moments and say goodbye to her granddaughter—if lucidity allowed. Luxury sheets and a handmade quilt didn't change facts.

"I almost forgot your meds." Mara strode to the corner table next to Sister Mary Clare where seven pill boxes rested on a crocheted doily and rejected each square until she found the one she wanted. She emptied the box into her grandmother's hand.

"Here we go," she said.

Olivia tried to swallow the assortment, but after she drank the water, they were still on her tongue. She kept drinking. Her mind knew what to do, but it was as though her body had forgotten how. By the third attempt, the tablets had disintegrated and washed away, leaving behind a chemical taste.

After Mara helped settle her grandmother into bed, she passed her the pink, stuffed monkey from the nightstand. "If you need anything, have Pinky ring the bell."

The light clicked off, and the nightlight activated. Olivia rolled over to see Sister Mary Clare peering between the blinds. She had told Olivia before that she didn't like the way the world had progressed—everything shone too bright, like it was ablaze. Olivia didn't blame her. One thing about being alive for almost a century is she'd seen a lot of things end. *Maybe the world is going down in flames*, she thought.

"Sister," Olivia said, patting the bed. Sister Mary Clare sat on the edge with perfect posture and gave her a doting smile. "I've been on this earth a long time. I know you can understand. I'm tired and need to rest now. So, if you're protecting me, it's time to stop."

The nun's face went blank. She closed her eyes and dipped her chin, making the sign of the cross. When she looked back at Olivia, those eyes—once a comfort—were hollow sockets; lifeless.

Olivia had experienced fear before, and had the usual "fight or flight" response. But physically, she didn't have a choice anymore. She couldn't run. And so she froze.

Hovering over the old woman, Sister Mary Clare whispered into her mind, "You should be here with us. Go back and see, special one."

Amy Hunter

The Great Storm: September 8, 1900

Strong winds blew in early from the north as waves slammed the waterfronts of Galveston. The gulf had risen at a steady rate all afternoon, submerging the island. St. Mary's Orphan Asylum was located on beachfront property, far from town.

Sister Mary Clare, one of ten Sisters of Mercy, was like an insect trapped in a spider's web, helpless. Heart racing, her first impulse was to fall on her knees and pray for wings, but she didn't want to frighten the children more. *The entire orphanage might be gone by dusk,* she thought.

An orphan tugged on Sister Mary Clare's tunic. The child couldn't have been three years old, yet she remained calm in the crisis, her face vacant. Certain they'd never met, the sister bent and took the girl's hand, inexplicably drawn to her.

"What is your name?" Sister Mary Clare worried about the child's small frame and lack of pigment.

"My name is Olivia. It's your time, Sister. Follow me and go to the hereafter." She held the nun's hand firmly, gazing into her eyes. The world slipped away, and nothing existed but their two hearts beating in unison. In the moment that passed between them, Sister Mary Clare's inner siren lulled to a hum. She was . . . warm. She released the girl's hand and stood, holding her head.

"Sister Mary Clare!" Sister Mary Katherine, the youngest nun, called. "The tide has reached the entrance, and it's still rising!"

"Where is Mother Superior?" Sister Mary Clare asked. The older nun would know what to do.

"She and two others brought a wagon into town for provisions hours ago, but they haven't returned." Sister Mary Katherine twisted the ring on her finger, the symbol of her new vows.

Olivia was still standing by Sister Mary Clare's side, hair aflame; her wild, green eyes watching.

"Come with me, special one." Sister Mary Clare lifted the orphan into her arms.

She walked to the podium and raised her free hand. "Sisters, we should move the children into the girls' dormitory at once."

To keep them from panicking, Sister Mary Clare gathered the orphans and asked them to sing her favorite hymn, "Queen of the Waves." Their a cappella voices, high and off-key, thin and full, resonated throughout the chapel to the beat of thunder.

Queen of the Waves, look forth across the ocean
From north to south, from east to stormy west,
See how the waters with tumultuous motion
Rise up and foam without a pause or rest.

After the initial verse, the structure shook on its platform. Sister Mary Clare tensed, crying out in panic. She turned toward the wall, using her body to shield the small red-headed girl from any imminent danger.

"The dunes!" A group of boys jumped up and ran to the windows, shouting. A line of sand dunes, the orphanage's main source of protection against natural forces, had been crushed. The salt cedar trees which protected them were blown parallel to the ground. The gulf now flooded every inch of land.

As Sister Mary Clare pulled the children away from the glass, a house drifted by as if on wheels. The scene was little more than a ceiling atop collapsed walls. And, God, there were people. She couldn't tell if they were alive or dead, but at least four men were on the roof.

Several sisters crossed themselves. The water that covered their shoes surged to their knees, rising higher by the second.

"Sisters, get the children to the second level!" Sister Mary Clare wasn't worried for herself; rather, she wanted to protect the child in her arms and those around her.

She pulled Sister Mary Katherine aside as the other sisters relocated the orphans.

"I need you to get rope from the utility closet. Will you do that for me?" Sister Mary Katherine, not much for words, nodded. Sister Mary Clare took her hand. "Be safe."

Upstairs, she watched Olivia sleeping on a bed next to another child her age. The special one had curled into the fetal position, and mumbled in her sleep with the arms of the other girl wrapped around her, "Follow me . . . "

Wind ripped the shutters off the building and panes of glass shattered from debris while the sisters hugged and rocked younger children. Prayers mingled with cries echoed throughout the rooms.

Sister Mary Katherine returned moments later with clothesline draped over her arms and around her neck. She handed the line and a large knife to Sister

Mary Clare. While one cut the rope into sections, the other went back for more. Both hoped there would be enough.

Each nun accepted eight to ten lengths, tying them to the cinctures they wore around their waists and then to the children themselves. The older kids climbed onto the roof of the orphanage.

"Olivia? Where are you?" Sister Mary Clare looked on the bed where Olivia had lain and underneath the frame, but the girl had disappeared.

"Sing, children!" Sister Mary Katherine cried over the groans of the building.

Moments later, the orphanage, which had been a sanctuary for the sisters and orphans, lifted off its foundation. Cracks spread like veins from the floorboards to the ceilings. When the bottom fell out, the roof collapsed, trapping everyone inside.

ᶜᵈᵉᶠᵍ

Less Than One Day Remained

Olivia woke clutching Pinky like a drowning woman clutches a raft. The nurse who stood beside her bed taking notes said nothing. *That's so she won't get attached.*

"Mara?" Olivia's voice was hoarse. She tried to sit up, but fell back onto her elbows. The nurse pressed the button to raise the mattress.

Mara rushed into the room carrying a half-packed suitcase. "Nana, thank God. You've been asleep for days."

. . . is the fastest forming hurricane the Gulf of Mexico has ever seen . . . Evacuations . . .

"Mrs. Post, would you turn off the television, please?" Mara dropped the bag, worry creasing her face. She took her nana's hand.

"What's going on?" Olivia's eyes were trained on the clothes spilling from the bag onto the floor.

"Please leave us, Mrs. Post. I think it's best if I speak to my grandmother alone." Mara looked down at the carpet as tears slid down her cheeks.

Olivia's granddaughter had never looked so much like a child to her. Even when she was younger, the girl was the first to do something brave, like jump a ditch on her bike when other kids were too afraid. Since Olivia was at last awake, Mara had lost her strength.

When Mrs. Post exited, Mara sat and held Olivia's hand to her face. "I wish I knew how to be what you need. You've always been so strong."

"What . . . ?" Olivia forced a smile. "You listen here. You've done your best. I won't hear anything else." *This must be it for me.*

Mara stroked her hair. "The nurse says you need more care than I can give you."

"Hogwash," she whispered. "That woman doesn't know the business end of a cotton swab."

"Nana, she's right. You need a nursing home."

Olivia held her hand up in protest, but before she could say anything, the door opened. When Mrs. Post entered, she clicked on the television, and a weatherman stood in front of a map of Texas, pointing west toward Galveston.

"We haven't been paying attention to the weather report, ladies. That rainmaker they've been talking about has turned into Hurricane Grace, and it looks like she's headed straight for us." Mrs. Post ran a hand through her pixie cut and sighed. "No one is going anywhere."

⸎⸎⸎

Grace was the first hurricane to hit the Gulf Coast in two years. With eighty-mile-per-hour winds, she landed as a Category One storm and had already killed one person in Louisiana.

While Mara drove into town for supplies, Mrs. Post taped windows, hoping for an easy cleanup. Olivia laid in bed halfway between sleep and consciousness, unable to achieve either thanks to her daily dose of Haldol.

A blurred shadow shifted into Olivia's field of vision and morphed into Sister Mary Clare. Olivia trembled, remembering the hollow lifelessness of the nun's eyes when they last met. She bit her lip to hold back a cry for help. The others would think she was crazy.

The nun sat on Olivia's bed and reached for the old woman's hand, but Olivia snatched it back before they touched.

"I would never hurt you, special one." Sister Mary Clare's voice dominated Olivia's mind; she couldn't hear anything else.

Olivia winced. "Why do you keep calling me that? What the hell do those memories mean?"

The sister clasped her hands, tilting her head. "We forever drown on this island because you live. You are meant to be with us, you see. You are an angel of death living a human life."

There was a beat of silence.

"You must sacrifice yourself, child. Shed your humanity and lead us all out of this hell. This is your divine purpose."

꧁꧂

Death shouldn't have been a big deal to Olivia, and it wasn't. The method is what she found hard to stomach. She had lived a long, full life and had family to show for it. She was ready to go, if that's what it took—even if Mara wouldn't understand.

Luckily, Mara and Mrs. Post were still busy. Olivia slipped over the guardrail, almost falling on her back. She needed to reach the medication box on the nurse's desk.

She reached for the Xanax—two milligrams—the kind shaped like bars. On a typical day, Mara would liquefy the pills for her. Today, Olivia needed to swallow as many as she could before the women returned.

Lightning struck nearby, followed by rolling thunder. Olivia flinched, dropping the sedative and several other bottles behind the desk. *Dammit.* She couldn't bend to pick the pills off the floor. If she did, she wouldn't be able to stand by herself.

Defeated, she trudged back to bed. Midway, the door swung open.

"What are you doing up?" Mara asked, her face pinched. "You'll fall. Get back in bed."

Olivia had no alternative but to break her oath and use her ability. She turned to Mara and took her hand. Seconds passed before a warm energy flowed, but when it did, the stress drained from Mara's face; it was like watching waves run still.

"Mara, you're calm. You're not worried about anything. Don't you want to lie down and rest?" Olivia's heart broke inside her chest as she said the words, but they were necessary. *Forgive me, darling. I'll see you on the other side.*

Mara crawled between the sheets, and Olivia tucked her in like she'd done for her as a child. Before she kissed her granddaughter's forehead, she crossed herself, something she hadn't done in years, and recited her favorite poem, "Four Corners, Four Angels."

After Mara was asleep, Olivia made her way to the kitchen, gasping and wheezing. Her guilt over leaving was immeasurable, but she had passed the point of no return. Determination carried her forward.

Thunder rumbled a moment after she opened the door. The wind blew her thin nightgown against her body; each step was an uphill battle she was ill-equipped to fight.

Horizontal raindrops stabbed Olivia's face like a million sewing needles threaded with the storm's force. She raised her hand above her brows to see. Nothing but gray. Her chest tightened, and she wanted to run screaming in the other direction. She laughed to herself. *Come on, Olivia. Don't be a coward.*

When she touched sand, her toes sank, and she fell to her knees. Hair sticking to her face, gown clinging to her body, she remained kneeling. Though she was in a downpour, she reached out, palms up, to cleanse her hands. As the grains rinsed away, she was struck by the simplicity of life: We were all just specks that could wash away with the tide.

Get up. Olivia's joints cracked the entire way to her feet. *A few more yards . . .*

"Nana! Where are you?" Mara's voice carried on the wind, like birdsong. Olivia had a matter of seconds before she was discovered.

But fear not, tho' storm clouds round us gather,
Thou art our Mother and thy little Child
Is the All Merciful, our loving Brother
God of the sea and the tempest wild.

Voices. Olivia could hear such sweet voices rising from the gulf. The closer she walked to the shore, the stronger the water's call.

Help, then sweet Queen, in our exceeding danger,
By thy seven griefs, in pity Lady save;
Think of the Babe that slept within the manger
And help us now, dear Lady of the Wave.

Olivia stepped into the water. The waves crashed into her, knocking her frail body sideways into the sandbar. She needed to find the riptide. She crawled on all fours through a foot-and-a-half of water until the violence of the current carried her out to sea.

This was it. A wave twice Olivia's height barreled over her, sending her into an underwater spin. *Let go. This is supposed to happen.* She couldn't see anything in the murky waters. Her nasal passages were on fire, her lungs near bursting. *Just let go.*

Queen of the Waves

Up to the shrine we look and see the glimmer
Thy votive lamp sheds down on us afar;
Light of our eyes, oh let it ne'er grow dimmer,
Till in the sky we hail the morning star.

Before everything dimmed, Olivia saw Sister Mary Clare singing with the orphans.

Then joyful hearts shall kneel around thine altar
And grateful psalms re-echo down the nave;
Never our faith in thy sweet power can falter,
Mother of God, our Lady of the Wave.

Monster in the Closet

Coriander Friess

"I love you, kiddo. Good night."

"Mom?"

"Yeah?"

"Mom . . . there's a monster in my closet."

"Babe, aren't you a little old to be worried about monsters? Have you been watching scary movies with your dad?"

"No." His tone is defensive. "Mom, really." I could hear intensity in the voice from the blankets.

"Benny, you know there's no such thing as monsters."

"Mom, what about sharks? I mean, if you'd never learned about them on TV and I told you about sharks, wouldn't they seem like monsters?"

"Maybe, but sharks aren't evil. It's just their nature—"

"What about scorpions? Or wasps?"

"Didn't you ask me for one of those blue scorpions for Christmas? Are you trying to leverage them into the 'educational' zone? Cause it won't work. Those things are creepy. Besides, if it got out, or if your sister

209

got ahold of it . . . How's about we just go to sleep, we'll get you something cool for Christmas, even if it's not a scorpion."

"But Mom! You don't understand."

"Do you want the light on? I could leave your door open a sliver."

"No, I just want the window open. Just a crack, please Mom?"

I sigh. I've got a lot to deal with yet tonight, and this is an easy concession. "Sure thing, kid."

He doesn't have teenager smell yet: feet, stale laundry, illicit cigarettes, spilled soda and spoiled food, all lurking under acrid cologne and minty gum wrappers. But this room smells. Not just the usual smells of pond water and cedar bedding. Something else. Something . . . dead.

I check guinea pigs, bird cage, lizards snoozing under heat lamps, frog spawn and aquariums. Nobody is belly up. But the smell is unmistakable. The breeze brings in the garden scent of dirt and leaves through the open window.

Our yard is the only one on the block buried under a foot and a half of leaves. Jackets, bikes, a Tonka dump truck and rakes, the ladder too, are all shamelessly strewn across the yard. Not a single leaf bagged, though there may have been a pile at some point. Tonight is pick-up night, and if I don't get out there, it's not going to get done. *Sigh.*

Did he notice the smell and just open the window? It's been a warm fall but not warm enough for the window to be open all night. *Oh, God!* Gagging into my shirt, I lift a dead rodent's small, desiccated corpse from the closet and fling it into the corner pail. I take the whole bag to the kitchen and empty that one, too.

I return to the scene of the crime with Lysol and offer a quick wipe of the closet floor . . . *eww*. I shudder. *What the Hell?* The crickets chirp in their plastic tub, placidly unaware of their purpose. The sparrow chatters and flutters about in her cage, feathers ruffled. Is she upset by my tidying? I suppose it would be disturbingly novel. When was the last time this room got cleaned? I wonder idly if birds can even smell as I swab various surfaces.

※ ❀ ❀ ❀ ❀

Not again. Not again. Dear God, not again. I sit there in the silent hull of a bedroom, cradling the sodden misshapen mass of dead bunny and I weep. Where did it go wrong? My bold adventurer, my National Geographic explorer, my own special zoologist . . . all the fond titles I gave Ben, my ten-year-old animal lover, felt ugly and marred in the face of this.

This wasn't the first time, even, but it was my wake-up call.

The first time, I had asked him to close the window. That was it. It was uncharacteristic, he was usually a pretty easygoing guy. The endless battle of wills was his brother's domain. My worries with Ben had always been his boundless energy and full-throttle pursuit of adventure.

All that evening he'd kept at it, though. First arguing, then pleading, finally tears and even foot

Coriander Friess

stomping. All the while I was in business mode, moving from dinner, to dishes, to laundry, to the bedtime routine. In that whole time, did I once pause to really see him? At nine o'clock I turned out his light. I shut the window and locked it.

I picked up some dirty clothes. "I love you, kiddo. Good night."

I heard tears in his voice. "You don't understand."

Puberty? It seems early; his brother was nearly thirteen before he turned moody. Ben's barely double digits.

Next morning, I tuned out his angry banging and thumping and stomping. I can't let myself get drawn into an emotional battle of wills. I've been a mom long enough to enough kids to know it won't help anything. But what has gotten into him?

I figure maybe if I just let him stew, we could discuss it after school when he'd calmed down. It has only escalated. He's upstairs trashing his room, and nobody can ignore the sound of shattering glass and forty gallons of water splashing onto the floor and cascading down the stairs.

I dump my coffee into the sink and focus on my Lamaze breaths. Fifteen years after the fact, I'm still struggling to create the illusion of control: If I can control my breath, maybe I can control my emotions. If I can control this inner turmoil, maybe I can control this chaos. Maybe I can control this irrepressible little bundle of life. Guide him, at least?

Wreckage. Window and tanks shattered. Water everywhere. One lizard drowned, one missing. But the worst . . . both guinea pigs dead, heads completely smashed to pulp. Where is this in those damn parenting books? There in the midst of it, looking dazed, frightened by what I could only guess was his own rage, is my Benny.

In that moment, I am afraid I have I lost him. I hold his two arms in my hands. On my knees, in the water, my forehead pressed to his chest. I hear the wild thumping of his heart. I looked up, searching his face. "Benny! Why?"

His chest heaving, he stutters, "You can't close the window, Mom. There's a monster in the closet."

I don't see any monster in that closet. I can only see the aftermath of blind fury. I see the mangled remains of his pets. I see the wildly dilated eyes of my ten-year-old son.

If there's a monster in this room, he's right here in my hands.

I slapped him, hard.

Or maybe the scariest thing in here is me.

This is too much. We need help.

His file landed on my desk with a solid *thwack*. Every kid I work with comes with a good three inches of paperwork. As a rule, I leave them there to simmer. The theory is to see the kid with unbiased eyes, let him make his own first impression just like any kid on their first day of school. Inside of ten minutes, I know who is going to try to bite me and who is going to pinch my ass. I haven't actually been bitten in years, but those damn ass grabbers can still manage it on occasion.

Truth be told, I've been doing this a little too long

and the papers just aren't that relevant. I don't read the files until I've worked with the kid for a while and if I'm desperate, then I'll comb through notes trying to brainstorm what else I might try.

All I really need for an intake is the right opener and the right mug. I have a whole collection of mugs with different designs. The mug is my power tie and ink blot test in one. The opener is a simple game. These kids are so done with adults talking at them, half of them play at lip service or sit silent in defiance. Either way, it's a cloak thrown over their fragile sense of self. The other half is completely baffled by their own actions and feelings, like powerless passengers in a vehicle careening into traffic.

Most of the boys I work with flat out reject coloring sheets. It doesn't make a difference if they feature dark comic book heroes, transformers, sharknados. Coloring smacks of kindergarten and adult desperation to enforce calm.

Drawing, on the other hand, is way too personal. We've all seen it: a tenured college professor mid lecture is brought low, shamed by scrawling a stick figure on the board, or adults doodling with a few crayons at a restaurant entertaining a small child will laugh nervously and protest, "I can't draw!" Drawing is guaranteed to make a kid self-conscious, something I don't need during an intake session.

Later, much later, once we've established trust, drawing can take us back to those early childhood days. When the deep chasm of raw, inarticulate emotion comes oozing from covered-over wounds, when we reach a point where words don't work, that's where drawing or paint therapy comes into play.

Monster in the Closet

There is something so satisfying about scrubbing blacks and reds over a clean white page, so soothing in the swirl of color created by mixing cheap temperas.

For most of my sessions, puzzles are my most reliable workhorse. They do well at focusing our mutual attention out and away so that our conversation can go interesting places. As a bonus, flipping a puzzle box with a hundred tiny cardboard pieces carries dramatic heft without the possibility any real physical harm. Everybody wins.

But to begin, I have a special selection of "openers," simple games with simple rules. The games are generally unfamiliar to the kids, this way I get to explain the rules, which means I set the tone. Flicking old-school paper footballs across the table is usually a hit—the game needs to have a physical aspect. Ben isn't much of a sports fan, so I settle on "Cross the River." The game has just a handful of cardboard pieces that we slide back and forth along the table. Outbursts aren't generally a worry during intake, but why provide ammo?

I'm parked on the couch, laptop open on my knees, warm mug nestled in my hands, files stacked along the coffee table. It's 9:30 PM and I've shipped my kids off to grandma's. I have a murder mystery cued up on Netflix. It's my reward if I can finish catching up on this paperwork in the next hour or so.

I'm stuck on this kid Ben. I can't get a read on him. Seems like we should be past the opening volleys yet

I'm still not sure what to think of him. I even spoke with his mother at length. Maybe that was my mistake. Am I getting locked into her perspective? A basic tenet of my profession is that how she sees him reflects more who she is than him. Her heartache and worry are compelling.

When reviewing my notes, I generally latch onto phrases with edges. Is that bitterness, there? Anger? These are great places to work down into, as habitual patterns of interaction mask old wounds. Picking away at family dynamics, so engrained they're just about Pavlovian, will typically uproot abscessed emotions buried deeply beneath the surface.

I'm not finding any of those places, though. Instead of festering resentments, pain and anger, this tastes like fresh fear. These aren't negative, established patterns or stress-induced dysfunctional coping strategies. What I'm seeing are run-of-the-mill family patterns interacting with some new and unspoken phenomenon or pressure.

No wonder I feel so out of my depth. My experience in the field of abnormal adolescent behavioral psychology has muddied the water. This kid, as far as I can tell, is "normal." In a case like this, where a kid is killing and mutilating animals without remorse, or even much acknowledgement, I'm expecting to find layers of dysfunction. This behavior usually has deep roots, or gets dredged up in the wake of profound trauma.

With Ben, it's much more random, like the sudden flip of a switch. What's going on with this kid?

Monster in the Closet

Something still isn't adding up here. It sounds silly, but I am having a consult with myself. I've got my file and notes spread across the table, iPad set up to record, and my best bright red mug. I'll review the footage and analyze my voice, my tone, and my own body language.

At its heart, my profession espouses the belief that truths are discovered by speaking them aloud. That's the art of my sessions. My patients can swear like sailors but overall, they're working with less than half the vocabulary and more than twice the baggage of their peers. I have to hear what they can't speak.

I clear my throat and decide to start with the most basic observations. "Benny isn't exactly my typical demographic. Usually, social workers, school counselors and administrators, or the juvenile court system refer these boys to me. In Ben's case, his family sought me out, and the school is largely unaware that he is here. What do I hope to accomplish? A paradox—do I give credence to his claims about a monster, or do I believe this boy is manifesting very serious maladaptive behaviors?

"Not sure how much progress we're actually making. He didn't go for puzzles, so we landed on drawing. The kid seems to have aptitude. I can see his posture and demeanor change as he settles into it. Take a look at these." I pull a pile of pages from the file, each covered in colored-pencil sketches. "We started with race cars and robots. Impersonal lines. These aren't what he wanted to be drawing, but he was so reserved and closed off at first."

Coriander Friess

I flip through a few more pages of his work. "These here are transitional. I'm gaining his trust. See, they're more naturalistic. A jungle scene . . . love this seascape. Never had a kid wax poetic over sea cucumbers." I chuckle and take a sip of tea, studying the next drawing. "Look at this one. These are his lizards, Fili and Kili. This is where he finally begins to open up. Just look at them! I can't get over the detail . . . these beautiful skin patterns." I pause, frowning. "He loved those lizards."

These drawings are helping me see Benny more clearly, but what I see is still confusing me. I rub my temples and continue. "His account of what happened to the lizards, the other little critters, it concerns me. His voice had all the control and objectivity of a nature program. And his insistence on his monster in the closet . . . it doesn't fit. Look at the realism of these drawings." Frustrated, I smack the pile of illustrations.

Here's where I need to stop myself. Stop talking. Forcing a pause (they do not come naturally to me) works. Kids raised amid screamed cuss words and hurled furniture, kids used to manipulating adults into reacting are taken aback by a well-placed pause. It hits me, too. Deep down we are all worried by silence, just like we're all afraid of the dark.

"So, what are we left with? Is he a budding sociopath able to fool adults into seeing a relatively well-adjusted boy while he murders small animals? If that's the case, you'd think he'd come up with something better than a monster in the closet. It's almost like it's completely ludicrous on purpose. There's no way anyone would believe that! Is that his way of being the misunderstood, injured party?"

Monster in the Closet

Okay, be professional. That's not a diagnosis, that's name calling. I set the drawings aside and look at my case notes. "ASPD . . . antisocial personality disorder . . . I'm not seeing the hallmark traits of impulsivity and rule breaking. Clearly, he has emotional depth and understanding.

"I'm going to back away from that label. It's too big and I'll lose him under it. Heisenberg's uncertainty principal applied to miscreants . . . once you define what a kid is, you'll never see who he is."

Still, my head swims, trying to place him. I'm muttering now, skimming through the things I've written down during our sessions. "I can rule out multiple personality disorder, too rare. Even if the entertainment industry loves it . . . adolescent schizophrenia doesn't fit either. There just aren't any of the comorbid disorders that go hand and glove with that one. No depression, none of the scattered thinking and processes."

I've finished playing back the video of my interview. Just like the image of me on the screen, I am resting my chin on interlaced fingers, brooding. I don't quite know what to make of this one.

※ ※ ※ ※ ※

School's all right, I guess. Aiden's always showing off. He wants everybody to think he knows all about animals. But he always picks the really popular animals so who cares. It bugs me that animals are fads. Like, four people wanted the platypus when we did Australian projects, when normal boring Australian animals like koalas and kangaroos are cool.

219

Coriander Friess

Just because we've known their names since kindergarten doesn't mean we really know that much about them. And all the girls used to have owls and foxes on their shirts last year but now they all have flamingos and llamas. Nobody even cares about any of it anyway. Animals are just another thing like the latest video game or movie, just something to put on your T-shirt to prove you're cool.

No, I'm not really mad at Aiden, or jealous or anything like that. I mean, when we're messing around, sometimes we talk about animals and he knows that I know all that stuff. He's come to my house and hung out in my room so he's seen my animals and all my books. Mostly when we're hanging out, we play video games or go down to the park. It's just during school he gets on my nerves, y'know? He's always trying to talk when Mrs. Brown's explaining things—like, she's doing the water cycle, so he adds stuff about rain forests and because it's kinda related so she adds that in and then it takes longer. Aiden thinks it's really fun to get her to move one topic over, and one topic over until we're way off topic. But that just means we start all over again with a "recap" before we actually start our work.

Yeah, I like animals, and I don't really have just one favorite. I did a project on pangolins for an exotic one. Exotic is like, strange and from far away. And when we did Australia I did compare and contrast circles about emus and ostriches, so I really did two animals not just one. On Tuesdays we have library. I always get animal information books. My mom lets me watch lots of documentaries. I probably get more TV time than Janna because she always picks cartoon shows. She hasn't figured out you get more turns if your shows are "educational."

One time me and Aiden were walking down to the corner store to get some chips and we found this dead raccoon in the alley. It was kinda weird cuz usually dead animals get all puffed out and stiff and there's flies, then they kinda deflate and it's not very long until they're just a patch of fur and bones. Most of the time somebody calls the city and like, garbage men or somebody comes and pick them up.

I'm not saying I like dead animals. I'm not saying anything other people don't know for themselves or can't see. Roadkill is a pretty ordinary thing. I haven't told you about this raccoon. I noticed him because it was just a little different, just . . . a little weird. He looked shriveled at first. He looked all shriveled and like parts of him were eaten, not just run over. But mostly, roadkill is gross so nobody really looks.

When Janna was real little, she used to have this picture book about raccoons and it was all lovey-dovey but I kinda liked it because it talked all about the raccoon's hands. Dogs and rabbits are always nosing around sniffing, and snakes always taste their environment and birds—owls and hawks especially—use super eyesight. But raccoons, I mean they have smell and they have night vision but they mostly learn by touching and messing with things with their hands. That's why they can always figure out how to get in the trash cans. I always thought I'd like a pet like that, an animal that would always be figuring things out. It could watch me do something and then repeat whatever I had done. But in the end that means it'll just get really good at getting in to all sorts of trouble.

Coriander Friess

The park near our house has a pond. I like to go there and catch frogs in the summer, or fish, even if you have to throw them back. They're mostly little blue gills anyway. Every year there are three or four duck families on the pond. I like how the babies follow their mamas. Or sometimes all the babies follow one mama duck like she is babysitting for the other mamas.

I like how all the babies hide in the reeds in the afternoon when the playground is noisy. You mostly see the babies really early in the morning. When they change from yellow to that fluffy gray then they stay in the middle of the pond in the afternoon, so nobody can get at them.

Janna and me used to leave for school early so we could go the long way through the park and see the ducklings. We would save our veggies from dinner to feed them. And we laughed because even the ducks hate cauliflower. There weren't very many ducklings this year so we didn't go so much to see them. This one time, I was late getting ready so Janna left without me. I was really mad at her and bummed about going to school. I already had a note my mom wrote me because I was going to be late, so I went through the pond way. Ten extra minutes wouldn't matter.

It made me even crankier because I only saw like, two ducks way in the middle of the pond. No babies, no families, only two males. This runner guy who always wears neon colors says, "That's global warming for you!" and runs off. But I just stood there looking at the empty pond and it made me sad the

222

way everything always changes. And all of a sudden, I realize I hadn't heard any frogs for a long time, either.

ᴇᴇᴊᴊᴊᴇ

Our neighbor Mrs. McPhearson can whistle like a cardinal. She can do a chickadee and almost a robin. And she has a super loud whistle she uses to call the squirrels. Every afternoon when she gets off work, she comes to the park with seeds and peanuts. All the squirrels know what she's gonna do. You can see them—they're already waiting for her in the trees by the pavilion and more come out of the woods by the path as she walks up. She whistles and they all rush out of the trees. It's this big crazy squirrel stampede!

She gives them the seeds and peanuts and all the squirrels scurry around and pretty soon they've eaten up all the food and then they just dwindle down until there's only a few and they settle down. Everything is all quiet and still and you wouldn't even know what had just happened if you walked up now except some birds are still upset and complaining and looking for leftovers.

I loved going with Mrs. McPhearson. I loved it so much my mom would ground me from going, instead of losing TV like Janna or phone privileges like Danny. Last time I went, Mrs. McPhearson cried. She got there the same time as usual but not even half the usual number of squirrels were there. When she whistled, none of the squirrels came down. They stayed up in the trees chattering squirrelly swear words and my favorite one that only has half a tail threw acorns at us.

Coriander Friess

Usually, Mrs. McPhearson takes a walk through the park after she feeds the squirrels but she just came back with me. She told me she started feeding the squirrels because they always used to ransack her bird feeders. Now no squirrels come to her feeders. Hardly any birds come either.

❦

At bedtime, Ben comes into the TV room, "Mom, have you seen Stormy recently?"

I look up from my knitting. I'm working hard on always making eye contact, always making a connection. "I'm not sure I have. Did you look in all her usual places?"

He holds up a bottle of veterinary topical antibiotic spray. "I need to put this on her. She has some pretty bad scrapes."

"Fighting with the neighbor's cat again? Maybe we should make sure she comes in at night."

"I don't think that's a good idea, Mom. She won't like that." His shoulders tense up, defensive.

"Well, we need to do something if she keeps fighting. Besides, there are other animals lurking about at night. Do you know coyotes still come into town from time to time? Or strange dogs, or skunks, or—I don't know, owls." I can see Ben shutting down, he's not listening anymore but I can't stop over explaining. "The more I think about it, the more I feel she should be in. Look at it from the other side. How many birds has she murdered and left on the doorstep?"

He shrugs on his way up the stairs.

Monster in the Closet

❦❦❦❦

From: Hodgekiss@htherapy.com
Date: 11/23/2003
To: summerhorses@att.net
Subject: A quick question
Email from Dr. Hodgekiss to Anna Fischer:
Dear Mrs. Fischer,
Recently, your cat has been the subject of much discussion during our sessions. Could you tell me about your cat? You don't have to "analyze," just run through the cat's history for me. Comparing your take on the cat with Ben's stories could be enlightening. Anything you tell me could be relevant and I know it's difficult for you to meet in person for an appointment, so feel free to go into as much detail as you can.

Sincerely,
Dr. Hodgekiss

❦❦❦❦

From: summerhorses@att.net
Date: 11/24/2003
To: Hodgekiss@htherapy.com
Subject: Re: A quick question
Dear Dr. Hodgekiss,
Oh, that damn cat. She's just a semi-feral barn cat from my dad's farm, but she's Benny's best friend and his security blanket too. The spring my mom died, Dad wasn't holding up so well. We went to visit over spring break and ended up staying for the summer.

225

When Dad had his stroke, we made arrangements to rent out our house so we could take care of things.

Things just fell into place. My dad's neighbors are a lovely family that we've known for years. Sam and Donna's kids are a little older than mine but overlapping in ages. Sam said if we let the kids roam wild we were sure to run into trouble. He had them hopping! Between the two farms, there were plenty of chores.

I was flabbergasted. My boys usually wouldn't even take the trash to the curb on garbage day and here they were running tractors, spraying manure, mucking out stables, and I don't even know what all else.

Sam projected movies onto his garage doors for them and let them run the ATVs. The radio never quit playing. They had bonfires and went fishing, so there was plenty of fun. Meanwhile, Donna and I ran garage sales almost every weekend. I sold the cows, too. I had to get things squared away because Dad was fading day by day. We found places for his sheep and goats. I gave Donna's youngest two of the lambs for 4H. Benny and Janna thought that was pretty unfair, but they roamed back and forth between the two houses and the barns nonstop so it's not like they missed anything.

My dad wouldn't hear of getting rid of his chickens. He'd never eaten a store-bought egg in his life, but we weren't hatching any more so I sold the incubator, and Donna and I fixed that tough old rooster in the crockpot for a Sunday dinner. Without the rooster protecting the flock, we lost a few hens to a raccoon or fox or something. Dad was hopping mad.

Monster in the Closet

Out of nowhere, the barn cats had this crazy population boom. I mean, there had always been a few around the place, but suddenly there were kittens everywhere. Benny and Janna were ecstatic. They gave all the kittens ridiculous names and made up elaborate stories about them. Let's see there was Martoch, Leonides and Menelaus, Fatty Lumpkin, Steeeve, Misty, El Guapo, Lollycat and her clone Lollycat II. There were more but I couldn't keep track of them all. I just scrambled to find homes for them.

Stormy is the one we brought home with us. What had happened is hurricane Sandy hit the coast and even though we're pretty far inland there was rain all through here for days, a lot of flooding too. Right in the middle of all this rain, this bulging, half-drowned, excessively pregnant cat shows up in our barn. She got up in the rafters and yowled and spit and hissed, cussing at everyone and everything. Janna climbed up to rescue her but that cat tore her up. Cat finally came down on her own, but didn't really warm up much to the other cats though. She never did get a name. Janna was too offended and then the cat didn't stick around long after her kittens were born. She had four, each a different color. She had them right in the chickens' laying box, which caused an uproar with the hens.

And just a few days later, that nasty old cat disappeared in the night, taking her kittens with her. As feral as she was, it came as no surprise to me when she disappeared. I explained to Benny sometimes mother cats will move their litters if they get spooked. Maybe he and Janna had handled the kittens too much, maybe even just been too close, who knows?

227

She was just following her instincts and trying to protect her babies.

But Benny found one kitten abandoned underneath the egg box. He bottle-fed it and named her Stormy. He carried her around with him everywhere in one of those canvas Carnie aprons, like a kangaroo. I was amazed she survived that kind of constant handling. As she got bigger she put up with that sort of thing less and less, but she'd chirrup and run to him whenever she saw him coming. In the fall she'd wait at the bus stop for him when he came home from school.

Dad passed in mid-January. We sold the land and the house separately which created a fiasco with the bank. All the business and divvying up and squaring away of a life time's worth of stuff took a long time. We stayed through the school year dealing with everything.

Re-reading this e-mail, I laughed that my voice got a little country. Guess my roots are showing! Too long to go back over and I know there's lots more in here than just the cat but it all jumbles together, with the feral cat becoming domesticated, the suburban boys becoming wild country teenagers, and Benny and Janna both growing like weeds that summer.

Thanks for the trip down memory lane. Hope it helps,

Anna

Monster in the Closet

From: Hodgekiss@htherapy.com
Date: 11/27/2003
To: summerhorses@att.net
Subject: Urgent, please call!
Dear Mrs. Fischer,
Please give me a call. I don't want to raise the alarm prematurely but I have immediate concerns regarding Ben's cat. He's fixating on her. I'm not sure why he is focusing so much energy worrying over the cat who is clearly not ill or in danger.

I would like to discuss subtle / non-invasive measures we could take to ensure the cat's safety. It is quite possible that I have misread indirect cues and that this will seem overly dramatic in a few days, I certainly hope so. Still, it's better safe than sorry. If we can be low key but protective that would be best all around.

Sincerely,
Dr. Hodgekiss

From: summerhorses@att.net
Date: 11/28/2003
To: Hodgekiss@htherapy.com
Subject: Re: A quick question
Hi Dr. H,
I got Sam and Donna to take Benny for the weekend. That will actually be a real treat for him. They have all sorts of animals on their farm and Sam assured me that he would put stuff together for the kids to do. Do you think Scouts or 4-H would help Benny. Wishful thinking, if only this would clear up with a stern

lecture and some extracurriculars. It's just that when we were out in the country, we didn't have any worries over him like this.

Anna

From: summerhorses@att.net
Date: 11/30/2003
To: Hodgekiss@htherapy.com
Subject: A sad update
Dr. Hodgekiss!
I took Stormy to the vet. He wanted to put her down immediately. He said it looked like she got caught in the engine block of a car. I guess sometimes cats climb up under the hood of a car to stay warm? Vet said she looks worse than some of the bait animals they find from that underground dog fighting ring. There's been a lot of them lately. It's been on the news.

   We don't know what happened to her . . . it's horrific. I don't know how she even got back to the house. I told him to do the best he could because the stupid cat is so important to Ben. His friend, a surgical resident from Children's, also assisted. (Please keep that confidential. They could get reprimands if it got out). So Stormy got the best care she could get, small comfort atm but they said I could pay half if she doesn't make it through the weekend. The bill is gonna clear out our Christmas savings for sure. I don't know what to do.

Anna

Monster in the Closet

꧁꧂

I'm curled on the couch, my tea has long since gone cold. Anna's email is still bright white on my computer screen while I'm rehashing facts and events.

Ben is forty miles away from his injured cat and still unaware of what has happened . . . presumably. But he said this would happen, didn't he? Our last session, he was practically hysterical. He was frenzied with the unshakable conviction that Stormy was going to get hurt. He's two counties over. He couldn't have hurt her.

But if he didn't hurt her, what did?

꧁꧂

Tuesday night is judo for both Benny and Janna. Janna has girl scouts immediately after, so I drop off Benny at home. There's just enough time to switch the laundry or unload the dishwasher before I head out to pick up Danny from his job at the burger joint, then I swing back to pick up Janna. It's one smooth, taxi driving feat of precise timing.

After work on this Tuesday afternoon, I stop at the grocery store for milk and stuff for lunches. Janna has a field trip coming up. I grab a couple frozen pizzas too. Danny had friends over and they finished off our stack. Tuesday is nearly always frozen pizzas for dinner. They're easy and more predictable than delivery. Heck, transportable if necessary.

That's where my mind was, spinning through the

logistics of the evening. The second I walked through the front door, though, I knew something was off, like the walls were holding their breath. Maybe I noticed that nobody did the greedy rush to inspect the groceries for goodies or because I couldn't hear the familiar squabbles over video games from the TV room.

Sharp shuffling and scraping noises came from upstairs, the tell-tale sign of roughhousing turned personal. Kids who are wildly hyped up brag loudly. They knock into things as they jump around. They yell loud meaningless taunts and threats. Kids intent on a real, no-holds-barred fight are quiet, except for that scuffling sound.

So I knew. I already knew before she screamed that something was terribly wrong.

And oh, that scream. It was no playful shriek. The sound Janna made was primal, desperate, panicked. As I charged up the staircase, I heard glass breaking. A dozen thoughts flashed through my head in an instant, recollections, observations, deductions.

Danny always seemed to punch dry wall or kick it in. The force it took to produce an angry, jagged hole satiated him and dissipated his teenage wrath, like the wall had absorbed his anger. He would calmly accept being grounded and repair the damage. I think he found the repair soothing, a chance to wipe the slate clean.

With Benny, it's always shattered glass, ever since that awful episode with the aquariums. Unlike Danny, who would fizzle after his outrage, Ben always seems filled with nervous energy, lost and flighty. He seems ready to dive through the window and run wild into the night. His restlessness reminds me of relatives in hospital waiting rooms. He doesn't even sleep well after one of these emotional incidents. I'll hear him tossing and turning late into the night.

Goes to show, you can get used to anything. In the space of a few deep breaths I switched gears, going from standard Tuesday maneuvering to managing a crisis mode before I was half way up the staircase.

I reach the top and take a split second to assess the situation. There's Benny, with a bat, standing in front of the broken window. Janna is cowering on the floor with her arms thrown up protectively over her head. There's blood. It's running down her arms and it's all over her face. I can't tell where it's coming from. She's still screaming.

"Janna, Janna I'm here. Hush now. Ben, Benny . . . Ben. Give me the bat." I already have him in a controlling hug, my hands taking the bat, my hands interspersed with his down the length of the bat. I frown, noticing that the bat is smooth and clean. No blood. Benny's eyes are glazed, wild and unfocused, while I absorb this information.

Gently, I pull him down to the floor into my lap. Janna stops screaming and is quiet for the space of a heartbeat. Then she is shaking, sobbing great big gulping hysterical sobs. She's in shock. I'm facing her with Ben in my arms. I'm praying. Both my babes are drowning right in front of me. How can I be holding him while she's bleeding and weeping? But how can I let him go? We are sitting here together, but we're all adrift in a seething, unseen, bottomless ocean.

"Janna, Janna sweetie, come here." She crawls into my arms. It's horrendous and joyous and broken and so damnably confusedly wrong. But she's on my right and he's there to her left on my lap and the three of us cling together under the broken window, next to the discarded bat.

Benny reaches across me and puts his hand on Janna's shoulder. She puts her hand on his. He starts sobbing a little, too.

Ten seconds we float there in the eye of the storm.

"Okay, guys. We've gotta hustle." Their eyes are wild and scared. I get to my knees, one arm still securing Ben, and check Janna's injuries. She has deep cuts along her arms, presumably from the glass. On her face, shoulder, and chest—just below her neck—she's bleeding.

Stitches, she needs stitches. I grab a crumpled t-shirt from the bed and give it a shake to knock loose any glass, then press it over the bleeding. I direct her to hold it in place. In one movement, I scoop up both of them, Janna on my right and Ben on my left, and we move together down the stairs.

I guide them through the house and out to the car. The whole time, my voice is running over the scene in a quiet, reassuring babble. "Everyone is safe. We just need to get you to the doctor. You'll be stitched up in no time, baby girl." I'm speaking the same monotonous nonsense that I poured out for my squalling inconsolable colicky babies, but these children are stunned silent.

I'm talking out loud, but my head is balancing facts and observations. The bat wasn't bloody. His hand on her shoulder, her hand on his. It wasn't even an "I'm sorry" squeeze. It was a consolation, a comfort . . . they'd been through something together.

Monster in the Closet

At the car, I pause for half a beat before putting Ben in the front seat. "Buckle in, Benny," I say before shutting his door. I settle Janna into the rear passenger seat. We make eye contact and all my words dry up in that instant.

There's no time for meaningful words or probing questions. I've got to move on to the next thing.

Emergency room. Psych ward. Phone calls.

At the hospital everybody talks weird. Their voices are too quiet and too slow. They sound like my mom's voice in the dark when Janna used to throw up on the bed late at night.

No one will tell me about Janna. They'll say she's okay, then they switch over to talk about something else. They use their too-quiet voices to ask me the same questions over and over. At first, I thought they didn't understand or maybe they just didn't listen, adults sometimes don't really listen if what you say doesn't match what they already think. After the first day, I knew they didn't believe me.

I'm glad Dr. Hodgekiss came to see me. I mean, it's always been kinda weird just talking about stuff with some grown up lady. I don't sit and talk like that with my friends, we do stuff. I don't even just talk like that with my mom. I guess we talk in the car and when we're doing the dishes on my kitchen night or at bedtime.

But it's nice that Dr. Hodgekiss knows me and her face isn't all tight and serious like when I'm in the principal's office or something bad. And it seems like she always already knows what I'm talking about.

Coriander Friess

Mom doesn't talk to me like I'm sick or somebody just died, either. She says she knows I didn't hurt Stormy and she knows I would never hurt Janna. Janna is afraid to sleep at home now, so Mom let her sleepover at Sam and Donna's even though it's not a weekend.

Then Mom told me that the neighbors' dog is missing. Actually, there are a lot of dogs missing on our block. Mom says there are pictures all over the telephone poles. The local news keeps talking about an underground dog fighting ring.

But I know they're wrong.

"Dr. Hodgekiss?" She looked up from her iPad. "How do you choose between two bad things? Breaking rules is wrong, but if I don't break the rules, I can't fix what I did." My mind was racing. I examined the window of the room, eyed the ceiling. That thing was out there. "I need to make sure things are safe. Maybe I can break out . . . or maybe I can bring her here?"

Dr. Hodgekiss's squinted and set the iPad down. "Ben, when you say 'her,' you don't mean Janna, do you?"

I looked down at my hands. I could feel her eyes on me and she was quiet for a long time. All this time I'd been telling her about the monster, and I knew she didn't believe me. Her and mom both just thought I was some sort of psycho kid.

Finally, she spoke up. "I've never asked you much about the monster. I'm sorry. I thought it was just a story that got too big for you to let go. I thought it was a delusion, so I was trying not to feed the idea."

I shrug. "Yeah. I named it Nelson, but started calling her Nellie when I figured out she was female . . . "

236

Monster in the Closet

Doctor Hodgekiss's eyes bulged when I said this so I shook my head. "No, no it's not like she laid eggs or had babies or anything. I googled it. It doesn't look like any of the pictures people put up. But the other information seems to match—stuff about its habits, behaviors, and instincts." I took a deep breath before I said it out loud. Here goes nothing. "El Chupacabra."

Her face was impossible to read. She does this thing where you can see her going through filing cabinets in her head, looking for something. Facts, ideas. Finally, she spoke. "Ben, you can't bring that thing here. Unsuspecting patients and staff would be helpless victims. There's a maternity ward!"

"But it could be days before I get released, and she's still out there! What if she goes after Janna again?" I squeezed my fists against my temples, thinking about Janna getting hurt. She shouldn't have been in my room, but she didn't deserve to get mauled for it. I screwed up pretty big this time.

Dr. Hodgekiss stood up and started pacing slowly. She was definitely processing this new information. I watched her putting facts and observations into those filing cabinets in her head. "Hang on a minute, Ben. Calm down. I can sign you out. Your mom's a smart lady. I'll call her, and the three of us can plan this out together. We're adults; we can help you navigate this. That's been my job from the very beginning, to understand what's happening with you and help you cope. Let's get started."

Benny leaned against the pillow in dazed relief. The poor kid had been telling us the truth the whole time, it was just too outrageous to accept. I feel pretty relieved too, though I'm sure in a different way. Now that I know the problem is environmental, not internal, fixing things is a whole lot simpler.

"What do you think, Ben? Once we get you out, how do we get rid of—of Nellie?" I have to smile a little at the fact he named his monster, and that he named it "Nellie" of all things.

Benny's eyebrows knit as he put together a plan. "I caught her in a live animal trap made for like, raccoons and cats. You know—small, pesky critters. But she's too big and too smart to get trapped that way again . . . " He trailed off, thinking some more. Then his face brightened. "She responds to my whistle. I learned that trick from Mrs. McPhearson. We could use that, and some hamburger meat . . . we lure her into Sam's truck and take her away."

I frowned. Take her away where? "I'm not sure you'll like this, Benny, but shouldn't we put her down? 'Away' just means giving the problem to someone else. Somebody else's Janna could be in danger."

Benny looked crestfallen. "But—but if she goes back to her natural environment, she'll just go back to hunting deer. That's what the websites said they usually eat, once they're full grown. That's why like, people don't really even know her species exist. If she has room to stay away from humans, she will."

If I'd learned anything from my sessions with Ben, and all the conversations I heard about his lizards, guinea pigs, and cat, I knew that I'd never convince him to put Nellie down, not without causing trauma.

Monster in the Closet

Nellie—the fact that he had given her a name, and referred to the monster by name even after she'd attacked his sister. And maybe there was nothing wrong with that.

Six months later, thirty miles east . . .

"This is Channel Thirteen Live Action News here with a breaking report: Residents in Hobbs, and Royalson Creek area are urged to keep their dogs and animals inside as there has been some unusual coyote activity in recent days. One local farm claims to have lost several new calves. On the scene now, our reporter Tyler Benton has an exclusive report. Over to you, Tyler . . . "

Repossessed

Christina Blanch

Never in my life would I have dreamed I'd be sitting in a police station trying to convince a detective that magic is real. But there I was.

"Are you saying it's haunted?" the man sitting across from me asked, trying to keep a straight face. He wasn't doing a very good job. His name was Detective Reeves. He had bags under his eyes like it had been a long day and those eyes were staring at me like I was a loon.

But I was telling the truth.

"Well, no. It's not haunted. Afflicted, maybe. Possessed. Vexed? These would be better terms."

"Thinks . . . it's . . . haunted," he muttered, scribbling something in his notebook. The scratching sound on the paper gave me goosebumps. I didn't like scratching noises.

Especially not after . . .

"This is not a normal situation." He made the comment like it was something I didn't know. I wasn't an idiot, even if my boyfriend Jeff thought I was. They were both wrong.

"And as I said, sir," placing my hand on top of his notebook, mostly to stop the scratching noise, "it's not haunted. You should write vexed."

He didn't seem happy about me touching his notebook. He pushed my hand away with the eraser end of the pencil, then used it to scratch his head.

"I'm not even sure why I'm here, sir," I said, maybe a little too impatiently.

Detective Reeves tapped his pencil against his forehead five or six times, and after exhaling loudly, he said, "There was a complaint. That's all I can say." He moved the pencil back down to the notebook. "Why don't you start at the beginning? Tell me about this . . . house."

So, there I was. In a dingy interrogation room at ten o'clock at night with a tired cop who didn't appear to have any wiggle room in the believability department. He seemed nice enough, but I'm not always the best judge of character. Pretty easy on the eyes, though. Maybe in his thirties. Nice eyes, a piercing green. But I digress.

I began. "The beginning . . . well, I had just graduated college—"

He stood up suddenly. "Oh boy. Let me get some coffee first. You want any?"

I was annoyed that he'd interrupted me, but coffee did sound like heaven. "Yes, I would. But first, you can apologize for being rude. And then, I take it black. Thank you."

He scoffed and stared at me for moment, but muttered a tiny "Yeah, sorry" before leaving the room.

I jumped two inches off my seat when the door clanked and I scowled, wondering if it had been a strategic move. I'd nearly fallen asleep by the time Detective Reeves returned with coffee. It is a powerful drink. The smell permeated my senses and made me forget, for just a split second, that things weren't normal.

"Okay," he said. "Please tell me about this haunted . . . " he trailed off, looking at his notes. "Excuse me. This *vexed* house. I'll be recording this." He pushed the record button on the device. That was my cue to begin.

"My story, well, it begins with a repossession and ends with a possession."

He leaned back with his hands folded on his chest, his eyes twinkling. "This sounds like a whale of a tale."

"Are you going to keep interrupting me, Officer Reeves?" I didn't know what to make of him. It was like he was good cop and bad cop all rolled into one.

"*Detective* Reeves. No, I'm sorry. I won't interrupt. Please continue, Ms. Manship."

Now it was my turn to correct him. "*Doctor* Manship."

He seemed taken aback slightly and said, "Please continue, Doctor Manship." He emphasized the doctor part—not sarcastically, but respectfully.

"Just call me Grace." I smiled a nice smile. You know that kind of smile. The one that means, "I'm not sure if we like each other but we're going to pretend we do to get through this." Now that our little dance was done, I continued.

After I finished my doctorate, I bought a beautiful Victorian home. Or at least, it had been beautiful once. It would be again, now that I owned it.

I *owned* it. An involuntary shiver went through me. I owned this dilapidated house! I have always loved old homes, and when I found this fixer upper for cheap, I just bought it. I was thrilled. My boyfriend Jeff? Not so much.

We had talked about moving in together, but he wasn't sure he wanted to live in a house I owned. He said he would help me work on it when he could, but opted to keep his apartment. Jeff pressed me to stay with him while I worked on it, but the house was habitable. Besides, I wanted to live there right away. I didn't care that it would be messy. That house had felt like home from the moment I stepped inside. I felt like I belonged there. That was a big deal for me.

I had never really felt like I belonged anywhere. This seems odd considering I never moved while growing up and went to the same school all through childhood. I held down basic jobs, went to college but never, never once, felt like I belonged. I mean, I don't even belong to a sign. My birthday is on a cusp, the solstice, and when I was young my brother told me I was a "Sagicorn" because no side wanted me. That might have something to do with it. It was almost like by calling me the name, it put a spell on me. But when I set foot in that house, I knew I belonged there.

Jeff watched me as I walked from room to room, making notes and planning along the way. He rolled his eyes and said, "You know nothing about this stuff, Grace! You can't do this."

Repossessed

I grabbed his hand and squeezed it, saying, "No, but we can."

"I just don't get what you see in this place." He pulled his hand away.

"Possibilities, that's what I see! The bones of the house are strong. And come on, it's not that bad! Remember my third college rental? That dumpster fire?" I pointed to the intricately carved woodwork. "Can you imagine what it's going to look like when we fix it up? Because I can." I was smiling so hard my cheeks hurt. I knew this was my home.

Jeff laughed a tiny bit and said, "You always can see things that aren't there."

But this house was there.

"I can picture myself years from now, sitting all cozy on the porch during a rainstorm drinking coffee."

Jeff frowned. "How come I'm not in that picture?"

I just laughed it off. "I'm sure I'll outlive you."

The day I took possession of the house, I started cleaning it up. It was already grueling work, and I hadn't even gotten to the difficult part. That night I decided to stay there. I didn't have any furniture there yet, but I took an overnight bag, a couple pillows and blankets and created a makeshift bed in what I'd decided would be my bedroom. It was perfect. Oh, I also brought a coffee maker because I didn't live in the Dark Ages.

That first night was the greatest night of sleep I'd ever had. Jeff wouldn't stay with me. He thought it was silly when there was a perfectly good bed a few miles away, but he'd never had much of a sense of adventure. Truth be told, I often wondered what I saw in him. Especially when he asked, "What if the house is haunted? If you hear spooky noises, you better call me to save you."

He was joking, but I thought it was rude. What could he do that I couldn't? And anyway, there weren't any noises.

Like, at all.

Usually old houses creak and groan as they tell the stories of their past, but not this one. It was silent. It was perfect.

The next few days were busy, but blissful. For me, anyway. I didn't start my new job at the library for three weeks, so I planned on getting a lot done. A few friends helped me move my stuff into the house. It looked so bare, trying to fill a huge Victorian home with all my stuff from a one-bedroom apartment. My parents surprised me with some recliners, and I bought a few things at Goodwill. It was coming together. Doing this work, I felt more alive than I'd felt . . . ever. Like I had really stepped into my own.

Jeff helped some, too, and even stayed over a few times. I thought he was becoming a little more tolerant of the house. I wished he could *see* things before he saw them. You know what I mean? I was able to picture a thing finished before I started it. He could not. When a room started coming together and he finally saw it, he would get excited and happy with me. Those were good moments, but they were few and far between the moments of him griping that the house took up so much of my time and energy.

The first week I scraped and sanded and painted and stained until I passed out at the end of each evening. Jeff's help was spotty at best, and he was becoming agitated.

"You never want to go do anything anymore," he complained.

I didn't understand what he meant. "Jeff," I said. I used my scraper to point at the walls. "It's been one week. Look around at this house! It already looks amazing!"

The library was complete, its shelves filled with books and trinkets; pictures and art hung on the wall. The floor was sanded and had a beautiful rug that, as "The Dude" would say, really tied the room together. Before winter was here, I would have the fireplace working. I gestured to the cozy room.

Jeff grunted and reached for his keys. "I'm going home."

⁓⁓⁋⁋⁋⁋

Detective Reeves cleared his throat. "Excuse me, but is there a point to all this? Sounds to me like your house was haunted by a bad boyfriend. I haven't heard anything out of the ordinary so far."

Apparently, I was the type of person that people like to talk down to because I don't appear confident. I had been told that I am too nice. I wasn't in the mood to play that game. I stood up and pointed at the detective. "You asked *me* here tonight. I came as a favor. This is inconveniencing *me*. You're getting paid for this while I am having my time taken away from me. I think you can show a little respect." The words just came out of me, and I was nearly shouting. I couldn't believe it.

He muttered a "sorry" and motioned to the chair. "That was rude. I'm sorry. I know you have had quite the day, but it's been a long day for me, too. Not an excuse, but I'm sorry."

"I appreciate that, Detective." I sat down and unruffled my feathers. "I'll skip ahead a few days to the first really odd find."

My handyman, Bruce, came over to do some jobs that I couldn't do myself. I wasn't any good at plumbing or putting in gas and electric lines.

Bruce seemed to be in a trance, staring at a wall in the theater room. "I think that's a fireplace behind there."

I squealed and hurried over to study the wall. There was a fireplace in the library already, so this would make two! I loved fireplaces. There's nothing better than curling up with a book in front of the fire on a chilly Midwestern evening. Throw in a cup of coffee and a dog and it's almost heaven.

Once again, I heard an "ahem" from the other side of the table. I smiled. "I sometimes get sidetracked, Detective. I apologize."

Detective Reeves smiled and took another sip of coffee.

Bruce and I both figured, "what the hell?" and we busted a hole in the wall. Sure enough, the drywall was covering another fireplace. We tore the drywall out and cleaned up the whole area.

Bruce studied the bricks and eyed the ceiling. "I imagine the chimney's blocked. You could probably get gas logs, though."

Just to be sure, I took a flashlight and wriggled myself under the chimney, shining the light up into the dark passage. The light bounced off the drywall dust and danced with the shadows on the brick. Then something caught my eye. There was something else reflecting the light. It looked like a bottle of some sort.

I was a little nervous, but it was so intriguing. I found the courage to reach up and touch it. It was smooth, like glass. I poked my finger around it until it started loosening. I prodded around some and felt some kind of string. When I pulled on it, the object came loose. Fortunately, I was able to grab it before it smashed on the bricks. Not knowing what to do next, I stood there a few moments, panting. I wanted to see it in the light and find out what it was, but it gave me an eerie feeling.

I squirmed out of the musty fireplace clutching my treasure. I held it up to the light coming in through the window and breathed, "Bruce, look what I found!"

"Huh." He peered at the glass bottle. "Never seen anything like that before."

I hadn't either. I snapped a picture with my phone, then Googled "glass bottle found in chimney." After scrolling through all the DIY articles on making wine bottles into oil lamps, I found the term "Witch bottle" and clicked on it.

None of them looked like the one in my hand. The pictures on the page were stoneware jugs and this was not that. However, it did say that later witch bottles were made of small glass vials. The one I was holding looked like a smaller version of a square Jim Beam bottle, but this had another smaller square on top of it. The bottle was corked at the top and there was something inside of it, but the glass was so grimy I couldn't see what.

Bruce broke the silence. "What's inside? Rolled-up money, I hope!"

I snickered. "I can't see."

I tried to move the cork, but it was pushed too far down into the glass and wouldn't budge. I stood up, dusted my pants off, and headed to the kitchen. It was the only room that didn't need work right away. Eventually, yes, but for right now, everything worked and I had so many other rooms that needed much more TLC. Priorities.

I turned on the faucet and thrust the glass bottle under the stream of water. I was rubbing it with my thumb, squinting my eyes as if that would help me see better, when I shrieked. Bruce came running in.

"You okay, doc?" That was his term of endearment for me. I kind of liked it.

"Yes," I answered, but I was breathing quick, shallow breaths. "I just . . . well . . . I think there's a finger in here."

I wiped off the bottle and set it down on a paper towel so it wouldn't drip all over. Bruce put on his reading glasses on and squinted at the glass the same way I had. After a few moments, he said, "Don't think it's a finger, but . . . eew. Those look like fingernails. And there's needles in there. And something roundish." He set it down and stared at the bottle, crossing his arms. "Weird. But nothing of value that I can see."

I picked it up again and held it up to the light. "Value can be more than money, Bruce. I think this is a witch bottle." I grinned. "And that's so cool."

When Jeff came over later that night, I told him all about the witch bottle we'd found, putting it in the light and yanking on his shirt sleeve so he'd look at its contents. Of course, he wasn't as excited as I was. He shrugged me off and glared at the bottle. "You should toss that thing out."

Like that was going to happen.

⁓ℓℓℓℓℓ

"Hang on." Detective Reeves leaned back in his chair. "He actually said to just get rid of it? I mean, isn't that how every horror story begins?"

I laughed. A real laugh. "He doesn't do horror. He's too scared." I smiled. "But I love it."

Detective Reeves nodded and pointed his thumb at his chest. "Me, too." It was a bonding moment. He sat up straight in his chair then, and asked, "So what did you do? You didn't open it, did you?"

I laughed again. "Of course I didn't. I'm not a fool! But I did want to know more about it, so I searched around until I found a curiosity shop a few towns over."

"The one in Pendleton?" he asked.

I blinked. "Yes," I answered. "You know it?"

He nodded.

I started telling him about my visit to the shop, but he stopped me. "I feel like I need some popcorn for this story."

I chuckled and told him I would wait if he wanted to make some. He paused for a moment as if in thought, then shook his head. "Continue, please, Doctor Manship." He leaned forward, intrigued.

Christina Blanch

I had no idea what to expect from the little shop in Pendleton. The closest I had been to this was when I watched a reality show about an oddities shop. This was real life, though. When I walked in, I was trembling slightly. The door chime startled me, but I relaxed when I detected the scent of sage. It reminded me of my mother.

There were rows and rows of shelves with bones and trinkets and all sorts of things I never knew existed. My heart was racing. I didn't see anyone but heard a rumbling at the back of the shop, so I headed that way.

A woman sat in an old, leather armchair in the corner, sipping what I guessed was tea from an ornate china cup. She didn't look up at me when I approached, her eyes gazing downward at an old book. I looked away for a moment to make sure my purse didn't hit any of the array of treasures packed on the shelves. Her voice startled me.

"You aren't looking for anything special on those shelves. How can I be of help?" The words were smooth and knowing, like Gandalf the Grey was talking to me from atop his horse. My body was shaking like jazz hands. Well, jazz hands are really stationary, so not jazz hands. More like how the floor feels when the washing machine is on spin cycle.

Repossessed

Detective Reeves clears his throat and I realized I was talking about jazz hands and spin cycles. He just raised an eyebrow and sipped his coffee.

⚬⚬⚬⚬⚬

I cautiously walked over to the old woman, holding the witch bottle out as tribute. "I looked it up and I think it's a witch bottle."

As soon as I said it, I felt silly. I realized I hadn't said hi or anything else. Just blurted out something about my Google search. *Smooth move*, I told myself.

But she stopped everything. It was like she was frozen, the teacup perched precariously at her lips. I wasn't even sure she was breathing. I mean, of course she was, but it was weird.

Then she looked at me. She didn't move her head. Just her eyes. Our eyes made brief contact before I looked away and it felt, well . . . scary. I could feel her fear.

After another few moments of standing there like a fool, I managed to speak. "I found it in my house. I found it in a chimney that had been walled over."

The woman still just looked at me. Finally, she put the teacup back down on the saucer. Who does that still? Using a saucer is just one more dish to wash. She seemed like such a caricature. But this was real. And to be honest, it was kind of cool.

She put her hands out, forming a small bowl with them. "Put it here, child." She motioned toward her hands with her head. I found her use of "child" rather comforting. Her hands were still, but mine were trembling as I placed the witch bottle in the cradle she

253

had created. As soon as the bottle touched her hand, her demeanor seemed to change. She was slightly more relaxed. I couldn't see this, but once again . . . I had felt it.

"You are correct. It is a witch bottle. Why did you remove it?" She asked me this like I should know better. It was a question, but I felt scolded, like a child.

"What do you mean? I didn't know what it was for sure until this very minute. And honestly, I'm still not sure why I took it. Why should I have left it there?" I was almost angry. Not angry, annoyed. Defensive. I was mentally going off on a tangent when her voice brought me back to the present.

"You haven't opened it, have you?" Her words were carefully articulated, each syllable weighted.

"No." I did not hesitate in my answer. "The cork is wedged way down there. And, I mean, that liquid in there could be rotten and sometimes those kinds of smells never go away." As soon as I said it, my shoulders slumped. That sounded stupid. Of course smells dissipate. Why do I let people make me feel like I'm moronic? Do I not have a PhD?

She could almost sense what I was feeling. "You were right not to open it," she said, not looking away from the bottle. "And it is a witch bottle, you can be sure of that." She gestured to the chair next to her, the chair I had not even noticed until then.

It was the twin of the one she was sitting in. They were those great high-backed chairs that make you feel like royalty when you sit in them. The small table between the chairs housed a teapot, her teacup and saucer, and an empty cup and saucer. Again, I didn't notice this until just that moment. It was almost like she'd been expecting me. I was still shaking when I sat down.

"Tea?"

I declined. At that, she looked up at me, finally taking her eyes off the bottle. "You should have some tea to calm your nerves." She poured some liquid from the teapot into the cup nearest me.

I took a polite sip, then smiled. "Oh, I love chamomile. It's my favorite."

She smiled back at me, like she already knew. Still cradling the witch bottle, she turned to me. "Tell me, what have you learned about witch bottles?"

I shrugged. The tea already seemed to have an immediate calming effect on me. "I don't know anything, really. Just what I read on the internet. That they were put in houses to keep bad luck away. Like a charm."

She laughed a throaty laugh very unlike the sweetness of her voice. "They are much more than charms. Witch bottles have been used for centuries. They aren't just for keeping bad luck away. They are to turn a curse back on the witch who made it. Sometimes it kills the witch, but many times they just remain dormant." She held the bottle up to the light coming in through the tiny windows. The glass fragmented the light, making it almost seem magical. That is, until you saw the contents inside.

"Well, did it work?" I asked the question in all seriousness, but the woman could not have rolled her eyes any harder.

When she remained silent, I started rambling. "I just moved into the house a little over a week ago. It had been in foreclosure, so I don't know the history of the house. All I know is that the lady who owned it died and had no relatives. The bank repossessed it and I bought it. I don't know much more yet. I was planning to research it later. Right now, I'm . . . "

She interrupted me. "That's a shame," she said. "While the past is simply in the past, it is also a roadmap to where you are. The people from the house's past are now in your story, too."

I gave her a confused frown.

"Witch bottles can contain many things. Urine, blood, nails, pins, nail clippings, needles, herbs. Rosemary is very common. This one has something I can't quite identify."

She got up from her chair, the chair groaning with relief like she had been there for quite some time. She made her way around the various shelves and small tables full of baubles, finally reaching the counter and using a magnifying glass to investigate the witch bottle; her eye looked huge in the glass, colors dancing around in the green of her iris. Her eyes had a life of their own.

The woman spoke her thoughts aloud. "Fingernails. And urine, most likely." I silently thanked myself for not opening it. She continued. "The needles are very normal, but this?" She shook the bottle. "It appears to be a ring of some type." She tutted some, and muttered, "Very strange. Very unusual."

I laughed. Not a funny laugh but the kind when you don't know what else to do. "Everything about this is unusual."

I got up and walked toward her, leaning over the counter to look at the witch bottle with her. It was mesmerizing. I couldn't help but ask, "How did they get the ring in there? The bottle aperture is smaller than the ring."

The woman looked at me and simply said, "Magic."

"But magic isn't real."

The corners of her mouth turned up slightly and I thought I heard a chuckle, but she spoke before I could be sure. "My child, magic is what makes the world go 'round. And it is real." She held the witch bottle up and gestured toward it. "Very real."

I hadn't really ever thought of magic as real, and wasn't sure I was buying it. Rather, I never thought magic would affect my life, but one can't be too careful. "So what do I do?"

She placed the witch bottle in my hands and covered them with hers, then spoke as she walked away. "Put it back. Don't open it. And hope for the best."

I stared after her in disbelief and a valid sense of frustration, but I was guessing she had said all she was going to, so I gathered my belongings to leave. "Thank you for your help." I glanced down and saw the empty teacup. "And thank you for the tea. May I pay you for your time?"

She turned back to me with her hands outstretched, clasping my hands in hers. "You may pay me when you return."

I tilted my head inquisitively. "Do you think I will . . . find more of these?"

Her response was a knowing smile. "I am not sure what you will find. But I know you will return."

It was creepy, I thought, and yet, I was sure that I

would return, too. Sure that I would need to. It was a strange feeling.

I turned to leave but before I could take a step, she took my hand and put something in it. "Please take this. Wear it. It will protect you."

I looked in my hand and saw a necklace there. It was a small bottle attached onto a silver chain. Inside the bottle were a few gemstones, a needle, what looked to be a sprig of rosemary, and a dark red liquid. My eyes widened and I glanced at the woman. "What . . . is this liquid?"

She laughed. "Relax, child. It's not blood. Just wine."

I was relieved, and I am sure it showed on my face. But then I frowned. "Protect me from what?"

The woman smiled another one of those infuriating, knowing smiles. "From whatever it is you need protection from, my child."

I nodded and had turned once again to leave when she called after me, "Don't open the bottle. And wear that necklace at all times."

I had no idea what was going on, and it all sounded ominous as all get-out. I put the necklace around my neck. Why take chances?

When I returned to the house, I was surprised to find Jeff there. He informed me that he had invited some friends over for pizza and a movie. I always tried to spin things like this, so I treated it as a positive step in our relationship. He was finally taking an interest in the house. I told myself to put on a smile and relax and have fun. I deserved fun. Not once did I stop and think that maybe he should have asked first, since it was my house.

Repossessed

I placed the witch bottle on the kitchen counter. Jeff saw it and rolled his eyes. "Are you still carrying on about that thing?"

There was no way for me to spin that statement. The man had no imagination or respect. "I'm going to put it back into the chimney where I found it."

"Another reason to not like this house."

It was my turn to roll my eyes and walk away. I grabbed the witch bottle and did just that.

I walked into the room where Bruce and I had found the fireplace and positioned myself under the chimney to put the witch bottle back. I made sure it was secure. Once it was returned to its place, I felt better. More calm. Everything was where it needed to be. I reached down and held the necklace firmly in my hand. Calm.

"More coffee?" Detective Reeves startled me.

"I'd love some. Thank you," I replied, handing my cup to him.

"Back in a sec." He smiled as he picked up the cup. He was much nicer, now. He probably felt sorry for me. The crazy lady. But I would take what I could get. I rested my head on my forearms that I had crossed over the table.

The opening of the door startled me out of my sleep. "Sorry," he said. "I'm sure you're tired. As soon as we are done with the statement, I'll drive you home."

That was nice of him. I told him I'd driven myself, but thanked him. "And thank you for the coffee," I added. "This will help. I'll try to hurry."

"No." He waved me off. "This is the most interesting this job has been in a while. Take your time."

I enjoyed the detective's new attitude. He was probably using some tactic to get me to say something I shouldn't. What he didn't realize is that I had nothing to hide.

"So," he said, "you had just put the witch bottle back. What happened when your boy—" he paused as if almost disgusted, "when your friends came over?"

It was about six o'clock when I put the bottle back into place. After that, I got changed and freshened up and tidied the house. We would only be in a few rooms, since I'd told Jeff I was not giving tours. He didn't hide his relief.

He left to grab pizza and beer and got back about a quarter til seven. Fifteen minutes later, I answered the knock at the door. Four friends of ours arrived; two couples with a lot more alcohol. I knew it would be a long night.

Jeff put on some movie with a lot of car chases and bad acting. I couldn't tell you the title. I voted for *John Wick*, but he liked this one better. The man had horrible taste. Everyone was eating and drinking, and drinking more. Especially Jeff. I left to use the restroom and when I got back, he was sliding out of the fireplace. The fireplace where I'd returned the witch bottle. I froze.

"What are you doing?" I yelled. I walked over and saw the witch bottle in his hand. I screamed at him to put it back. He just laughed. His drunk laugh. Great. I bent down to his level and asked him nicely to give me the bottle.

"Let's play keep-away. Remember that game?" Jeff struggled with the few words he managed to put together.

"Jeff," I said once again, trying to be calm. "Give me the bottle." While the word 'bottle' was still hanging in the air like a speech balloon, Jeff heaved it into the air. I tried to catch it but missed.

Glass shattered on the floor and the rancid liquid seeped out on my freshly sanded and stained floors. The worst part was the smell. It was so foul you could almost taste it.

I stood there, my back to Jeff and our guests, my chest heaving. Finally, I said in a low voice, "Everyone get out of my house." I turned and pointed to Jeff. "And take this ass with you!"

I stormed into the bathroom, where I splashed some water on my face and looked in the mirror. My mascara was smeared and I realized I was crying. I stayed there in front of the sink until I heard the front door shut, then opened the door cautiously and looked around. They all seemed to be gone. I couldn't hear anything. But I could smell something. And it smelled terrible.

I got some Clorox, a small bowl, and some paper towels, then put on a pair of rubber dish gloves and headed toward the source of that putrid smell. I was shaking, I was so angry. And what would I tell . . . I didn't even know her name. The lady from the shop. Why was I even worrying about that?

Holding my breath, I got down on all fours and

picked up what I guessed was hair, a few pins, some type of plant, and the ring. I sprayed the Clorox on the spot, noting that the stain was a perfect circle. I sprayed a few more times for good measure and started cleaning up the liquid.

I shuddered. It felt like I was just moving a thick pile of mucus around on the floor. I'm sure it only took few minutes, but it felt like hours. It was the strangest substance.

After I had cleaned everything up, I put the small bowl and all the items from the bottle in a Ziplock bag, which I set on the front porch. The smell radiating from it was enough to choke a donkey. I sprayed some air freshener all around the room and shut the door in an attempt to keep the smell somewhat contained.

When I was all finished, I threw up several times. I could still taste that smell. I showered to try to get it off of me, but didn't think I could ever bathe enough to get that odor to go back from whence it came.

That night, I doublechecked the house locks before I started up the stairs to bed. On the way to my room I noticed a squeaking I hadn't heard before. "Great, more to fix." I decided to take a sleeping pill since I was still angry over the events of the night. I wouldn't be able to sleep and I desperately needed to after a day like that.

And to be honest, I was a little worried. I held the bottle necklace in my hand while the pill started to work its magic. As I was drifting off, I heard strange noises, like bricks scraping against each other. "That's new," I muttered.

I hadn't remembered hearing noises before tonight. Any noises. I thought about getting up to investigate, but before I had finished that thought, I was asleep.

When I woke up the next morning, I felt pretty good. I reached up, felt the bottle necklace in my hand, and for a moment I was at peace. Then I remembered the night before.

The witch bottle. My friends. The mess.

And Jeff.

What was I going to do about Jeff? I thought about going back to sleep and hoping my problems would just go away. That never works. It only means I wake up later with the problems still there, and then I chastise myself all day because I wasted so much time.

I threw on my robe and slippers and went downstairs to get coffee. While it was brewing, I checked on the room. I opened the door and sniffed slightly, readying myself to slam it shut and run for fresh air. To my surprise, the odor was gone. I inhaled again. Not a trace of the putrid scent could be detected.

I walked to the spot where the bottle had broken and studied the stain on the wood, in the shape of a perfect circle. "Nothing like doing the same work over again." I tilted my head. "At least it's kind of a pretty stain. I might keep it."

I drank my coffee and piddled around downstairs until I decided it was time to get to work. It was already noon. Today was the day I planned to remove the tile in the downstairs bathroom. It was usable, but really needed to be updated and have some pipes replaced. Bruce told me I could save money by removing the tile myself. After watching some YouTube videos, I felt vaguely confident. I walked into the room ready to HGTV that baby, carrying a newly purchased sledgehammer which made me feel super cool. What could go wrong?

I put on my protective glasses and dragged the hammer behind me. Glancing in the mirror, I snorted at the sight. Maybe it was time to think about my life choices? I decided to not go down that path. I was still pretty angry at Jeff, so I decided to use that anger. I heaved the hammer up and brought it down on the tiles, which crumpled under the force of the blow.

It was a great feeling. I felt like John Wick digging up his guns and coins. I took a few more swings and was feeling pretty badass until I got a little overzealous and brought the hammer up too high. It hit the ceiling and busted a hole in it. That's not the only thing that got busted: so too did my dreams of being a badass.

Setting the hammer down, I looked up at the ceiling with a heavy sigh. Seriously? Small bits of drywall were raining on me, making me feel slightly defeated. Whatever. I was going to finish this. I thought about Jeff, lifted the hammer, and continued my chore until it was completed.

When it was all in pieces, I looked at the mess. Kind of like my life at the moment. I grabbed the stepstool to assess the damage to the ceiling, though dust from the drywall made it hard to see. It was just a small hole and it should be easy to fix, I thought, without really knowing for sure. *I guess I'll be attending another class at the University of YouTube*, I thought to myself, reaching up to soften the edges of the hole a bit. Another piece of the ceiling came loose and fell to the ground. Then I shrieked.

Repossessed

I looked at Detective Reeves. "You remember that movie *The Money Pit*?" He raised an eyebrow and nodded knowingly.

"That is what it was starting to feel like."

"But with magic," he added.

I smiled. "Yes, but with magic."

He smiled back at me. It was nice.

❧₰₰₰₰₰

When the dust settled, I peered inside the hole. Something was in there. *Please don't let it be another witch bottle.* It wasn't.

It was worse.

I poked at the drywall with my gloved finger and more broke off. This time, though, whatever was up there fell out and landed on the floor with a *thud*. I couldn't see what it was until the mushroom cloud of dust settled.

There on the floor was the mummified carcass of a cat. I poked at it with the end of a broom and turned it over. Its claws and teeth were still intact. It had sunken eye sockets, protruding ribs, and its tail looked like a magic wand. The desiccated mouth gaped open, as if it was trying to tell me its secrets. The thing was scary and amazing at the same time, like a train wreck. I wanted to look away but I couldn't.

I reached out to touch it, almost expecting it to meow at me. Thank goodness, it didn't. I picked up the cat and placed it gently in a box. Poor baby. I wonder if it got stuck up there. It didn't look like it was in a natural position. It almost looked like it had been posed after death. And had it been mummified naturally, or did someone do it?

To be honest, I may not have thought much about the cat if I hadn't already found the witch bottle. And although I had returned the witch bottle to its original resting place, I didn't think I could leave a dead cat in the wall. I decided I would bury it in the backyard later that day. I hadn't started on the landscaping yet, but everyone deserved a burial.

I looked at the cat again and felt sorry for it. How had the poor thing ended up like that? Instinctively, I grabbed for my phone to Google "mummified cats in walls," then I realized I didn't have it. I must have left it upstairs.

It felt strange not having my phone, but liberating. The truth was, I always carried it with me because, well, if I didn't answer Jeff right away, he got mad.

Today, I didn't seem to care.

The Detective snorted and I answered him with a quizzical look. "Are you okay?"

He smiled a one-sided smile and said, "Oh yeah. I'm just trying to figure out why someone like you would be with someone like that guy."

I laughed out loud at that. "I am, too." Then I added, "I'm pretty sure it's over. Having me brought in for questioning is as good an end to any relationship as any."

Repossessed

This time it was his turn to laugh out loud. He took a sip of coffee and asked me to continue. Motioning at his clothing, he joked, "But wait, should I change for the cat funeral first?" His green eyes twinkled and we both laughed. It felt good.

"What you're wearing is fine, Detective. Because there was no funeral."

"Another twist! Can't wait."

⠿⠿⠿

I carried Winston, tucked away in his box, and put him on the kitchen counter then went upstairs to get my phone. Little specks of drywall followed me up the stairs, a breadcrumb trail leading back to the bathroom. At least I wouldn't get lost.

⠿⠿⠿

"Yeah, I named the cat." I was answering the amused look on Detective Reeves' face. He was doing a bad job of hiding it.

"I had always wanted to have a cat but my mother was allergic so we couldn't have one. And Jeff hates cats, so I just put it out of my head. But now I had Winston. And he had been doing a fine job protecting this house. He absolutely deserved a burial."

Detective Reeves raised his hand, like he had a question.

I laughed. "Can I . . . help you?"

"Yeah, Doctor Manship?" he said. "I was just wondering how you knew it was male. Or did you just assume? Most people assume dogs are boys and cats are girls."

267

I gave a wrinkled smile with a shrug. "He just . . . looked like a Winston. I didn't think much about the sex. I have always wanted a grumpy-looking cat to name Winston."

"Desiccated cat would be pretty grumpy, I think." He shook his head, snickering.

When I retrieved my phone, there were over twenty texts and seven missed phone calls. Mostly from Jeff. His messages ranged from "I'm sorry" to "Answer me!" I didn't feel like responding, so I didn't. I searched for information about the cat instead.

Google informed me that sometimes mummified cats were put into the walls of houses for protection against all sorts of things, but especially rodents. I had never seen any trace of mice or rats, which seemed odd in a house that had been sitting empty for this long. Apparently Winston had done his job.

I laid down on the bed for a minute to play a game of Rummy on my phone while I processed the morning's events. The next thing I knew, someone was banging on the door downstairs. I glanced at the clock on my phone. It was six in the evening! I had fallen asleep. There were about twenty more unread texts. It was probably Jeff at the door.

Getting off the bed, I caught my reflection in the mirror. With the white flakes nestled in my black hair, it looked like the worst case of dandruff ever recorded. I shook it out the best I could, creating more of a mess to clean up. The knocking came again. "Coming!" I yelled before I had started for the door. I brushed my hair with my fingers, trying to get it in some semblance of order, but finally gave up. It didn't matter anyway. I was who I was, no matter how I appeared.

The knocking was much more persistent by the time I swung the door open. "Sorry, I was . . . " I trailed off as the visitor was revealed to be, of course, Jeff.

He stood there, sheepish, holding flowers, burgers from my favorite place around the corner, and beer. "Are you okay?"

I just stared at him, shaking my head. I motioned toward the beer. "You didn't have enough last night?"

"I'm so sorry, baby."

Here it comes, I thought.

"I'm *so* sorry."

This wasn't new; I knew the pattern. It goes like this: Jeff is a jerk—sometimes alcohol is involved and sometimes it isn't—we fight, he shows up with flowers, sometimes food depending on how bad it was, and a mouth full of apologies. It usually worked, but this time, I wasn't so sure. He seemed to sense that, too, and he was desperate.

"What exactly are you *so* sorry for, Jeff? That you were a jerk? That you were drunk? That you damaged my property? That you disrespected me in front of our friends? Tell me, what are you sorry for?"

After I said this, I couldn't believe I did. I had never spoken to him like that. I was usually the passive one but this time, I felt free. Like it was okay to know I had worth. I had found myself.

Jeff looked shocked, but quickly recovered. "Baby," he said. Hearing him call me that made me want to throw up. "I'm sorry for all of it. I've been a jerk." He got down on one knee.

I saw him reach for his pocket and pull out a ring box. *Dear god, no,* I thought to myself. I needed to stop this. I yanked him up and told him to come in.

"Wait!" he yelled, but I was already gone, heading to the kitchen. He followed me and handed me the flowers. "Baby," he said again, starting to kneel down. "I have something to . . . " He stopped short. "WHAT IN THE HOLY HELL IS THAT?" Jeff's eyes were huge as he stared at the cat in the box.

I tried not to laugh. "Oh, that's just the cat mummy I found in the bathroom wall today," I said nonchalantly. There was no way I was going to let him know I had screamed when I discovered the thing. "I call him Winston."

Jeff was walking toward the cat box but when I said this, he stopped and gave me the same incredulous look he'd given the cat. "You may be the strangest person I have ever met."

After a silent moment staring at Winston, he came over and tried to hug me. I pushed him away.

"Hold on there, Tex. You are in no way out of the doghouse."

"But, baby . . . " His face was close to mine and I could tell he had already started drinking. I closed my eyes, shook my head, and pushed him away.

That's when the smell of the burgers made its way to me, and I realized I was starving. I hadn't eaten all day. I was still angry at him, but I wasn't going to let the food go to waste. I told Jeff to come on, grabbed the food, and headed to the couch. I figured if I put on a movie we wouldn't have to talk and he wouldn't attempt to propose. I didn't have anything to say to him at the moment.

I selected an Edgar Wright movie, started it, and got out the food. Biting into the burger—and it was one tasty burger—I heard a beer open. Of course Jeff was having a beer.

About halfway through the movie, when the food was gone, a thunder clap startled me. It was pouring rain outside. I hit "pause" on the remote and poked at Jeff who seemed to be dozing in and out. I loved thunderstorms. "I'm going to the front porch to watch the storm." He dragged himself off the couch to follow me and I avoided his attempt to grab my hand.

"Coffee?"

He shook his head.

That's right, I thought to myself, *he has his beer.* There were only two left. I made coffee and went outside to the front porch. Jeff was already there.

We sat there silently, me drinking my coffee and him drinking his beer. "So," he asked, "what are you doing with that disgusting cat? Are you going to keep it?"

I really didn't like him today. "I am going to bury him," I answered. "I was going to do it tonight, but it's too muddy. I'll do it in the morning."

Jeff gave me another look. "You are one odd duck, as my gramma would say."

I shrugged. "To each their own. I think all living creatures should be respected." Then I swatted a mosquito. "Except mosquitos."

It was getting late by now. Jeff was drunk. Not sloppy drunk, but sleepy drunk. He asked if he could stay over. I told him he could sleep on the couch. He wasn't happy with that answer but he was too drunk to do anything about it, so he agreed. I got him a pillow and blanket and said good night. He was nearly asleep before I left the room.

I went upstairs, chastising myself along the way that I hadn't swept up my path of drywall crumbs. Following the trail to my bedroom, I locked the door behind me. It wasn't a matter of being scared, I just didn't want Jeff to wander in.

What did I really expect from a man like that? I needed to break up with him, but kept thinking he would change and treat me like an equal. He thought I wanted a commitment. I looked at my hands and realized they were trembling with my anger. Knowing I wouldn't be able to sleep, I took a sleeping pill again, promising myself this was the last one for a while.

I was falling asleep when I heard faint, unpleasant noises. *Scritch. Scritch.* It occurred to me to investigate but the pill was starting to take effect. Instead I reached up to hold my necklace as I made my way to slumber.

I slept hard that night. I rarely sleep past seven but by the time I'd rubbed my eyes awake, it was after nine AM. I stretched and looked out the window. A beautiful day, and I felt rested. I would bury Winston that morning. It was a good start to a Sunday.

Humming "Easy" on my way down the stairs, I noticed parts of my drywall trail were gone. Jeff better not have tried to get in my room last night. Good thing I locked the door. I made coffee and said "Good morning, Winston." But when I turned to his spot on the counter, Winston wasn't there. He was gone. The box was gone.

I ran to where Jeff was sleeping and tried to shake him awake. "Jeff, wake up." He was completely covered by the blanket. I shook him harder. When he didn't wake up, I pulled the blanket back and immediately gasped. He was covered in tiny red splotches, almost like bite marks.

"What happened to you, Jeff? You have red marks all over you!" I shook him again and he finally woke up. His eyes fluttered open and when he could focus, he saw the marks.

He sat up on the couch in a panic. "What the hell?"

I left to get a warm washcloth to clean him up and he followed me. I wheeled around, suddenly remembering the cat. "Jeff, Winston is gone."

He pointed at the marks all over his arms and chest. "That's probably what this is! A rash from that damn cat carcass! I'm glad I burned it last night."

His words were still hanging in the air when I yelled, "You *what?*"

Jeff looked smug. "I burned it. It was gross." He looked down his arm, rubbing one of the many red spots. "You should be thanking me. That thing was diseased."

"Get out." I said it calmly.

"Are you serious? I'm hurt!"

"Get. Out." My tone was angrier this time.

He turned on his heel and started walking, yelling over his shoulder, "You are a crazy bitch!"

Then he was gone, and that was a relief. But so was poor Winston.

Not really knowing what to do with myself now that my morning burial plans were rendered unnecessary, I wandered absently into the bathroom to look at the hole in the ceiling. I snapped back to reality when I stepped in liquid. There was water all over the floor. I wondered vaguely if I had busted something yesterday without realizing it, but on closer inspection the water looked like it had splashed out of the toilet.

Jeff.

God, that man was an idiot.

I went outside to view the remains of Winston and his box. Such a sad little pile. I raked up the ashes, dug a small hole in the corner of the yard, and buried what was left of him. "I'm sure you were a good cat, Winston. Rest in peace." I shivered involuntarily as I said the words, though it was a peaceful moment.

⤜⸆⸆⸆⸆⸊

I looked directly at Detective Reeves. "Have you ever had the shivers? Where your arm hair is standing on edge?"

His eyebrows raised, startled. He'd been pretty into the story, apparently. He thought for a moment, then said, "Once, at a gruesome crime scene. Also, I'm sorry," he added. "That had to be awful."

⤜⸆⸆⸆⸆⸊

The lady in the shop had said I would return, and she was right. When I arrived, it was almost like she was waiting for me. I greeted her and she motioned me to sit. Same chair, the tea already waiting.

I told her everything. She hadn't said a word since I walked in and was silent the whole time I spoke, only moving to take a few sips of tea. When I was finished, I said, " . . . and now I am here."

She spoke for the first time. "And what do you want?"

I handed her the remains of the witch bottle.

"You know what is happening," she told me.

I frowned. I didn't know. That's why I had come back to her shop.

"You want protection from what is harming you."

"Yes, like, from whatever made all those marks on Jeff."

The woman let out a throaty laugh. "You need not fear that. It won't harm you because you were kind to your protector. There is a greater evil you need to concern yourself with, my child."

A cold chill trickled down my spine at her words. She carried the bag with the broken witch bottle to the counter and took the small ring from it. As soon as she opened it, I held my breath. However, it didn't smell at all. She placed the ring inside a new bottle she'd pulled from her apron pocket. It shouldn't have fit, but it did.

"You know what to do with this. It will protect you. What could harm you is not in your home right now, but you need to keep that evil away."

Confused, I took the new bottle and thanked her. I asked what I should do with the broken bottle and she said she would return it to where it needed to go. I studied her face. "What do I owe you?"

Without a word, she reached out with a pair of scissors and snipped off a piece of my hair. "You are paid in full." She took the broken witch bottle and walked away.

I stared after her for a moment before gathering my things. As I was leaving, she called after me, "You know what you need to do."

And suddenly, I did.

The next two days were uneventful. I placed the new bottle back in the fireplace, and I wore the necklace. I got a marker for Winston's grave, and things were back to normal.

Not extraordinary, just normal. Normal minus Jeff. The stained circle was still on the floor by the fireplace, but it was fading. Every day it was lighter. My spirit was lighter, too.

Late in the evening, I got a call from the police saying they had some questions for me. They told me Jeff was hospitalized and claimed that I caused it. I told them I would be in later that day and hung up. I tried calling Jeff to find out what was happening, but he didn't answer.

I took a chance and headed to the local hospital. He was sleeping when I entered his room, and he was covered with patches of small, red bumps. I peeked at his chart: fever, violent vomiting, muscle pain, bleeding from his ears, and skin rash, "possible RBF."

I glanced at the bumps on his skin. They looked painful. A quick Google search and I was rolling my eyes. Rat Bite Fever? Really?

At that moment Jeff woke up, saw me, and started screaming "WITCH!" Two nurses rushed in and while one tried to calm him, the other one asked me to leave. I did, and I knew he was gone from my life.

And I felt nothing.

Repossessed

"Then I came here, talked to you, and now you are all caught up."

Detective Reeves was silent. I sat and watched him ponder the story he'd just heard. "That is quite the story," he finally said.

"I'm sure you don't believe me." My hands on my necklace, I stared at the floor.

"I can tell you one thing that I believe," he said. Then he paused. It was a long pause. Did he think I attempted to kill Jeff? That I did this to him? I started to shake.

"I am sure that you have nothing to do with his condition."

The relief I felt when I heard those words was almost audible. I realized that I was holding on to my necklace so tightly that I might break it. I loosened my grip, and gave him an embarrassed look. "So . . . can I go?"

Detective Reeves stood up with a warm smile. "You absolutely can go."

I thanked him and headed for the door, stopping when he spoke again.

"And Dr. Manship?"

I turned to look at him.

"Thank you. It's been a pleasure. A . . . really strange pleasure."

I laughed and said, "Yes. Yes it has."

When I arrived home, the house felt right. It was late when I trudged up the stairs. I threw water on my face and quickly brushed my teeth, then collapsed into bed. I hadn't even thought about the day before I was out. No sleeping pill needed.

Eight o'clock the next morning, I felt great. I got coffee, showered, dressed. All the normal things. It was Monday. Just one more week until work started. My break hadn't gone how I planned it, but I felt free. Like I was allowed to be myself. Jeff thought he owned me, but I had repossessed myself. I could almost feel the house embracing me.

Refilling my coffee, I noticed the flowers Jeff brought me had wilted. They were in water and should have still been beautiful, but they were wilted. I threw them in the trash, which is what I should have done in the first place. Coffee in hand, I headed to the front porch to sit and watch the blue butterflies dance around the flowers that seemed to have bloomed overnight.

The car pulling up in my driveway knocked me out of my reverie. A cop car. Inwardly, I groaned. And here I'd thought the incident with Jeff was over.

My heart did a funny thing when I saw Detective Reeves get out of the car. He waved and held up his finger, telling me to hold on a minute. He took something from the passenger side of the car and set it on the ground, then did this again with something in the back seat.

My thoughts raced. What is this? Evidence kits? But it couldn't be. He was dressed in casual clothes and looked very different. Relaxed.

He made his way up to the house with a bag and an animal carrier. Neither of us had spoken a word. He set the carrier down, opened it and brought out a grumpy-looking cat. Still not saying a word, he handed it to me.

Repossessed

"Grace. Meet Winston, Jr. Winston, Jr., meet your new mom."

I stared at him, then the cat. Him, then the cat. "Are you serious?"

Detective Reeves looked shocked. "You don't have to keep him," he said, his face reddening.

I hugged the cat, who wasn't quite sure what was going on, close to my chest. "Don't you even try to take Winston away."

There was relief on his face. "Wouldn't dream of it." He motioned to the bag. "There's food, bowls, litter box, toys. Everything you should need is in there."

Winston Jr. purred gravel in his throat when I rubbed his ears. "Would you like some coffee, Detective Reeves?" I asked.

There was more relief on his face, and something else. He seemed familiar to me. Not just from the previous evening at the police station, but from somewhere else. "Sure."

I smiled a smile so big it hurt. "Come on in." I motioned him to the door.

"Meow." Winston put in his two cents.

I rubbed my face against his. "Welcome to your new home, Winston. I think we'll be happy here."

When I looked up again, I saw it. Detective Reeves was wearing a necklace very similar to mine. I looked into his eyes and then peered at the necklace, stepping in for a closer look. It contained what looked like rosemary, a few needles, and a lock of very dark hair.

"Where did you get this?"

I knew it before he spoke. "My mother."

They Never Left

Leah McNaughton Lederman

Skyler shivered against the cold. Her body was shutting down. She'd managed to free her arm from where it had twisted underneath her body. It took some effort, but she knew it'd be worth it.

Investigating with clumsy fingers, she touched along her scalp and felt her skull. Immediately, she thought of the ceramic mug her brother had broken when they were kids. Their mother had screamed at them when she saw the shards on the floor.

The blood flowing from the wound was still warm, and Skyler knew with a grim, resigned certainty that it was the last warmth she'd ever know—her own pulse, drumming out its final beats against the gravel.

She drank in the sight of the massive metal structure towering over her. Dad used to laugh, calling himself a "pile-on" in mimicry of the pylons that overlooked their backyard. In the spring, eagles used them as artificial trees, watching for prey. Mom told Skyler and her brother Josh to keep the cat indoors.

There was no eagle perched on this one, but its aircraft warning light gazed upon her with a malignant blink and Skyler knew she was done for. It was like she'd waited her whole life for this.

It was time to die.

She looked up at the pylon imposed against the hazy dusk and wondered, not for the first time but very nearly for the last, if the demons had ever truly left.

She couldn't help but think of Dustin. It made sense, when faced with her death, that she'd remember that stolen moment in the street.

Wes had given a few of them a ride home, and she was in the backseat with Dustin. He was pressed up against her because they were riding with Jean and Alisha, and when the car slowed to stop in front of her house, he'd stepped out into the street with her.

The air was crisp, with a February full moon peeking through the limbs of the old sycamore. Skyler knew this because her neck was bent back, staring at the cerulean sky, doing her damndest to memorize everything about this moment. She knew it was the start of a whole new life.

She'd left the neighborhood kids behind and was turning over a new leaf, volunteering at the Community Center. She had good friends now, not just the available social deviants. She was bringing herself up.

Dustin took her in, his happy teenage arms around her waist. Their happy teenage mouths kissed and she felt like something had reached down into her insides and taken all the sparkles she felt there and thrown them into the sky to mix with the stars and the moon. She was at once embarrassed by her giddiness but also aware she had joined with the eternal bliss of young lovers written about in Greek poetry . . . and she knew her life was over.

It could never get better than this moment.

Skyler knew before she went that it was a bad idea to go to Charlie's party. It put her in the way of too many temptations. After class was over that day, she'd ridden home on her bike. It was a gift from Dustin before he left for college. He told her it was better exercise than riding the bus. So she got her exercise. And she had prayed, like he taught her.

Maybe the party was no good but it was so nice to see some faces from the neighborhood, real people, not those college posers with their hands shooting up in the air to answer a question, or sidling up to someone trying to get into a sorority. Skyler saw through all that fake stuff, and knew Lacie did, too.

That's why she'd agreed to show up. A lot of people were in town for Thanksgiving, so she'd be sure to see a lot of old faces. It would be nice to be where people knew her. Really knew her. She could cut out the competitive crap for an evening.

She wasn't going to lie to herself, even if she lied to everyone else about it: she knew Brian Woz was going to be there. She'd been exchanging heart-fluttering glances at him for the better part of two years but he was always dating someone else. This time, she was the one tangled up, but she wasn't going to let that stop her.

Dustin wasn't happy when she told him she was going. He'd warned her against drinking beer and all the trouble it could cause. She'd flipped into the "mmhmms" and acquiescent silences normally reserved for speaking to her parents. He could worry all he wanted. She needed this. She was going to do something for herself.

Besides . . . beer? In the year that had gone by since their first kiss, the longest she'd ever been in a relationship with anyone, Dustin had tried to let his prep-school upbringing rub off on her. He actually thought beer was the worst thing he had to worry about. Alcohol was the real enemy, he'd say to her.

Lacie cut lines on the back of a Green Day CD case and offered them to her. Skyler took them quietly, reminding herself it was just the one night. A throwback to sophomore year, then it was the straight and narrow again.

It had been a long day of classes and Skyler was hungry. She also felt strangely lonely. She found herself missing Dustin, or at least the barrage of friends he brought with him. Sometimes it was nice to get lost in a crowd, albeit a small one.

Smiley's Café had always been a haven. Each time Skyler opened the door, she savored the thick aroma of freshly ground coffee, the inevitable classic rock playing on repeat. It got to where she always knew what song was going to come up next on their jukebox rotation.

She pulled out her chemistry textbook and set her pens down. A bit of reading and a few equations on a Friday night was a nice way to wrap up the week. It was early, but she knew that before long the other regulars would arrive, and she'd get to chatting and having a great time. It would be a good night. She'd even ordered one of their grilled chicken salads with the feta cheese, her end of the week treat.

The doors to the kitchen swung open and Charlie approached her table.

"What are you having to drink with that salad?" he asked.

Skyler tucked her hair behind her ear and tried to look coy without being obvious about it. He was cute. "Mountain Dew. A lot of studying tonight."

He gave a perfunctory nod, and she watched him head to the busser's station and pull out a to-go cup. He stalked back to her table and slammed the cup down. "You'll take your order to go."

Skyler felt her mouth drop open and she blinked, searching for words. Charlie stood there, glowering. After a moment's struggle she managed to say, "I don't understand."

"No? You don't understand what it costs to replace a door that's been kicked in?"

Her face crumpled in confusion. So much for looking pretty. "What?"

"Really? You're going to play it like that." Charlie crossed his arms. "Your stupid friends took my shit. That whole bottle."

Dave, the other cook, emerged from the kitchen

with her salad in a Styrofoam box and gave her a menacing look as he set it down in front of her. Rapid-fire thoughts burst through Skyler's brain. She knew what Charlie meant by the "bottle." He'd been selling it off for weeks, a few sips of mushroom tea at a time. And she knew without asking questions, just like he did, that it had been Troy and Lacie who took it. It was the sort of thing they would do.

"Those kids are dead, next time I see them." Charlie stared at her for a minute. His face almost seemed to soften. "I've known you a long time and you're a decent kid. But those fucks? As long as you're hanging out with them, you're not hanging out here."

The words cracked against her sternum. Smiley's had been hers long before Charlie had ever worked there, but she was just a regular, a teenaged one at that. She couldn't hope to hold the sort of social capital that he did.

Skyler gathered her things, balancing her Mountain Dew on top of her salad box, and walked out to the bus stop just a few yards from the café's front door. Naturally, she spilled her Mountain Dew all over her salad and drenched the front of her coat. "Really, God?" she cursed under her breath.

She sat down on the bus stop bench, a deflated balloon, and did her best to arrange her bookbag and coat so that they would block her from view of people entering or exiting the restaurant. The bus wasn't due to arrive for another forty-five minutes. If anyone saw her, they'd want to know why she was leaving so early in the evening, and Skyler didn't have the stomach to explain.

She set to work on her chicken salad, balancing it on her lap while she opened her biology textbook. It wasn't a surprise to her when she turned the page and heard the reedy clink of her plastic fork dropping on the sidewalk beneath the bench.

She bent over to pick it up and froze. Someone's shadow passed over her, and she groaned inwardly. One of the regulars must have spotted her and wandered over to ask questions. She sat up slowly and looked around. Nothing. Just the automotive susurrus of traffic passing by.

Skyler frowned, but relief outweighed her curiosity, so she ate the rest of her salad, hunkered down behind the makeshift tower of her coat and bookbag, then boarded the bus when it whined to a stop in front of her. She didn't see the second shadow that followed her onto the bus.

The bus crunched through potholes and debris on the road and the city yawned out in front of her, reaching toward the hazy towers of downtown. Her parents lived a few blocks from city center.

A little old lady was searching through her grocery bags on the next seat over and Skyler watched her. Her own problems were smaller, somehow. At least she wasn't carting a load of groceries home. At least her coat didn't have holes in it, even if it was soaked with Mountain Dew.

Skyler froze. She kept her eyes on the old woman but there, right there, in her peripheral vision she caught sight of something. It made her chest run cold even before she fully identified it. She remembered the shadow at the bus stop. She thought of an earlier memory, one she'd buried from so many years ago.

There in the window, the reflection of the old woman was staring at her.

But it wasn't the woman's face.

The reptile wore a crown positioned on top of its scaly head. It gave her a toothy grimace and licked its lips with a forked, whiplike tongue.

Skyler jumped up and yanked the bell cord. The old woman blinked at her, confused, watching Skyler stumble toward the front of the bus as it slowed to a stop. She'd left her bookbag on the seat and managed to hop off the bus before she threw up on the curb.

⚬⚬⚬⚬⚬

The wait was always excruciating. Skyler hated when Lacie made her sit in the car. Still, it was probably better than being in the old folk's home. She couldn't take the adrenaline rush.

Grandma Vicki had been living there for about five years. When she mentioned it once in front of Lacie and Troy, their ears had perked up and the plans started. After the mushroom tea incident, Skyler had learned this was the sort of thing that they did.

They'd taken turns casing out the place while she visited her grandmother in the home, figuring out where they kept the meds. And now Skyler just had to wait in the car across the street.

The pavement looked greasy from the rain; reflections from the streetlights stretched across the asphalt like smeared lightning bugs. Skyler heard a sound in the backseat and whipped her head around. There was nothing there.

Lookout duty always made her paranoid. That's why they gave her the job, she supposed. She leaned back against the headrest and closed her eyes.

When she opened them again, she saw the eyes staring at her. Some thing, some figure, was in the backseat. She saw it in the rear-view mirror, reaching toward her. It wasn't a hand, just a cloud, just a blackness. An absence of light.

Skyler lurched away from the foul thing, hugging the steering wheel and squeezing her eyes shut. *It's not there,* she told herself. *Too many drugs, Sky.* When she opened her eyes again, carefully, one at a time, she was alone in the car. No malignant presence.

She exhaled and took a look around the car and out the windows. Still nothing. Except . . .

The water droplets weren't right. They were changing as they pinged against the car. The rain, it was marching, like . . . like little insects.

Skyler leaned forward and studied the hood of the car. There they were, tiny squadrons of clear-shelled beetles, making their way toward the windshield. Toward her.

She clicked out of her seatbelt and had her hand on the door latch when the passenger door opened. "Now that's what I call a payload!"

Troy was grinning and dripping with rain. He handed a canvas bag to Lacie, who had opened the door to the backseat and let out a squeal of delight.

"Sky, you are not going to BELIEVE what we scored!"

Skyler smiled with her mouth, but her eyes were wild. She tried to keep her cool, giving a casual, sweeping look back at the hood of the car.

Water droplets. Just the rain.

No beetles. No marching bugs.

She shifted the car into gear and pulled away, turning on the windshield wipers and laughing while her friends made up a ridiculous song about Oxycontin and Darvocet cocktails.

Lacie rolled down her window and shrieked their chorus, "Don't forget the blue footballs! Hut, Hut, HIKE!"

Too many drugs, Sky. She smiled to herself and shook her head.

When she had talked to Dustin about it, Skyler blamed the cheating on the alcohol because that would make more sense to him, to anybody. The truth is, she'd felt nothing. There was some sort of disconnect in her. Some switch went off in her head and, just like that, her affection for Dustin was all used up. Just like that, she was thinking of him in terms of his usefulness.

She tried to get back her feelings. She pored over snapshots of them together: at homecoming, at a neighborhood clean-up, at a party. She even listened to their favorite songs but it was like someone had scooped out the part of her that loved him.

Contrary to what she'd told him, there hadn't been any beer. She really didn't care for the stuff; didn't like the way it slurred her mind. It was so much simpler than that, so simple Skyler couldn't make sense of it. Her feelings for him had died. The stuff about stardust under the sycamore tree? Garbage. She made a deliberate choice to move on, and calculated her way out of the relationship.

They Never Left

The simplest thing was to cheat on him. That way, the cut would be a clean one. She knew, clearly and coldly, that she had to make herself an unbearable, filthy thought in his mind. Something worth hating. The kind of person who could go to a party, get drunk, and cheat on her steady beau.

It worked.

Brian Woz was simply a convenient bonus. A feather in her cap.

Dustin was so lame he told his mom everything, and then his mom called her mom and told her all about her daughter's misdeeds. Skyler stared blankly at her purple biology notebook when her mother entered her room to speak to her. It was typical mom-to-wayward-teenage-daughter talk, life lessons. Skyler queued tears and sniffed her nose in the appropriate places.

But then she had caught a chill. Her mom stared right through all of it and said, simply, "This isn't like you. Is my daughter somewhere in there?"

Skyler jumped up from her bed and hurled the purple notebook at her mother. "You BITCH!" The movements came from her body, but she didn't feel them. It was like someone else went through the motions for her, and she allowed it.

Penciled sketches of the Krebs Cycle and color-coded, outlined notes rained down on both of them and her mother panted, holding the corner of her mouth where the spiraled end of the notebook had caught her skin. When she pulled her hand away, it was smeared with blood.

It didn't make any sense to her. All of this cold detachment, this rage. Her mother was right—where was she? Skyler closed her eyes and bit down on the inside of her cheek, getting ready to speak. She wasn't even sure what she was going to say.

"What is going on in here?" Josh's voice was low and clipped, menacing. Her older brother took two strides over to their mother and examined her face. Silent tears had mixed in with the bit of blood and made little red rivulets on her chin. He stepped across the hall and wet a hand towel, then brought it their mom, putting an arm over her shoulder and ushering her out of the room. He glanced at Skyler as he passed by. "Get your things and get out."

Biology papers fluttered while Skyler stomped through the room, shoving items into her school bag. A sheet of paper shot underneath her bed. It was probably from her blustering around the room so much, but the movement still struck her as odd, almost like an invisible hand had snatched the paper.

She knelt down and reached along the floor beneath the box spring, pawing between old shoeboxes and other weird crap she'd forgotten was under there. The paper rustled when her hand bumped it, and she drew out a crumpled ball of college-ruled notebook paper. She unrolled it and her breath caught.

It was the illustration she'd made last quarter in AP Bio, a full-page rendering of the human heart with all of its ventricles and atria. What startled her was that, even though this was clearly the drawing she'd made—she remembered it, and it was her handwriting labeling all of the different parts—this heart wasn't shaded in with the red colored pencil she'd used. This heart was black.

They Never Left

Skyler crushed the paper back into a ball and frowned. It must have been something she'd done but couldn't remember. It was weird, that was for sure, but now wasn't the time to dwell on it. She tossed it into her bag before zipping it up and heading for the door.

Their laughter rang out like a flock of starlings alighting on a tree branch on a summer evening, chattering and echoing against the sky in a brilliant show of bliss. Skyler threw her head back and laughed again, watching the birds escape her open mouth, chirping their happiness and darting into the farm field.

They weren't far from where Skyler lived—or at least, where she had lived her whole life until a few weeks ago. She threw an empty beer can down by her feet in the truck bed and reached for another. Troy had parked the F-150 in a giant field where a transmission tower loomed in the semi-distance.

It made her think of the one in the backyard where she'd grown up. Her mother and brother were probably sitting there in that stupid house now, on the couch after dinner watching reruns of some sitcom right now.

For the first time ever, she found herself missing the canned audience sound of a laugh track. It told you what was funny, what had gone too far. It told you your parents were in the room with you, or just in the next room, putting dishes away.

She hadn't been there in weeks. Hadn't had a

homecooked meal in longer. The last time she'd sat at a table and eaten a meal her mother had asked, softly, "Sky, what's going on?" Her mom had just watched her daughter stare out the window for five minutes straight—she knew because she timed it—frozen in motion with the fork halfway to her mouth.

Something had snapped inside of Skyler, like a dry twig. She blew up, throwing the fork and her plate at the wall behind her mother. She caught a glimpse of her twisted face in the hallway mirror and screamed in rage. Grabbing the red ceramic pitcher of water from the table, she hurled it at the mirror. Shards of mirrored glass and red pottery exploded against the wall.

Her brother Josh launched himself at her and threw her, bodily, from the house. Their mother walked out to the porch, wiping her face on her sleeve.

"Skyler," her mother cried, "What is this? What demon has a hold of you?"

Skyler stood in the yard, glaring up at her mother and brother. She saw her mother's runny nose, her tears, and felt nothing but contempt. Something in her, a small, faraway voice, told her she was being unfair, that her family didn't deserve this after all they'd been through. Something else overpowered that voice, though, and Skyler spat on the ground before walking away.

Josh stood with his arms wrapped around his mother, watching his little sister calling out curses as she stormed down the street. He stroked his mother's brittle hair while she sobbed.

"What has happened to this family?" Her words came out already strangled, dead on her lips, and it made him weep.

They Never Left

Skyler had watched them from the shadow of the trees in their yard, panting from the exertion of the last few moments. Aside from that, though, she'd felt nothing. A disconnect. The plug pulled from caring about her family.

Skyler, Troy, and Lacie were out celebrating their latest conquest, and that's why they were laughing now. Troy had sold the rest of Charlie's mushroom tea (after they'd each taken hearty gulps from the jug) and was treating them to a Chinese buffet. Lacie stared, mesmerized by the rainbow beams shooting off of the heat lamps, while Skyler ate rolls of sushi directly from the buffet table.

"Miss? Miss? You canna do dah." The waiter was standing across from her, frowning at her moonpie stare and pointing at her.

Lacie grinned at him, absentmindedly shoving hush puppies into her coat pockets.

"You canna do dah! I call manager!" His finger shook as he pointed at her and he cast a worried look toward the kitchen. He didn't seem sure if he should leave her there unsupervised while he went to fetch help.

Skyler snorted with laughter and grabbed Troy from where he was overfilling a bowl with soft serve ice cream. "We need to leave." She wiped tears from her eyes. "I can't take you assholes anywhere!"

"YOU CANNA DO DAH!" Lacie shrieked, pulling another hushpuppy from her pocket. They had driven to the nearby field and were sitting in the bed of Troy's F-150. Every silence brought with it another fit of the giggles, and the hushpuppy sent them over the edge.

Skyler threw back her head and howled with laughter, tears streaming down her face. The huge pylon spread across her vision. At the tip of one of its outstretched arms, she saw something. It was dark, like a shadow of itself, and moved in short, unnatural jerks. Startled, her breath caught in her chest. With her torso already angled back, the small movement was all it took to send her reeling to the ground, her arms flapping like a cartoon as she fell.

"Oh my god. Dude!" Troy had spit out his beer and was peering over the side of the truck, wiping spittle from the edge of his mouth. He couldn't wipe the grin off, though. He fell back into the bed, holding his sides and laughing.

Lacie jumped off the end of the truck and stumbled over to Skyler. She was giggling when she held her hand out to her friend, but faltered when she saw Skyler's face up close.

"Troy . . . Tr—" she stammered, falling back a few steps. "Troy. This is not good. She is not okay." She weaved closer again, brushing her long hair out of the way to take a closer, more focused look. She was sobering by the second. "Skyler! *Skyler? Can you hear me?* Oh shit, Troy . . . "

He had come off of the truck by then, and clutched Lacie's elbows while he stared down at Skyler. The blood was moving in ruby streams through the crabgrassy sand. It was surprisingly red, and wine-dark where it had already soaked into the sand and dirt. Skyler's eyes were glassy and her mouth open, like she wanted to say something. Her face was tilted upward, held there by the unfortunate cinder-block pillow beneath her.

They Never Left

"Lacie . . . oh my god . . . What?" Troy brought a fist to his mouth and bit down, his eyes spastically scanning their surroundings. He turned away and made sick all over the truck tire, then stayed there, bent over and gasping for breath. When he turned around again, his face was stone. "Lacie, we need to get out of here."

Lacie was stroking Skyler's cheek, muttering to herself in a high-pitched, desperate whine. She whipped around and glared at him. "What are you talking about? Just leave her here?" Spittle flew from her mouth as her words broke into frantic sobs.

Troy lurched forward and grabbed her up by an elbow. "Lace, there's half a retirement home's worth of downers in the truck, and we're too fucked up to deal with this. We gotta get out of here."

Lacie yanked her arm out of his grasp but she nodded. She wiped her eyes with the insides of her wrist and sniffed a few times, trying to compose herself. "Okay." Her words came out in breathy gusts. "You're right. Oh, Sky. Baby . . . " Her face crumpled again and she ran to the truck. "Let's go, Troy. We need to go."

※※※※※

Skyler could hear the twangy bass of *Seinfeld* coming from down the hall. She couldn't sleep. Her parents' voices blurred through the walls, but she squeezed her new "Year of the Rooster" pillow and took some comfort in listening to them. Dad had come home from China the week before, and their lives would return to normal now that he was finished teaching there.

Leah McNaughton Lederman

The last few nights—since her dad had come home, really—she'd been having nightmares. The first night it was spiders. The size of quarters, they were fuzzy with black and yellow stripes. They covered the floor of her bedroom, churning and clicking, all three feet deep of them. To make matters worse, her brother appeared in the hallway outside her room and picked up one of the hissing arachnids, inspected it with some curiosity, and proceeded to place it on her arm. Robot-like, he repeated this action several times until not just her arms, but her legs, stomach, neck, and face were covered in hairy black and yellow spiders.

That was the first night. The dreams continued every night, though, and she was afraid to go to sleep. Skyler hugged her pillow again and burrowed deeper into the bed, determined to calm herself, to control herself. Her parents were so tired, she knew, and she didn't need to give them more to worry about. Besides, she was entering the eighth grade in a month. Way too old to be running to her parents about a crummy dream.

Her favorite self-soother at bedtime were the schools of little fish she summoned from memories of trips to the aquarium. She mentioned introducing a fish tank at home, but her dad vetoed it, not wanting to deal with weeping children when the fish floated to the top. She contented herself imagining schools of tiny fish gliding about the room at night, when no one else would know.

Sometimes she rubbed her eyeballs until she saw green and yellow against the backs of her eyelids, a fluorescent tunnel boring into the back of her head.

Then, when she opened them, the room would bounce back with renewed edges and sometimes, if she'd done it just right, everything her eyes fell on was surrounded with a fuzzy haze.

And then she saw it—something new. Something she hadn't brought into the room.

A large, circular spiderweb, round like the school of fish, with wispy edges where the web had trailed off. The whole thing pulsed; energy emanated from its center.

There, at the heart of the feathery cobweb, was some sort of rounded beetle. It looked exactly like one of the buttons from her dad's vintage camel trenchcoat: a deep brown, rounded from its flat base and ridged, faintly, into various sections.

The trenchcoat button beetle floated above her bed, a silent mass of stretched cotton strings. It hovered there for many moments, long enough that she wondered why her imagination hadn't driven it somewhere else. The button beetle must have sensed the thought, because at that moment she was aware of its movement closing in on her. The fish had long since scurried away, and now she missed them and their erratic float pattern.

Slowly, the beetle advanced toward her face on the pillow. She wondered what it might feel like against her cheeks. Would it stick to her eyelids? It didn't stop moving closer. This was not some imaginary school of fish; she did not have the ability to control it.

At the last moment, just before its spiny legs would have grazed her face, she rolled to the side and sat up, watching as it dropped to the pillow and gripped the soft indent where her head had been. It pierced the fabric with bladed legs.

Skyler jumped out of bed, sheets and blankets trailing after her. "DADDY!" The rooster pillow rolled after her until inertia slowed it and it wobbled to a stop like a discarded coin. She hazarded a look behind her and saw, out of the piles of bedding, smaller cobwebs were emerging and . . . standing? They were walking after her.

Her dad was sitting bolt upright when she sprinted into his room, his arms outstretched to her. "What is it, baby girl?"

Skyler's words sputtered out in incoherent syllables between her sobs. Finally, she lifted a trembling finger to the cobweb creatures trailing into the room. She turned away from the sight of them, bunching his t-shirt with fists that could squeeze charcoal into diamonds.

That's when she saw them coming from the other direction, peeling themselves out of the corners of the window and hopping onto the side of his bed. They stood on flimsy legs and walked with their arms outstretched, reaching. They looked just like the pylon that loomed over their backyard.

Her scream was silent, a desperate wail. "They're everywhere!"

A laugh track was blaring on the television down the hall. She heard her dad call out to her mom, but there was no answer. She was pretty good at falling asleep in front of the TV.

Skyler's father stroked her hair and kissed the top of her head. He looked everywhere his daughter looked, and where she had pointed, but saw nothing there, nothing out of the ordinary. Nothing that would cause a young woman, nearly in the eighth grade, to huddle into his chest and sob, terrified.

He ran through a list of explanations in his head. It wasn't the first time he'd thought of it that week. All of these nightmares, it wasn't like her.

Skyler was a level-headed, reasonable girl and had always been that way. Since he'd come home, though, something had been wrong. Something felt wrong about the whole house.

Joe took a deep breath. As he exhaled, he formed the words, a low grumble issuing out into the room. "Oh, Lord Jesus." He said it again and again, not knowing what else to do, and noticing the tension in Skyler's shoulders easing slightly. "Baby girl, it's okay. *Shhh.*"

He held his daughter close until her breathing had slowed, even if her eyes were still stretched wide open, seeing things that weren't there.

"Daddy?" She was whispering.

"Hm?"

"They don't like that. You praying like that."

Joe paused, considering this. "Good. You do it with me now, okay?"

Together the two of them prayed, calling on the Lord like his mother had taught him to do.

He kissed her head again. "Show me where they came from, will you? I know you're scared. I'm trying to figure out how to help."

Skyler nodded and, with a snuffle, unfolded herself from his lap. The two of them padded cautiously to her room. Her sheets and blankets were strewn about all over the place. Joe shrugged, not knowing what to make of the scene before him. He realized that Skyler had gone stiff in the shoulders again.

"What is it, Sky? What's wrong?"

Ashen-faced, she pointed to the bed. Joe looked. Nothing unusual, her pillows still at the head of the bed. She really liked the Year of the Rooster pillow he'd bought for her in China, and had slept with it every night since he'd come home.

"That pillow shouldn't be there." Skyler's voice was hoarse. "It fell off the bed when I ran to your room. Why is it back on the bed?"

Joe's face darkened. It took him three long strides to get to the bed and pick up the pillow. It was warm to the touch. Frowning, he put his hand on the bed and her other pillow. Cool. The rooster pillow was emanating its own heat. He felt a wave of dizziness, standing there holding it. The air was thick, like he was sitting too close to the heater vent in a car.

Without really understanding why, he reached for the garbage can on the floor and pulled out the plastic bag. He stuffed the pillow inside it. Once he was able to hold the pillow from the handles of the plastic bag, the carsick feeling left him.

"Go on and sit with your mom, Sky. I think I've got the problem right here." He didn't want to come near her with the pillow, even it was in a trash bag.

～՛℘℘ℓ℘℘℘ℓ℘

Joe took a knife from the kitchen drawer and plunged it into the pillow. Then he did it again, and again, until there was nothing but scraps of fabric swimming in a sea of white feathers inside the metal bucket he'd placed it in. He took a moment to make sure none of the feathers had landed on the ground outside of the bucket, or anywhere else. Then he lit a match and tossed it in.

He prayed the whole time the fire licked upwards, prayed when he doused the charred remains with water and buried the bucket in the shadow of the pylon. Even in the middle of the night, the giant metal structure cast a shadow from the stardust above it.

"What's going on, Joe?" Linda asked him. He turned to find his wife standing in the doorway, her arms crossed against the evening's chill. The light from the kitchen illuminated the worry on her face.

She walked over to him, where he was digging a hole in the corner of the yard. In sentences punctuated by his huffing breath and the sound of shoveling, he told his wife everything that had happened that night. He told her about his confirmed suspicions that something hadn't been right since he'd come home.

Linda listened, nodding occasionally. Finally, she said, "I didn't know you believed in demons. I don't even know if I do. A pillow?"

Joe scoffed. She hadn't seen Skyler, hadn't held her trembling body. He rested on the shovel and bit the inside of his cheek.

When it was clear to Linda that he was done speaking to her, she turned and trudged back into the house. She went to where Skyler was still sleeping on the couch and sat next to her, pushing a few strands of hair out of her daughter's face.

Jay Leno was finishing up with his monologue when Joe came around the corner, resting a muddy hand on the door jamb.

"It doesn't matter that you don't believe in demons, Lin. The person who made it does."

Leah McNaughton Lederman

Joe Montaigne had only ever wanted to tour the world. Instead, he got a family, a farm, and a few decent pets. The farm had gotten away from him, though, and the cat was questionable. But he had a resilient wife who humored his restless spirit, taking care of the children while he wandered the earth.

He figured he'd stay home a while, this time around. This latest trip to China had taken its toll. Josh was old enough, busy with school and sports, but Skyler . . . clearly something was wrong, there. He still wasn't sure what had happened the week before, and his mind was starting to tell him it had been less about the pillow and more about his absence around the house. Inwardly, he vowed to change that. But how the hell does a pillow cause nightmares and hallucinations?

His brother Mike, divinity school dropout, had offered his two cents when Joe called him. "Sometimes when people worship critters, those critters get a big head and cause a little trouble. They might tag along for the ride across the ocean as a stowaway. We don't respond well to it because we're not used to that sort of critter. But the treatment is the same. Just stomp them out."

Joe scratched his chin thoughtfully on his way to retrieve the mail. The old mailbox was slanted at an angle from all the times the snowplows had bumped it during the winter months. Linda was always bugging him to set it in concrete, or put up one of those plywood walls.

They Never Left

He tugged open the box—it was always jammed—and reeled back, cringing. Yellow and black spiders were spilling out of the metal container; some of them had jettisoned onto him from the force of opening the mailbox. Joe brushed them off with terrified strokes and continued flailing backward.

His own ragged, panicked breathing was so loud in his ears he never heard the truck coming down the street, and certainly never saw it.

The driver of the truck never slept well again, though, and his wife silently cursed the suicidal stranger. Taking your own life is one thing, she'd mutter. But you don't have to force a stranger to get involved.

❧ℓℓℓℓ

With mute horror on her face, Skyler watched her friends get in the truck and drive away.

Don't leave me, she whispered. But no sound came out. She was alone, and absolutely helpless. She stared up at the pylon, feeling the tears roll down the side of her face, pooling cold in her ears and neck.

Her parents never knew she had heard them talking about that stupid pillow, out there in the yard. She'd hurried inside and feigned sleep on the couch. She understood her mother's incredulity. None of it made any sense.

What her dad had done—burning the pillow and burying it—it didn't work. He died a week later, hit by a truck on his way back from getting the mail.

She'd been suspicious then of what she was sure of now, watching the dark figure make its way down the pylon. Clumps of sand formed their way into pincered arachnids and inched toward her.

The demons, they were real.

And they had never left.

Author and Artist Bios

Jennifer Barnett has been active in a variety of artforms for over thirty years. Her creations are usually pen and ink on card stock in a standard 8 1/2 x 11 format. Jennifer feels most at home surrounded by nature and her happiest place is under the trees and by a river in her favorite park. Most of Jennifer's art centers on multiple faces and eyes, giving a variety of windows into different fractures of the soul. Jennifer has three children and lives with her husband on Indianapolis's northwest side. Naturally prolific, she typically creates two hundred works in a single year.

Christina Blanch is a relative newcomer to the world of creating comics but not to reading them or teaching with them. An educator who uses comic books to teach in the higher education classroom and the force behind the online SuperMOOC courses, Blanch has now produced her first comic series, *The Damnation of Charlie Wormwood*, with co-writer Chris Carr and artist Chee, coming this year from Source Point Press. Her work is also

featured in Aw Yeah Comics and Papercutz, including *Tales from the Crypt*. Blanch owns Aw Yeah Comics in Muncie, Indiana, moderates at Comic Conventions, and is penning several chapters and comic-related books, one which is based on her doctoral dissertation, "Searching for the Comic Book Scholar." Follow her at @christyblanch.

Autumn Nicole Brown uses multiple artistic approaches to explore the quiet moments of life, those fleeting minutes that pass by so many of us. For years, she has struggled against the mainstream current rushing us through this life. By creating art, and through her art's content, she is finding that the slower, down-to-earth version of life is more appealing. Autumn lives in Oklahoma with her husband and three daughters. When she's not trying to balance family, homeschool, and art, she's following the trend of eating too many tacos.

Isabella Christiana is a debut author from Ohio. She has always had a passion for writing stories that capture the reader's attention. Izzy hopes to be a more involved writer and plans on reaching a wide audience with different types of writing. She wants to make a difference with her writing and wants to connect her writings to issues seen today. Izzy is already continuing many projects and this will most certainly not be the last time you will see her name.

Sanda Cook is Romanian-born, and studied art at the Brasor School of Arts in Bucharest. She strives to brings

worlds together each time her brush touches canvas. Her art serves as a window to her journeys through Europe, Japan, and the United States. She is listed among the "Most Prolific Painters in Metro Detroit" by the *Detroit Free Press*. Her work has been featured on several mass media platforms, including PBS's "Detroit Performs." She has also been shown on "Live on D" and "Detroit's Local Four Today." Her work is displayed at The Scarab Club, The River's Edge Gallery, Downriver Council of the Arts, the Carr Center for the Arts, the Detroit Artist Market, Grosse Point Art Center, Ariana Gallery, 4731 Studios, and the Padzieski Art Gallery. You can find her online at USartboutique.com, fineartamerica.com, and artistsofmichigan.org. Sanda is also heavily involved in local charity events and donates her work wherever the opportunity presents itself. Art, for her, is a way of being alive, of connecting to the mysteries of the universe, nature, and the magnificent human soul.

Coriander Friess is the mother of five and holds a degree in special education. She is an avid knitter and voracious reader, occasionally doing both simultaneously. She endures a multitude of scary movies because her husband of twenty-two years loves them. This is her short story debut.

Michelle Joy Gallagher is a poet from Sacramento, CA. She enjoys mixing poetry with other artistic mediums, and pushing her own artistic comfort zones in the process.

When she is using visceral imagery and playing with the elasticity of language, she is happiest. Michelle is author of poetry chapbooks *A New Mourning* and *S=K log W*, and her poetry also makes appearances in *The Rejected #1* and *#2* by Stan Konopka (Source Point Press), and *Siren's Call Ezine*. Her spoken word poetry is featured on Boneman's Tattoo Room, from their album *The Dogwood Tree*.

Dani Herrera is a mixed media artist who likes to work with unconventional materials such as old clothes, damaged books, even dryer lint! She loves the saying, "One man's junk is another man's treasure" and always tries to put it into action.

Amy Hunter lives in southeast Texas. Born in 1983, she wanted to be a professional karaoke singer until the stories in her mind became more interesting than music. Writing since her early teens, she now has three published short stories: "Core," appearing in Scout Media's *A Journey of Words*, "Salted Ground," appearing in *A Haunting of Words*, and her

312

latest, "Queen of the Waves," appearing in *Café Macabre*. To learn more about Amy, you can visit her Facebook page.

Cora Linden is a contemporary mixed media artist residing in London, ON. She has been participating in group and solo art shows since 1983. Cora is a lifelong student of psychology and sociology. She is fascinated by what goes on in people's heads as well as how they relate to and communicate with each other.

Cora's works are 2D and 3D mixed media interpretations of her observations and experiences. She incorporates re-purposed objects, specialty papers, and different textural elements to tell the story. You can see more of Cora's work at
https://www.facebook.com/coralindenartworks/

Stefani Manard is a writer and podcaster from Detroit. She has written several books and comics, including *Secrets Best Kept*, *Aeonian*, *The Last Heist*, and *Psycho Path*. While predominantly a horror writer, she is currently working on the superhero comic *Vigilance* with Freestyle Komics, as well as several short comics for anthologies of different genres. She hosts a show that highlights indie creators of all types on the Podcast Detroit network called "The Way Station," as well as a history podcast called "Shot of History."

When not writing she enjoys petting every dog she sees, binge watching *Black Books* on the regular, and

Arting in any way that she can. She is a novice painter, piano player, and singer who frequently annoys her dogs with her musical antics.

Leah McNaughton Lederman is a writer and freelance editor from the Indianapolis area, where she lives with her husband, three kids, three cats, and dumb dog. Her poems and short stories have been published in Scout Media's *A Matter of Words, A Contract of Words,* Clarendon House's *Fireburst* and *Cadence,* and Indie Author's Press *Issues of Tomorrow: A Sci-fi Anthology.* As an editor, she has worked in fiction, nonfiction, poetry.

Kari McElroy is an author and artist, her primary project the award-winning graphic series, *Regarding Dandelions* (running for over five years! Available every Wednesday at Comic Fury, Smackjeeves, The Duck Webcomics, and Tapas). She's a traveler and a lover of music, art and all things storytelling. She lives in Indianapolis with her husband and two dogs. Find out more at www.karimcelroy.com.

Scarlett Driscoll Once upon a time her evil twin sister forced her to write down all her nightmares for a sinister book of horrors. She composed this under duress. Her sister cured her writer's block only by the prospect of certain doom.

Crystal O'Rourke dabbles in photography, with her #creepyhalls collection, and worked in journalism as the Indie Huntress. She lives in Ann Arbor, where she dabbles in watercolor.

Marianna Pescosta lives in Italy, where she has drawn and colored several comics, winning both scholarships and awards in the process. Her American comic book work includes stories in *Tales of Mr. Rhee* and *Nightmare World* with writer Dirk Manning (Devil's Due Publishing) and she is also the illustrator of *Haunted High-ons* with the hip-hop band Twiztid from Source Point Press. When she has time to use social media she posts on Instagram @maripescosta.

Kasey Pierce is an author from the Metro Detroit area. Her horror short story collection *Pieces of Madness* (Rocket Ink Studios) gave her residency on the comic convention circuit in 2015. She joined the ranks of Source Point Press shortly after and it was her acclaimed sci-fi comic series *Norah* that made her a household name in indie comics—eventually becoming a flagship creator for the company. Since then, Kasey has toured throughout the US giving her panel on marketing and selling indie comics, "Good Luck with That." Her Viking-horror comic series *Seeress* and indigenous sci-fi *Mexica* are both projected to release May 2019. She's currently in the works on a paranormal space opera, *The Other People Who Live Here.* To find out more, visit facebook.com/kosmickasey.

Corinne Roberts writes and illustrates the ongoing web comic series *Out and About*. She has also written/illustrated *Trip to Trekka* and *Imaginary Sea 1,2,3!* Along with her books, she illustrated the web comic, *Kitty Game* and the card game, *Unreal Estate*. You can see more of her work at: www.corinneroberts.net

K. Lynn Smith is an artist and writer from Michigan. Her artwork has won the Michigan Press Award, as well as the Helen Victoria Haynes World Peace Cartoon Contest. She

is the writer and artist of the western comic *Plume*, published by Devil's Due Comics, and has been involved with projects such as *Garfield*, the Strength in Numbers Studios's video game *Tuebor*, *Afterglow* written by Pat Shand, and *Hope*, co-created with Dirk Manning.

Harlow West is a New York based author, illustrator, and professional hot mess with resting grumpy cat face. From her humble beginnings of writing short stories about boys that lived in pumpkins and the painfully awful poetry written for her high school poetry club to writing about nerds and their naughty bits, Harlow has written everything from horror to fantasy to nerdy, nerdy romance. Because

hey, nerds need love too! When not covered up to her elbows in one kind of ink or another, Harlow spends more time than is probably socially acceptable with her nose buried between the pages of one book or another. Like, seriously guys, it's a problem. Harlow currently lives in a compartment in the city with "the hubs" and her two geriatric, codependent kitties, Princess Bitch-face and Squishy.

Behind the Scenes of
Café Macabre

The idea for *Café Macabre* came to me at about two in the morning in the summer of 2016. The fantastic horror stories I was editing at that time had melted together in my tired mind and the result was, I was taking the puppy out for one last piddle and found myself checking over my shoulder in classic "I'm pretty freaked out right now" fashion.

Push come to shove, that puppy would be no protection against whatever was watching me from the shadows.

Up to my elbows in the stories of several talented writers, at the same time exchanging emails with each of them regarding their work, it was clear to me I had access to a goldmine of talent. The different writers' voices complemented one another so thoroughly, in life and in prose, I knew it was something special. It was a crime not to share it.

I gathered my writers with the goal of creating a prose party where I could sit back at the table and listen to these different voices go back and forth. Throughout the compilation process, I thought of the Algonquin circle and of the famous late-night party with Byron and the Shelleys that birthed *Frankenstein*.

Okay, but when I invite people to my house to sit at my table and talk, I don't mandate what they talk about. That's why I didn't call for a theme when I requested stories for this collection. I chose each writer specifically because I wanted their voice at my party, and I really wanted to see what they came up with without any further prompting than "write something scary." At times I regretted this as a potentially neophyte move, but when I finished reading each of the contributions, I knew I was right to trust my gut.

Why all-female? I really don't have an axe to grind. Bottom line is, as someone with five brothers and, at the inception of this book, the only woman living in a household of males, I wanted to hear more women's voices.

Whether women fear different things, or express that fear differently in their art, is the stuff of thesis papers and dissertations. In other words, I'm not touching it with a ten-foot pole. Not here.

I will say this, however, citing the anecdotal evidence afforded me by my work on this anthology and in freelance editing: Certain themes emerge; ideas overlap spontaneously.

Animals were pets, protectors, or monsters. Men? Absent, deadbeat, dismissive, or threatening. Houses were either malevolent or inviting, and certainly more than mere dwelling places. They were characters in the stories.

And then, memories. Obviously, anything haunted is going to deal with the past, but these stories ask deeper question. Do we write our own pasts, or do our pasts write us? If we can't remember our sins, will the guilt consume us anyway? What happens when the crimes against our ancestors haunt us?

In each step of putting this book together, from its

inception to the Kickstarter, I asked for input and advice from these ladies. In the inaugural, invitational email I sent out, I wrote, "'Reply All' this shit to the max—it will be good to hear from one another, as I hope to make this a collaborative effort. Lord knows I need all the help I can get!"

So, we collaborated. We read each other's work and offered feedback based on some peer-reviewy-type questions I'd put together (once an English teacher . . .). I didn't want a "top-down" mentality and, although I was editing the collection, I didn't want too much of my stink all over every story. I wanted *all* of our stinks on every story.

The collaborative process of the book is most clearly manifested in the cover K Lynn Smith produced. The lynchpin for all of the stories, it was the very table I'd been working to create from the start of the project.

My prompt to the group regarding the cover was this: "There's a table at a gathering. On the table are representative items from each story. What is the image from your story?"

There was fun back and forth on that. My mantra throughout was, "I want people to look at this and say, 'how do I get invited to *that* party?'"

When (the incredible) K Lynn sent me the finalized piece I was a little verklempt. I shared it with the *Café Macabre* team and told them, "Y'all know this project was a long time coming. I'm a different person now than I was when this project started."

It was true. I had edited nine novels in as many months, several comic scripts and short stories, and given birth to a baby girl. Plus, I had walked through the process of compiling and editing this book. Life was different, now. I learned things about myself.

The idea for accompanying illustrations was not my own. For that, I credit a non-female source, one Dirk Manning. It was an invaluable suggestion for which I wish him to receive full credit. He said it best: "I think it's important to remind people once in a while that I do have some limited use in their lives."

I have always been interested in the ways literature intersects with art. Heck, I've choreographed to Emily Dickinson poetry. Here was a fantastic opportunity to add more voices to the mix, and create a three-dimensional quality to the collection.

It was a wonderful new experience for me to work with artists. In doing so, I happily took Dirk Manning's advice from *Write or Wrong: A Writer's Guide to Creating Comics* about how to approach the elusive artist unicorn. Thus, my involvement with each writer/artist pair varied as needed, from "can you make it look like this?" to "will you read the story and come up with something based on what YOU see?"

(Shameless plug: You should buy *Write or Wrong* if you're interested in writing and in collaborating with artists.)

The House Awoke
Written by Leah McNaughton Lederman
Photography by Crystal O'Rourke

I was pregnant with my second child, alone in my house, editing. My long-time cat companion, Midi, was sleeping on the coffee table and I was laying on the floor. Out of nowhere, I felt a light gust of wind; the unmistakable feeling of air being disturbed as someone—particularly someone little, like a child— runs past.

There was nothing there, in the direction the person/thing would have gone (given my split second, instinctive mathematical calculations on trajectory, etc.), but when I looked back at the cat for confirmation that something odd had just happened, she gave it to me.

Midi was sitting up, alert, her pupils fully dilated, staring in the same direction I'd looked.

I got up and left the house immediately, pacing on the sidewalk like it was a fire drill and I was in kindergarten. It was a long time before I could catch my breath and calm myself down.

At least once a year, a picture frame falls off the wall in that same area. It's always struck me as a playful thing the house does, even though I'm not prone to believe in that sort of thing. It was intriguing enough that my brain teased out the story. One day, I sat down and typed it out. It was the first piece written for *Café Macabre*.

Based on the photography work she does in her #creepyhalls collection, I wanted Crystal O'Rourke to compose and edit the photo. Crystal remarked, "My photo for this reflects the same silence I try to capture in my "Creepy Halls" collection. I like to think it caught the moment and reflected a weary mother's side table but also captured the horror and pain of the story, which is left largely unspoken for the reader to experience on a more visceral level."

I knew we needed a baby monitor to complete the look, and it just so happened my super awesome neighbor had a really old (I mean, *old)* baby monitor that she was willing to donate. The baby monitor is the item I included for this story on the cover.

Also on that nightstand? Aside from the obligatory glass of wine, there's a baby "tag" blanket purchased for me at 2016 Toledo Fantasticon by Kasey Pierce. There's also the Scout Media anthology, *A Contract of Words*, which includes my story "The Women No One Sees." Its cover design was Amy Hunter's, who contributed a story and art for this collection.

The Eleventh Hour
Written by Kasey Pierce
Photography by Sanda Cook

Kasey and I forged a friendship through editorial notes and the emails exchanged while we worked together on her short story collection *Pieces of Madness*. She was one of the first voices I heard at the *Café Macabre* table.

For this collection, we both wrote stories centered on a common interest of ours: memory, individual and cultural. The item she chose for the tabletop was the copy of the Latin Vulgate (*Biblia Sacra Vulgata)*. Initially we tried Seamore the Seal, but that was a little weird, even for my party.

Her story is an intensely personal one, and she told me, "This story was inspired by the time I went way too far down a rabbit hole. I went full Sarah Connor and it caused problems in my relationships and at home. Even my brother had to come over and talk me down. I didn't sleep."

The photograph featured in Kasey's story was taken by Sanda Cook and owned by Kasey, though she sent it to me as a gift. She told me it was a memento for me, and that she wanted me to have it "as a reminder of your ideas coming to life."

Steps
Written by Kari McElroy
Art by Kari McElroy

Kari and I met because she was my oldest son's librarian. I didn't know her all that well when I asked her to contribute a story, I just knew she was really awesome, plus a disciplined writer and artist. Every Wednesday she gives us more of her brilliant coming-of-age/slice-of-life webcomic, "Regarding Dandelions."

Over the course of this collection, Kari became dear to me. We talked about story ideas over microbrew growlers in her backyard; we exchanged emails while she lived across the world for months at a time.

When it comes to her story and its accompanying art, her words are best: "My story is about a woman in an emotionally abusive relationship who finds dark escape in her sleeping mind. That said, my inspiration is going to sound TERRIBLE: my partner partially inspired this one. Bear with me. He didn't inspire the husband character—he has the liveliest sleep life I've ever witnessed. I've seen him wander around, play on his phone, have conversations, everything. The man is a sleeping marvel. At times, though, the stuff he sleep-chatters about is downright terrifying. Spending years witnessing this sort of separate sleep life with no waking awareness definitely played into the inspiration for this story."

When I asked her to comment on the art she produced for this collection, she said, "This one stressed me out a little bit. Most of my artistic energy is spent on graphic novel work, but I didn't want this to feel cartoony in any way. I spent a lot of time looking through the art from *Scary Stories to Tell in the Dark*. Remember those books? They scared the hell out of me when I was a kid (and maybe a little now? Are we being that honest?). I don't have the skill set to emulate the work—I still don't know how the artist does it—but I tried to get that creepy vibe in my mind as I went forward with my piece."

"Steps" is represented on the cover in the Fitbit one of the guests is wearing. The curly-haired one. I'll only add one boring editorial note—normally, numerals are typed out. Given the nature of this story, I left them all as numerals, even when it was a non-Fitbit number.

Manifestation
Written by Stefani Manard
Art by Autumn Nicole Smith

Stefani was also one of the first *Café Macabre* voices, and another writer I have befriended via emails and Microsoft Word comments. We worked together on her stellar collection of horror stories with Jason Chmielewski, *Secrets Best Kept*.

Regarding her story "Manifestation" (represented on the cover by the crow) she writes, "I did lose my cat, who was my first pet, and I did kinda go batshit for a bit, but not on this level. I tried to write out some of my residual grief in this story, probably for catharsis. But most of it is fiction, thankfully. This is kind of my love letter to him, as weird as that sounds."

What I like best about Stefani's contribution to *Café Macabre* is the stillness of the story. A maddening silence and desperate loneliness. This is what I saw captured beautifully in the artwork of Autumn Nicole Brown. I am a huge fan of her paintings and installation pieces, and knew she'd be perfect for Stefani's story.

She definitely was. In her own words, "I wanted to convey more than just information on the details of the story. One of the things that the story left me with was a hollow, sad feeling. So with my composition I wanted to evoke that somewhat. I wanted to depict the character in one of her most desperate moments that might be visually (in someone's mind) overlooked. Yet, also one that could be a real moment in someone's life. All of that but in a very convoluted way. It's never a linear process."

Autumn and I have never met in person, but we have exchanged enough Facebook messages and posts that I call her a friend, and know that we "get" each other. Strangers from across the country, we are both in the trenches as creative moms. There's a special slice of pie for us.

Beating a Dead Dog
Written by Scarlett Driscoll
Art by Jennifer Barnett

I first read this only a few days after finishing Stefani Manard's "Manifestation" and always knew these two would have to be side by side in the collection, if for no other reason than my own dark humor.

On the inspiration for this story, my sister says, "This story was a dark fantasy. My dog pissed on the floor while I was PMSing." The dog collar on the cover belongs to this story.

As for the art, I had been a long-time fan of Jennifer Barnett's work since we met at the Alley Cat (a renowned dive bar in Indianapolis) and bonded over a mutual appreciation of the boots I'd glued bottlecaps to (I still have them).

I knew this would be the perfect story for Jennifer because her art is so abstract, and a story this dark and violent needed to be farther removed from realism. Still, this piece created a challenge for her. She later told me, "Anything based in realism or anything created as a request (rather something that came more through organic inspiration) can be a challenge."

Jennifer has this to say about her process: "While reading the story, the energy from the piece was absorbed into my being. From there, through my pen, that energy transferred itself (through me) into the creation."

Red Woman
Written by Michelle Joy Gallagher
Photograph from the Grant Foreman Collection, used with slight alteration with permission from The Oklahoma Historical Society

Michelle is someone I knew from social media and hadn't interacted with in real life, though for a long time I had convinced myself I met her at Fantasticon Toledo in 2016. She assured me that wasn't her. (It was some other stunning, formidable woman.)

Michelle's biting wit, combined with the compelling way she arranged words and emotions in the poetry she posted online, convinced me to ask her to write me some prose. I knew she was a perfect fit before she did.

When I asked her about this story, Michelle said, "We were asked to give our voice and perspective to the horror genre and to me, the most horrific things have been actual events human beings have perpetrated against human beings. I wanted to portray this event in a way that could connect the past with the present and to also show the generational impact the colonization of the US and the trail of tears had and is still having on modern natives."

Michelle found this photograph of Crazy Snakes campground and obtained permission for its use. We then altered it, throwing in the modern day medical IV stand. We both thought it mixed the two worlds in a compelling, haunting way. Similarly, the choice she made for her story's objects on the cover—a syringe and stone-carved ceremonial knife—blend historic violence with present day.

Hardly a Scratch
Written by Leah McNaughton Lederman
Art by Marianna Pescosta

This story was inspired by a violently jarring nightmare. When I woke up from it, I was in the throes of an anxiety attack severe enough to make me worry I was having a heart attack. My arm hurt and was tingly, the whole bit.

329

The gist of the nightmare was that something so ghastly had occurred to someone I loved, and I'd gone crazy. Members of my family were trying to bring me back around to sanity.

That's the kernel of it in this story: Cathleen has made a grave error, and in order to protect herself from the guilt and horror, her brain has shut off certain parts of itself.

The idea of the gas explosion came from a real-life insurance fraud scheme gone wrong here in Indianapolis. Nearly an entire housing block was destroyed, and people died as a result.

I was racing against the clock to finish this before the birth of my third child. I didn't make it. This story came with me to the hospital and I worked on it there after my daughter was born.

As frustrating as it was to have a delay (stupid baby!), having to fuss over it and re-work it showed me there was a way to incorporate my old friend Esther into the story. The deranged cleaning lady is included in three of my published stories: "Dust to Dust," "Lithium Sandwich," and "The Women No One Sees."

Marianna Pescosta loved the cognitive dissonance in the story, and composed artwork that blew me out of the water. She said, "These are ghost-like characters with no face (like when you use long exposure for a portrait and you move your head), all compenetrating, and Cathleen is in the middle, overwhelmed by noises and fuzzy memories."

(I will tell you all that I had to look up "compenetrate.")

Marianna also observed, aptly, that "making an illustration for a writer is like being a tailor. We do pieces that fit perfectly for that writer."

Send in the Clowns
Written by Harlow West
Art by Harlow West

Harlow and I have never met in person, but I have been so charmed by her in my interactions with her online in several writing groups that she was one of the first people I thought of as an addition to this collection. She did not disappoint!

Regarding her contribution, she writes: "The story is about an ethereal carnival and was inspired by, well, the circus obviously. One day while working on something completely random I came across that old saying about running away with the circus. It made me think about language and how one person can interpret a phrase completely different than another person. So I thought of all the weird ways that the saying could be interpreted. My story is just one of them.

Harlow is also one of infuriatingly talented people who can draw as well as write. I didn't quite realize it when I initially asked her to contribute a story, but then I saw her posting about artwork she was doing, and asked if she wouldn't mind coming up for something to accompany her story.

About the artwork, she said, "I wanted to capture the innate creepiness of clowns with a throwback to those old school funhouses that you don't really see anymore." The clown on the cover, of course, belongs to Harlow's story.

Queen of the Waves
Written by Amy Hunter
Art by Amy Hunter

This story was one of the first completed because it wasn't initially intended for *Café Macabre*. Amy had written this to submit to another anthology (one of Scout Media's "Of Words" series). She ended up using a different story for that anthology, I didn't waste time capitalizing on the situation and giving her story a home.

Amy wrote "Queen of the Waves" about a bit of local history. She says, "It's part of local history. I live about an hour from Galveston, so I grew up hearing it. Galveston Island is known for its haunted history. There are museums on the island dedicated to the storm and memorial statues. There's also a small theater that plays short films about it."

In preparation for writing this piece, she listened to several first-hand accounts of Hurricane Katrina survivors.

I know from my interactions with her on social media that Amy is a graphic designer and has put together covers for several books—including *A Contract of Words* (which includes my story "The Women No One Sees" and is shown on the nightstand in Crystal O'Rourke's photograph for "The House Awoke"). She had the best idea for capturing the essence of her story in an image, and I was elated when she agreed to provide the image for this collection.

Oh, and Amy's chosen item for the table? The rosary.

Lover to the Unknown
Written by Isabella Christiana
Art by Corinne Roberts

I am a sucker for a good diary story, and this one hits the spot! Isabella's story, represented on the cover by the open journal, is a haunting story about isolation and victimization. The journal-entry format perfectly captures the gnawing resentments and pressures of high school. Because our personal writing doesn't follow the same strictures of grammar and spelling, there are intentional grammatic mistakes.

Corinne's watercolors are breathtaking, and often whimsical. Her watercolors reflect the lonely desperation of the story. While she was going through the steps to put this image together, I was really impressed with how carefully she planned out each color to be included. Through the process of compiling this book, I've become a huge fan of Corinne's art, process, and outlook. Her advice to new artists has been a comfort to me several times over: "If at the end of a very long tiring day, the worst thing that happened to you was creating a piece of art that goes in the trash . . . then life is good and try again the next day."

Monster in the Closet
Written by Coriander Friess
Art by Ashley Jagodzinski

This is another story written by my brilliant seester. After I'd approached her about writing a story for this collection and she'd read "The House Awoke," the idea came to her fairly spontaneously: "My own children are no longer babes in arms but increasingly independent. My biggest fear was that I had failed to do thoroughly as a mother, and that a son I loved and had raised would be a monster. I came at that thought slantwise. Monsters in the closet or under the bed are perennial childhood fears. Raising a serial killer is a harder feat to tackle."

Cori and I have worked together on resumes and work emails for years, and while she has often given me feedback on stories, this was the first time I ever edited a story for her. To be honest, I was a little nervous. You can imagine my relief when she said my edits were like Photoshop—it brought out the best version of the story (she paraphrased Tina Fey's quote on Photoshop, "it's okay to make a photo look as if you were caught on your best day in the best light.")

For the artwork on this story, I approached Ashley Jagodzinski, whom I'd always admired in graduate school. I knew she was smart as a whip but had never known she had mad pencil skills until she posted a few portraits on Facebook. I knew, immediately, that her work would fit this collection perfectly.

Repossessed
Written by Christina Blanch
Art by Dani Herrera

I can't tell you how excited I was to work with a woman of Christina Blanch's caliber, and elated that she agreed to provide the thirteenth story for *Café Macabre* as a Kickstarter bonus.

She and I have never met but I've become a fan of hers. In emails, she told me about her writing process for this story: "This was the first time I wrote a horror short story. I've written comics, academic articles, contributed articles to websites, and a dissertation among other things, but not short stories. So, I stepped out of my comfort zone to do this. And I was panicked. I had so many ideas but kept thinking "this would be a great comic!" so I would think of something else. When time was running out, I panicked and read some of Ray Bradbury's *Zen in the Art of Writing* and it was inspiring. I decided to read a book which I now call my secret weapon (sorry, it's a secret!) and as soon as I read about mummified cats, I knew where to start. When I was remodeling a room in my "old" house, I also found a covered-up fireplace but it contained a mummified cat in it. That's all it took. I just started writing. I didn't know the ending at all. In fact, a friend of mine read the first half and said that they couldn't wait to see how it ended. I said, "me, too!"

To accompany the story, Dani Herrera created the fireplace and witch bottle using silk, cotton, and corduroy. I love the corduroy paneling! I met Dani in 2010; in fact, her husband was one of my first students. I have a visceral response to her artwork—the textures, the colors, the contrasts—they sing to me. I own seven of her original pieces, as well as a few prints.

Dani is an unstoppable force in the art world, and when I thought of her as an artist for the second bonus story, I was almost embarrassed to ask her because I hadn't asked her sooner.

They Never Left
Written by Leah McNaughton Lederman
Art by Cora Linden

When I was around four years old, my dad came home from a gospel-preaching trip to China (it's illegal to preach the gospel there, so he posed as an English teacher. He even dropped off suitcases filled with bibles at the airport).

I vaguely recall having several nightmares, including the one with the yellow and black spiders which my brother was putting on me. I very distinctly recall the trenchcoat button beetle landing on my pillow—I was not asleep at the time—and then running to my dad's room. I watched the cobweb pylons climb up the side of his bed and come toward me.

It never occurred to me until several years later that my dad hadn't seen the creatures, but he did pray with me. He left the room and got rid of a specific pillow that he'd brought home (this I know from speaking to older brothers). I don't know how he knew it was the pillow, since he'd brought lots of things home, and I don't know what he did with it, but the nightmares stopped after that.

I always wanted to capture this strange episode in my life and was grateful that *Café Macabre* afforded me the opportunity to do so. Since it is a bonus story and written after the cover was completed, there's no object on the table. But if I could bring something to the party for this one, it would probably be the rooster pillow.

The fact that Cora Linden was able and willing to contribute to this project still amazes me. I'm a huge fan of her work, and love what she came up with as a response to my story. We went back and forth on whether to have an airplane light on the pylon—indeed, I worried about including it in the story, as my research indicated specific height requirements for airplane lights—but ultimately, we both felt it added something that needed to be there.

In Cora's words, this is "a multi-step mixed media piece. First, I paint the canvas. Next, I sketch out the key elements for the picture on textured paper. I cut out the pieces and collage them in layer onto the canvas. Once that's cured, I add detail with pens and pencils." In our email exchanges, Cora told me about a recurring thought she had while working on this piece: "It's that moment when you admit to yourself that you need help, you reach out, and then you realize that no one's there for you."

Leah McNaughton Lederman's Tips on Self-Editing

Editing is more than spotting typos in restaurant menus, more than disdainfully correcting the grammar of people you disagree with on the internet.

It involves looking at the flow of the story, the believability of the characters (likeability, maybe), the accuracy of information, the overall tone.

Does the narrative keep you interested, or are there tangents in there, inappropriate soapboxes? Strange appearances of a character for one chapter that you forgot to weave more fully into the story . . . ? (I've done it.)

Does the story jerk you around? No one wants to be jerked around.

That's what I'm talking about with editing.

So, there's a few different steps to go through when editing your own story.

Take some time away.

Deadlines and personal preferences will dictate

exactly how much time you can spend working on something else (or nothing else, whatevs. I'm not your mom.)

Regardless, once you've completed the work, spend some time away from it. A few days minimum, preferably a few weeks. Return to it with fresh eyes and give it a going-over.

Save it as a new draft before you edit.

Before you make changes to your work, save it as a new draft so you have an untouched/unrevised copy to return to in case you make changes you're unhappy with.

- (Note: I don't think I've EVER gone back to the way things were in a previous draft, but it gives me peace of mind knowing I have the option)
- Keep it simple: "Story draft 2." Maybe add a date, that sort of thing.
- You should always have a copy of your story stored in your email, Dropbox, or cloud. Computers crash. It's a lot of time, work, and soul lost if you haven't backed up your work.

Read your work OUT LOUD.

This is the number one piece of advice I give to every single student and writer, and probably the least heeded. I get it, it's painful and awkward. So is your face. Deal with it!

- Print it out, if that's a manageable option. There's

definitely a switch in how we read something on the screen versus in print.

- o If you can't print it, send it to your e-reader.
- o If you don't have an e-reader, then change the font on your computer, plus enlarge it at least twice over.
- o Some people have told me they have their computer read it to them.

Point to each word as you read it.

If you've snuck in extra words or omitted any, this is how you'll find those mistakes.

At the word level:

- Look for "extra" words. The usual culprits are "very," "just," "that," and "only." Remove them if at all possible. (It's usually possible.)
- Here's a word I see overused often quite often, from writers at all different levels, and while everyone's wringing their hands about adverbs and words like "just," no one is talking about "AS."

Example:

As I walked to the refrigerator my hand reached out to open the door. I shifted my weight from one foot to the other as I tried to make my choice. I was as hungry as a bear and needed to eat something as soon as possible. Using my knee to hold the door open as I rooted through the refrigerator's contents, I saw the candy bar hidden behind the eggs.

Leah McNaughton Lederman

Edited:

I walked to the refrigerator, my hand reaching to open the door. I shifted my weight from one foot to the other while I tried to make my choice. I was hungry as a bear and needed something to eat, like now. Using my knee to hold open the door, I rooted through the shelves. That's when I saw the candy bar hidden behind the eggs.

- Look for your personal, preferred "repeat" words, phrases, and sentence structures.
- We all have them. It's what gives our writing its unique flavor—we have a voice. But that means we tend to use the same words and the same sentence structure throughout our writing. Find out what your tics are and be prepared to work around them.
- Having edited and graded the writing of hundreds of people, I can tell you that many people cannot see it for themselves. That's why they do it.
- Once someone has pointed out your repeat word/structure, it's up to you to find them.
  - ○ In Microsoft Word, hit "Ctrl + H" and a "find and replace" dialogue box will come up. Look for your word and observe how many times you use it. Replace it with something better— not necessarily some weird obscurism from the thesaurus. Often, simple is best.
  - ○ Sometimes you might have to rework a sentence to avoid the word. Don't resist this type of change. It's called revision. It's good for you.

Tips on Self Editing

At the sentence level

Check your sentence length for variation
- If it's handwritten/printed out, circle or highlight each period. If it's typed, hit the return key after each sentence so you can see them all on the page.
- Are they all the same length/same structure? This can be mundane to read, so switch it up!
- Don't just check for varied sentence *length* but also the style of sentence.
    - Often you'll see the same words starts several sentences in a row (pronouns are usually guilty).
    - Also, vary the sentence structure you use. If every sentence starts with the same Noun/Verb setup, even if you're using different words and characters, you have redundancy.

Example: Noah begged her to listen to him. She turned to him. It was not going to be easy. His eyes were glued to her. He studied her every move. She sighed.

Change: Noah begged her to listen to him. Hearing the urgency in his voice, she turned to him. Both of them knew it wasn't going to be easy. Noah studied her face, her every move, looking for some sign that she might relent. Finally, she sighed.

At the paragraph level

- **"Reverse outline"** to check paragraph order and content:
  - Read each paragraph one by one. On a sheet of paper, make a little outline, just a dash or a bullet for each paragraph, or the words "Paragraph 1, 2, 3 . . ."
  - Beside each one, jot a few words explaining what that paragraph is about.
    - This shows you if the flow of paragraphs makes sense, that they're not spread all over the place or too repetitive.
    - It also lets you know if there's a sentence within a particular paragraph that might be better suited somewhere else.
- Check the length of your paragraphs using print preview (or just zoom out)
  - Is it just one giant paragraph? No one wants to read a solid brick of text. Unless they're Anglo-Saxons. But that's different.
  - Is one paragraph noticeably shorter than the others? (This can be okay—but make sure it's intentional, and not just an out-of-place thought).
- Zoom out and do the same thing with your chapters—are they about the same length throughout?

Don't let the record skip.

The most generic advice ever, but what I rely on most: When you get to a spot where the CD "skips," STOP.

- Something didn't flow well, and that's what made

you hesitate, made your brain skip like your 90s Discman on a speedbump. Maybe your wording is chunky or bumbly (technical terms) or you realize you never developed this character outside of this particular chapter and that's pretty awkward . . .

- Don't beat yourself up for your mistakes. Thank yourself for reading through your work before submitting it.
- Stop to make changes as you go along:
- If it's just a minor error, circle it.
- If it's a slightly more involved sentence-level change, don't count on yourself to remember later what you wanted to change. Write yourself a little note as to how you want to reword things—either in the margins or in a MS Word comment.

Don't be boring.

Openings don't always have to have shouted dialogue or intense action. We can't all write *Lethal Weapon*. But the whole "grab your readers" thing is real. Get your reader's attention with crisp detail and new perspectives. Don't start off with a long soliloquy or some sort of recap.

Throughout the story, ask yourself, "Do my readers need to know this? Am I furthering the story or just adding words?"

Endings can't just fizzle out. Endings must always leave the readers wanting more—why else would they turn the page, read the next chapter, or buy your next book?

Leah McNaughton Lederman

Is your salad proportioned?

I'm a bit of an OCD salad maker. The ratio of lettuce to cucumbers to tomatoes to dressing needs to be perfectly balanced or my life is ruined. Same with your story.

As you're reading, make sure there's a balance between dialogue, a character's thoughts, description, action, etc. Too much of one thing and you no longer have a story, you have a script, or you have a giant info-dump.

Balance the elements of your story. Parse out your information, spread it along like breadcrumbs (croutons?).

Make your dialogue and action tags work for the story.

Some people will tell you to only ever use "said" as a dialogue tag. I'm in the camp where the occasional "replied," "answered," "whispered," or "shouted" is okay, but sparingly.

What is *not* okay is when characters are gurgling, blubbering, chortling, chuckling, crying, sniffling, or beelzebubbing every single utterance. It's distracting.

I am a fan of the action beat, myself. Patrick Rothfuss perfected the form in his *Name of the Wind* series, so go read that, I'll wait . . . Okay, no I won't.

But here's a sample of what I'm talking about:

Dialogue tag: "Hey," Jack said.

Tips on Self Editing

Action beat: "Hey." Jack didn't look up from the paper he was writing on.

Lastly, let me just say this: If you didn't know that there are specific rules regarding the formatting of dialogue, I'm going to let you in on a little secret: *there are specific rules regarding the formatting of dialogue.* Yes, they can be broken. But before you go breaking a rule you didn't know existed, *learn* the rules.

"KILL YOUR BABIES*"
*not my line

Just because you wrote it doesn't mean it's going to stay.

- Is there something that doesn't fit? A paragraph that disrupts the flow?
- A problem I have, and one I see often in other people's writing, is the repeat sentence—you've said the same thing two different ways. Likely, you couldn't decide which one was better so you left them both in, thinking no one would notice.
  o (We noticed.)
- If you wrote the best sentence ever written (I can relate. I've written a fair few, myself) but you know it doesn't fit, or it's repetitive, open a separate file and name it "Title of Story JUNK DRAWER."
  o This is where you keep the beautiful golden nuggets of wisdom and high literature you've written. They didn't make it to your story, but

somehow knowing they're safe in a junk drawer file makes it easier to cut them out.

Get some readers.

This is where you're going to find out who your real friends are.

Part of taking your writing seriously is surrounding yourself with writing and with writers, online and in your community. Many libraries and coffeeshops have open mics or workshops, and check "your local listings" if there are writer's groups in the area.

Thousands of online communities exist online to talk about writing—genre specific, even! In the past year I've had tons of help, inspiration, and opportunity from online groups.

Yes, there are nasty trolls in comment threads and high schoolers pawning off their homework. Sift through and find the right voices. They are there. It's how I met several of the contributors to this very collection!

Notes on readers:

- You'll have to read theirs if you want to read yours.
- It helps if your readers are familiar with your genre, and have some writing or editing experience.
- Don't be satisfied with responses like, "it was good." What was good? Did it work when I transitioned from daytime to nighttime, etc. You need to give them more prompting and things to focus on, or you need to find more confident and experienced readers.

Tips on Self Editing

- You will never get better if everyone just tells you how great you are. No one is that great.
- On the other hand, don't throw out advice or criticism or mistake those things for personal attacks on your writing. Put on your big-kid pants.
- Okay, you're allowed to get a little mad at first (especially if it's not in person). "What? These people wouldn't know a decent story if it slapped them in the face!" Now, once you've gotten over yourself, recognize the very helpful criticism you've been given and use it to make your story better.
- Do NOT give someone a draft to read and then make changes to the document so you have to send them the REVISED COPY ("Read this one, not that one").
  - That is the absolute worst thing you can do to someone trying to help you revise. It will make them not want to work with you. Revise it yourself first, THEN send it along.
    - And NEVER do it to your editor.

Write down your game plan.

You've followed the steps. With any luck, you've got your margins filled with notes and questions, there's arrows connecting paragraphs across pages, and you've got emails from readers asking for clarification . . .

Oy.

Leah McNaughton Lederman

BEFORE YOU START REVISING:

- Map out your plan of attack. What steps are you going to take to implement all of the suggested changes?
- If you're not careful and you just dive in, it's easy to get lost in the woods and lose track of what needed to get done. It creates a lot more work in the long run. Be organized.

  Sample Plan of attack:

  o Tighten dialogue in first chapter
  o Figure out what happened to "S" character in fight scene
  o Research hippocampus and incorporate in "L"'s dialogue at end of chapter 2
  o Make bigger cliffhanger at end of chapter 5

Leah McNaughton Lederman's Tips on Proofreading

This is what most people skip to immediately after they've written their story. Truth is, it's the last thing you should do, and it gives your work a polish, not an overhaul—that's editing, which should already be completed. There are similarities in the two processes, but they are not the same.

Proofreading comes late in the process, after your work has gone through a few different readers, and hopefully an editor. It's when you polish the story and doublecheck your style guides.

Having said that proofreading comes last, I hope

Tips on Self Editing

I don't confuse you when I say it also needs to happen a before you submit to an editor. What injustice is this? You have to proofread twice? Let me remind you: the writing process is not linear. Some steps happen more than once.

I've said it once and I'll say it again—it is *not* the editor's job to clean up your entire rough draft. If you're going through the trouble of hiring an editor, make absolutely certain they are seeing your best work.

At all times, you need to be dealing with as clean a piece of literature as possible. Don't just regurgitate your thoughts on the page and expect anyone, yourself included, to be able to make sense of them. The less your editor is distracted by fixing minor typos or other surface errors, the more time they have to focus on the "big picture" issues within the text.

So, you've been through several drafts, had other people read your work, and gone through the self-editing checklist. Now it's time to proofread.

Ideally, get someone else (someone qualified) to proofread your work and pay them to do it for you. You're too close to this baby.

But you might not have the funds for a proofreader. I get it. The first few steps are identical to the steps in editing, but you're scraping at the top layer of text once the dust has settled from the edits.

Get time away from it.
Save it as a new draft.
Start reading—OUT LOUD.

- Just like in editing, print it out, send it to your e-reader, change and embiggen the font. This way, errors will jump out at you more readily.

Stop to make changes as you go.

- Don't think "I'll remember where I needed to make changes." Circle grammar/spelling errors and typos, and make small notes to yourself.
- Is there something that still doesn't fit? At this point, get out the axe.
- If you're making notes like, "develop Dineen's voice more clearly here" or "Whatever happened to Mike?" then you might need to return to the editing phase. You're still doing heavy lifting, creating verbal dust, and the work isn't ready to be polished.

Read it backward.

- Quite often, we get caught up in the story (yeah, I know you're that good).
- Start at the end and read the final sentence, then read the one before it, and so on.
- This forces you to pay closer attention to the mechanical end of the story, to each individual sentence, rather than the image and story the words create.